MW00440248

THE TRAP

GREGG DUNNETT

This is a work of fiction. Names, characters, business, events and incidents are the products of the author's imagination. Any resemblance to actual persons, living or dead, or actual events is purely coincidental.

Copyright © Gregg Dunnett, 2023

The moral right of the author has been asserted.

All rights reserved. No part of this book may be reproduced or used in any manner without the prior written permission of the copyright owner.

To request permissions, contact the publisher at rights@stormpublishing.co

Ebook ISBN: 978-1-80508-159-3
Paperback ISBN: 978-1-80508-161-6

Cover design: Emma Graves
Cover images: Trevillion, Shutterstock

Published by Storm Publishing.
For further information, visit:
www.stormpublishing.co

ALSO BY GREGG DUNNETT

Erica Sands Series

The Cove

The Trap

Standalone thrillers

Little Ghosts

The Wave at Hanging Rock

The Glass Tower

The Girl on the Burning Boat

The Desert Run

The Rockpools Series

1. *The Things You Find in Rockpools*

2. *The Lornea Island Detective Agency*

3. *The Appearance of Mystery*

4. *The Island of Dragons*

ONE

A violent gust of wind rocked the car. Outside, the branches of the trees, already stripped of their leaves, clawed at the air like the stunted arms of ghouls. Up ahead, the road plunged into a hollow. Detective Chief Inspector Erica Sands flicked on the full-beam headlights, illuminating the greasy wetness outside.

She was still a few minutes from the murder house, and not for the first time she wondered if she ought to have brought another officer with her. But they were short of staff in the MID – the South West Murder Investigation Department – and it would have been a waste of resources for two people to check on a minor detail like this. She pressed the thought away, as the wipers swept rain from the windscreen.

Besides, there was something about this minor detail that had made her want to deal with it alone.

The call had come in from Commander Black, the most senior officer in the South West police force. He had started by telling her that his interest was routine, a claim that was so obviously untrue she'd wondered if he'd meant for her to be suspicious, but if so, she didn't know why. Then he'd asked her about the Jane Smith case.

The heavy car crested the edge of the hollow, momentarily weightless, as the road dropped away. At the bottom, Sands felt the forces push her into the seat. Automatically she relaxed her grip on the wheel as the powerful engine surged back up the other side. She ran through the case in her mind.

Jane Smith had died three months previously, aged fifty-five years. She had lived alone, with few close neighbours, and her cottage was in a particularly tucked-away corner of this already rural part of Black Dorset. A local garage mechanic had discovered her body after becoming concerned when she'd failed to collect her car. Demonstrating the kind of personal service that was fast going out of fashion, the man had visited to check if she was OK. Looking through the window of the cottage, he'd seen that she wasn't – her body was lying at the foot of the stairs.

The subsequent police investigation quickly established the basic facts:

Ms Smith's cottage showed clear signs of a break-in. A single-glazed window in the kitchen had been broken from the outside, and whoever had broken it had presumably then reached inside to open the kitchen door, which was discovered undamaged but unlocked. The cottage had been ransacked – drawers and cupboards emptied, their contents spread about on the floor. It didn't look like the culprit or culprits had been looking for anything in particular, but some higher-value items were missing. Smith's post-mortem revealed bruising around the upper arm, a broken neck and a deep cut to the back of her head.

The picture that emerged was of a burglary gone horribly wrong. With no car on the driveway, the house would have looked empty, and therefore presented an easy target. In such an isolated location, the thief might not have been concerned about making much noise, which in turn could have woken Smith. With the cottage's only landline telephone downstairs in the hallway, and her mobile phone apparently left in the kitchen (as indicated by the location of the charging cable; the mobile itself was missing), she would have had no means to call for help. Perhaps she tried to escape from her assailant, or perhaps she tried to confront them? It wasn't clear. Nor was it easy to say whether her fall down the stairs was the deliberate work of the intruder, or simply an accident. What was clear was that her injuries were enough to kill her – she would have died instantly when her neck was broken.

No unaccounted-for fingerprints were found in the cottage; there *were* footprints in the yard outside, but they were poorly defined, suggesting that whoever had left them had taken the trouble to tie a plastic bag over their boots. The only real clues were the tyre marks thought to be left by the intruder's vehicle, but even this did little to narrow the field of potential culprits. The tyres were large, probably belonging to a van or a 4x4, and worn in a way that suggested the vehicle was old and probably poorly maintained.

Gloves, sturdy boots covered by plastic, an old panel van – all standard issue for a burglar or team of burglars. It was likely that whoever broke in would also have worn a balaclava – a terrifying final image for Smith to be confronted with.

Sands had given the case to her deputy, Detective Inspector John Lindham. And though she'd been kept abreast of developments, she hadn't been devoting much attention to it. She agreed with Lindham's hypothesis that they were searching for a burglar or burglars, albeit one who could turn violent when challenged or surprised. And she shared his pessimism regarding any hope of identifying the culprit. Budget cuts meant burglaries were barely investigated these days and lists of potential suspects were hopelessly out of date. Moreover, professional burglary had advanced considerably in recent years. Teams of thieves tended to move around the country or even overseas. It was highly likely that whoever had killed Jane Smith was already abroad, anywhere from Romania to Russia.

With so little to go on, and such a slim expectation of success, the case was more about accurately logging the facts and hoping for a break than actively investigating. The only member of Smith's family that Lindham had been able to identify was a sister who'd lived in Canada for many years, and she wasn't pushing that hard for justice to be served.

All of which told Sands that this wasn't a case that would usually warrant interest from Commander Black. And yet he *was* interested, and apparently willing to lie about it too, given his pretence that his question was merely routine. That alone might have worried Sands enough to go out to the murder house right away, even in the teeth of the approaching storm. But what he'd gone on to say had sealed the deal.

The trees had thinned now and the road stretched out ahead, the wet tarmac reflecting what little light was left in the sky. Sands had visited the house once before, when scene of crime officers were combing through the wreckage of Smith's cottage. She'd watched as Lindham gave his orders, she'd studied the body and considered how the dead woman's final moments might have played out, but then returned to her own workload, satisfied that Lindham was investigating the case to the best of his ability, which was all she could ask of her staff.

Her thoughts almost distracted her enough to miss the turn, a narrow track that led a few hundred metres off the main road, hidden behind a stand of already-wintry trees. But she braked hard, made the turn and let the Alfa coast down a track pock-marked with water-filled holes. Her headlights illuminated the little cottage.

A creeping sense of neglect already emanated from the cottage. Smith's relatives were apparently wealthy enough – or just too far away – to have gotten around to selling the place; in fact they hadn't even arranged to have the cottage cleaned up, despite having been given the all-clear to do so many weeks before. Blue police tape was still stretched over the front door, and the broken window where the killer had gained entry was poorly secured with cardboard, sodden from this storm and the others that had raged through the area before it.

It was so dark that Sands left the headlights on as she walked across to unlock the front door. Once inside she tried the light switch but her heart sank when she realised the power was off. The bills probably hadn't been paid, or the wind may have brought the power lines down. Whichever, she would have to find her way around in the dark. Sands swore under her breath, then returned to her car to get the flashlight she always carried in the boot. This time she reluctantly turned off the headlights, not wanting to risk running the car's battery flat.

She stepped into the kitchen first. To her left was the window where the intruder had gained access, the cardboard flapping and sucking against the window frame, pushed by the wind outside, as if some kind of creature were trying to get in. She watched it for a second then swung the beam of light around the room. The whole place was a mess. Broken crockery and ripped-open food packets were strewn across the floor. Most of the cupboard doors were open, and drawers also hung open and empty, some broken where they'd been pulled out too violently. The walls were stained with the white powder they used to pull off fingerprints. She sniffed – though she barely needed to. A foul smell of decay sat heavy in the room. She shone the light into the sink and then checked the fridge, gagging as the door swung open. It still contained food from Jane Smith's last trip to the supermarket. For a second Sands could picture her there, perhaps choosing her purchases carefully to fit a tight budget. The food had rotted inside its packaging. Everything sealed had swelled up from the decay, and several items – she identified one as a tray of chicken thighs – had burst open and were writhing with maggots. Shutting the fridge, Sands pulled a tissue from her pocket and used it to cover her nose.

She stepped carefully over the mess towards the small living room which looked less disturbed. A sofa faced the empty space where a TV had once stood. The intruder had either taken it before killing Smith, or had felt comfortable enough to finish the job while she lay dead at the foot of the stairs. Sands was more interested in the hallway, where Smith's body had been found.

There was a different smell there. A stale odour of old blood. She shone the light on the floor to see the blood stain that had soaked into the carpet. Stepping around it she looked up at the walls, finally allowing herself to consider the strange question that Black had asked her earlier that day.

Was there anything to do with chess in the hallway? Chess and animals?

She'd asked him where the question came from, but he wouldn't tell her. That was fair enough – she'd presumed it meant a link to another investigation she was unaware of, but instead he'd been evasive, and tried to distract her with further details of the Smith case. Irrelevant details. Another hint that something about his question was anything but routine. Her mind had wandered first to Smith's cottage and anything that might fit at the crime scene. But then somewhere else – the childhood bedroom she'd lived in until the age of twelve. The chess set she'd loved and played with daily, until her circumstances changed. Each piece represented by a different African animal. She'd liked the queen the most, a proud broad-faced lioness carved from Padauk wood, golden-brown. Chess and animals?

As soon as Black had rung off she'd pulled the file and studied the scene of crime photographs, but there was nothing obvious. But by now something was niggling at her memory, a fragment that wouldn't quite come back to her. This was why she'd headed to the cottage straightaway.

She shone the torch around, trying to consider the hallway

in its entirety before focusing on the detail she'd come to see. The few items in a coat and shoe rack made it obvious Smith lived alone. Sands had something similarly sparse in her own hallway. There was a very old-looking phone on a small table. Nothing seemed unusual, so she turned to the photograph on the wall. Her memory of it had clarified as she drove there, but she noticed some details for the first time. It was the largest image in the hallway, its frame simple, its location prominent. Nothing suggested it bore any relation to the crime that had taken place; that was why it hadn't been included in the case file. She had no idea why she'd even noticed it herself, except perhaps that it was such a memorable image. Whatever, she felt oddly satisfied to see it there, almost exactly as she'd eventually recalled it.

Smith had kept two cats, one black and one white, the choice of colour presumably a reference to her interest in chess. Certainly the photograph suggested so. It showed the two animals sitting either side of a chessboard, as if playing a game. Sands now noticed the checkmate position of the famous "Opera game". Somehow, Smith – or whoever had taken the photograph – had managed to get the white cat to place its paw on black's doomed king, and it really did look as if it was about to knock it over. It should have been a fun, light-hearted photograph celebrating the romantic heyday of the game, but something about it – perhaps its suggestion that Smith devoted so much of her attention to her animals instead of other people – gave it an undertone of sadness.

She shone the torch beam on the photograph, again hearing Black's question in her mind.

Was there anything to do with chess in the hallway? Chess and animals?

She felt only ongoing disquiet at her discovery, but she couldn't quite place why. She tried to dismiss it, concentrating instead on the photograph, noting further details. It had been taken in the living room of the cottage, with the window used as a backdrop, dressed with houseplants. It also wasn't the only thing in the frame. In the bottom right corner was a newspaper clipping, with the headline: *Local Woman Wins Photography Competition*. The text was brief, but it confirmed that Jane Smith herself had won the competition, with this photograph. The original photograph and the newspaper clipping had been framed together, and given pride of place in the hallway.

Fine. So how did Commander Black know about it? And why was it relevant?

Sands played the beam at the other pictures hung along the wall, mostly pencil drawings of flowers and watercolours of harbours with boats at anchor. She returned to the cats. Then, balancing the torch on the telephone table so its beam shone roughly in the right direction, she pulled on a pair of forensic gloves, then gently lifted the photograph off the wall. There was nothing behind it. She turned it, inspecting it all the way around. And this time she noticed a trace of white somewhere between the frame and the backing card, as if something had been slipped in there. It was difficult to grip with the gloves, so she began to lift the little metal tabs that held the frame together and then carefully pulled the backing card away. As she did so, something slipped out and, twisting through the air, fell onto the floor.

At first she thought it was the newspaper clipping, but as she turned the frame again, she saw it was still in place. This was something else. She aimed her torch at the floor, where a slip of paper had landed in the bloodstain. When she picked it up she thought the carpet still felt wet, but it was probably just her mind playing tricks.

She had to crouch a little to hold the paper in the light from the torch – just a single slip of paper, apparently torn from a small notebook. Hastily scrawled and smudged, the black ink was difficult to read:

The crossroads of time approach.
The eternal journey begins with the spilling of one innocent's blood.
It will not end until blood flows like the Nile in flood.
I kill to save! The world will be reborn!

As Sands moved the scrap of paper closer, she saw the words weren't written in black after all, but a dark maroon colour, and then she realised it wasn't ink at all.

The note was written in dried blood.

TWO

The next morning Sands pulled up outside DI John Lindham's house at 7:38 and dialled his number as she glanced through the kitchen window, taking in the snapshot of a family getting ready to start their day. There were flashes of children, Lindham's wife at the sink pretending not to notice the conspicuously red Alfa waiting outside. Sands had met Sarah Lindham a couple of times, but little about the woman had interested her. She'd seemed somewhat cold, presumably a result of all the time he spent complaining about her. That thought interested Sands even less.

Lindham finally appeared at the front door and was followed immediately by Sarah and two little blond boys in their school uniforms. Sands watched as her colleague bent down to kiss them goodbye.

"Sorry about that ma'am," Lindham said when he finally got in the car. "Elliot's having a bit of trouble at school. You know how it is."

Sands briefly wondered which one was Elliot before accelerating away. The journey was only an hour and half, although they both knew Sands would get them there quicker than that.

. . .

The meeting took place in a glass-walled room on the third floor of the impressively new Yeovil Police Station. Commander Black turned up ten minutes late. He was tall and his heavy frame filled out his neatly presented uniform. The man who arrived with him wore a grey suit that hung off his narrow frame and accentuated how he was all angles. It took Sands a moment to place him, but when she did, her frown deepened.

Before Black sat down he pressed a button on the wall, and the glass walls turned opaque.

"DCI Sands, thank you for coming up," Black began, but he paused at once, glancing at Lindham. "And this is...?"

"DI John Lindham, sir," he replied. Black nodded thoughtfully, then turned back to Sands.

"I wasn't expecting you to bring anyone else."

"Neither was I," Sands replied, looking pointedly at the man in the suit. Neither he nor Black replied, but they glanced at each other. Sands sighed, and continued. "Detective Lindham is leading the investigation into the Jane Smith murder. He ought to be here. And we should get on with whatever this is." She looked pointedly at a clock on the wall, and then opened the bag she was carrying. She pulled out the hidden note along with the original photograph, now back in its frame. Both items were secured in plastic evidence bags.

"I don't understand how you knew about this, but it's highly relevant to Lindham's enquiry."

Black inhaled carefully. "What we have to talk about is of a... sensitive nature. You might prefer it if he waits outside."

"If it's relevant to solving the crime, I shouldn't need to keep it from my officers. I'd prefer him to stay. Sir."

Black exchanged another look with the thin civilian, then shrugged very slightly. "As you wish." He held out a hand, indicating the note. "May I?" Sands slid the smaller of the bags across to Black, who studied the note, first one side, then the other.

"How did you know about it?" Sands pressed, as Black finally looked up. He didn't reply, instead reading the words out loud, frowning deeply. "'The crossroads of time approach. The eternal journey begins with the spilling of one innocent's blood. It will not end until blood flows like the Nile in flood. I kill to save! The world will be reborn!'"

He paused. "Lots of blood. And it's actually written in blood? Is it hers? Jane Smith's?"

"No," Sands replied. "The lab says it's from a bird, most likely a chicken."

"Can they get anything from that? Anything helpful?"

Sands shook her head. "No. They say whoever wrote it could have got a bird from any supermarket."

"What about the actual text? I have to say, it sounds to me like the words of a lunatic." Black passed the note to the thin man.

After a few moments, Lindham answered on Sands' behalf. "Yeah, we're not really sure what it refers to. The 'spilling of one innocent's blood': that could be taken as an admission of guilt for killing Smith. And then the line about it not ending until blood flows like the Nile in flood. Clearly that sounds like there might be more to come. A lot more."

"Why the Nile?" Black asked, but no one answered him.

"How did you know we'd find it there, or something like it?" Sands asked again, but again Black acted as though she hadn't spoken. He continued questioning Lindham. "Fingerprints? Fibres?"

Lindham shook his head.

"Was there anything else about the scene that seemed out of place? Especially now this has been uncovered?"

"No sir. We thought it was a burglary gone wrong." Lindham cleared his throat. "Until this."

Black sat back in his chair. "It still might be. This could have been placed there before the murder. Or afterwards. It may not be relevant at all."

"But clearly you knew it was there," Sands cut in. "Or something like it. How did you know?"

"I didn't *know* exactly..." Black began.

"You called me to ask if there was anything in the hallway related to *chess and animals*. This note was hidden behind a photograph of two cats sitting by a chess board. That's not a coincidence."

"I agree."

"So who told you?"

Again, Black exchanged a look with the man in the suit. Sands glanced at him too, and Black shook his head.

"I haven't introduced you. This is James Mc—"

"I know who it is. He's James McDonald." Sands turned to look at the man. "The Director General of Highmoor Prison."

McDonald smiled in a somewhat sickly way.

"So it's a tip then? From someone inside?" Lindham asked, his frown suggesting he knew he was missing something.

Black was watching Sands. "Are you sure you wouldn't like to continue this without DI Lindham present?"

Sands took a breath, and then turned to her deputy. "As you probably know, HM Highmoor is the UK's highest-security prison, where the most dangerous male prisoners are kept. As such, it's where Charles Sterling, the man who was my father, has been held for the last twenty-five years – ever since he was convicted of the murder of eight women, including my mother and my sister." She turned to Black. "I assume this concerns him in some way?"

"Yes. It does."

"Well?" Sands pressed. "What exactly does Sterling have to do with this?" She held up the note.

Black paused before explaining. "Detective Sands, your

father claims to have information which might identify the perpetrator of this crime. And he wants to give it to us."

"What information?" Sands shot back.

"Unfortunately, he won't tell us."

Now it was Lindham who broke the silence. "I don't understand! You just said he wanted to—"

"Perhaps it's better if the director explains," Black interrupted. "He's got more of a handle on the situation."

After a moment McDonald took over, his voice sounding raspy after Black's deep tones. "As you're no doubt aware, over the years your father has made repeated attempts to reconnect with you..."

"Please don't call him that."

"I'm sorry?"

"*My father.* I don't consider him that anymore. His name is Charles Sterling and I'd rather you refer to him that way."

"Of course. I understand how you must feel," McDonald continued soothingly. "But the fact remains he *is* your father. And throughout his incarceration he has tried to maintain a familial connection with you, his sole surviving relative. On many occasions he has tried to persuade you to visit him, or to answer his letters—"

"All of which I've refused to accept, or thrown away unread when you've allowed them to be sent," Sands replied. She sat back now, arms folded, glaring angrily at the director.

"Yes – as you say. But your father – sorry, Sterling – hasn't given up hope. What he appears to be proposing here is to trade the information on the killer's identity. But only if you'll agree to see him in person. He'll only give the information to you."

Sands knew she ought to control her anger, but she felt ambushed. She stared at the prison director, hating him for his association with that man, yet knowing the hatred was irrational. Unfair. She turned to the commander instead.

"With respect, sir, you need to understand this is bullshit."

Black seemed taken aback but Sands pressed him. "You cannot believe him. He won't have anything of value. This will be a trick. A waste of our time."

"That may be his intention. But clearly he knows something. He told us about the note."

Sands paused. He had a point. She blinked, trying to make sense of this. "What *exactly* did he say? How did he tell you?"

Again it was McDonald who explained. "Your father asked for a message to be sent to me two weeks ago claiming to know the perpetrator of a recent crime. The murder of a woman named Jane Smith. These things happen from time to time – prisoners hoping to exchange what they know for a reduction in their sentence. Obviously, that doesn't apply in your father's case..."

"Will you please use the man's name?"

McDonald gave his thin smile of apology. "Of course." He carried on. "In such cases we ask for the information up front, but your..." – his hands came up again in apology – "*Sterling* refused. He said he would only give the information to you, and with your very clearly-stated refusal to have anything to do with him, we deemed it inappropriate to contact you. When we communicated that to Sterling, he said he would give us one piece of information to demonstrate the veracity of what he was saying. He told us to look for the chess and animals connection in the hallway."

"Just that?"

"Just that."

Sands fell quiet. Black turned to Lindham again. "Did we say anything about Smith being a chess player? Any way he could have known?"

Lindham appeared to consider but then held up his hands. "It never seemed relevant. Smith was an amateur player. A member of a local chess club, but it wasn't anything we put out; no reason to."

"We might not have put it out there, but *she* did." Sands pushed the photo across the table to Black, her finger resting on the newspaper cutting with the headline *Local woman wins photography competition*. "I assume Sterling is still allowed a generous choice of newspaper subscriptions?" She looked scornfully at McDonald.

"He's entitled to receive them," the director replied. "We consider it important that all our inmates receive their basic human rights. All of them. It's also the law."

"So you're saying," – Black appeared not to notice the animosity between McDonald and Sands – "Sterling could have seen this article, and known that Smith had this photograph. But how would he have known about the note behind the picture?"

Sands opened her mouth to reply, but she had no answer. Neither did anyone else. McDonald broke the silence. "There's a simple way to solve the mystery." He shrugged lightly. "Sterling's psychiatric assessments have been saying for some time that he's a very different man from when he went in. I do believe he'll tell you. If you go and see him." Again the room fell quiet.

"No. I'm not seeing him." Sands seemed a little surprised to hear her words spoken out loud. "I don't want to see him."

"I can understand your reticence," McDonald replied. His voice had returned to its previous butter-like smoothness. "But in my opinion, his motives for wishing to speak with you are entirely human and positive. A need to heal. He has undergone a great many changes..."

"No, he hasn't." Sands voice was husky, quiet. "He's not different at all."

The director shook his head. "With great respect, Detective, I don't see how you could possibly know that, given how you haven't seen—"

"*No*." Sands interrupted him, angering again. "This is a

trick. *A con.* However he got this information, he's using it to blackmail me to come and see him. That sounds *exactly* like the man I remember."

McDonald winced slightly. "He is attempting to use leverage, I agree. But you must understand, he has very limited options. You don't answer his letters, you haven't *ever* been to see him, in nearly twenty-five years..."

"Oh spare me, please. The man murdered my mother and sister. He waited for me to come home and discover what he'd done, just so he could tell me the only reason he didn't kill *me* was because he thought I was like him. Why would I go to see him? Tell me, why would I want to do that?"

It took a long while for anyone else to speak. It was Black who finally did so. "Do you have any suspects at present in the Jane Smith case?"

Sands used the ensuing silence to try and pull herself together. She wasn't handling this well.

"No sir," Lindham answered for her. "We're focusing on people with burglary records. Trying to find someone who was in the area at the time."

"And how's that going?"

Lindham ran a hand through his thinning hair. "About as well as can be expected. With budget cuts... we don't have a full picture to work from." He shrugged.

"Quite." Black looked at Sands. "You have a difficult investigation on your hands. And if this *is* relevant," – he tapped a finger on the note – "Then it's possible you're looking in entirely the wrong place."

For a few moments they all looked down at the note, still in its plastic sheet, until Sands abruptly picked it up, reread it and turned it over to inspect the back, holding it up to the light. Finally, she shook her head. "Maybe he doesn't have to tell us," she said. "Perhaps we can find out how he got the information directly. The photograph and the newspaper article are three years old. And Sterling's been in prison for nearly twenty-five years, so *he* clearly didn't put them here. Which means someone else did, and then told him about it. Or at least told him to look there for something." She looked around. "Well, *how* did they tell him? He's kept in a soundproofed, isolated environment in a maximum-security prison, with zero contact with other prisoners." Sands turned to McDonald. "I assume that's still the case? If not, I should have been informed." There was an accusatory tone to her words.

"Of course it's still the case." McDonald nodded quickly. "Your father was ordered to serve a whole life sentence in a segregation unit. That hasn't changed."

"So he's entirely isolated." Sands spoke with a bitter edge to her voice. "Good. Then it's most likely the letters."

Lindham turned to her, not understanding, and Black looked confused as well. Only McDonald seemed to understand.

Sands explained, directing her words towards Lindham. "When Sterling was caught, he wasn't ashamed of what he'd done, quite the opposite. He showboated his way through the trial, and it gave him publicity. He became a kind of ghoulish celebrity. Since then, books and films have been made about what he did. That much you already know. What's less known is just how much of an opportunist he is. As the director said, he has a legal right to correspondence, so that's what he does. He corresponds. And it turns out there's plenty of crazy people out there who jump at the chance of having a caged sociopath as a penfriend." She paused, her lips thin. "And then there's the *other* letters of course." She didn't elaborate, but turned instead to McDonald. "How many is he getting these days? Is it still dozens a week?"

McDonald hesitated, then nodded. "He gets a steady flow of mail, yes."

"And you're still passing them onto him?"

"As you've just said, we have an obligation under the law to allow prisoners to receive mail."

"And as *you* know, it can be restricted in certain exceptional circumstances, which I've argued several times applies in Sterling's case." Sands sighed. "If it's in his mail, just go through the letters and find it. Then I don't have to speak to him."

McDonald shifted uncomfortably in his chair. "Of course we open and photocopy all mail that he sends and receives. But as I think you are aware, the nature of some of the correspondence makes it a difficult task…"

"But you have it all? You have photocopies of everything he's received and sent?"

"Yes."

"And you actually *read* it?"

Another pause.

"We've seen nothing that leads us to believe it's coming from his mail."

Sands breathed heavily, then spoke under her breath, the words seemingly for her alone. "It's definitely his mail."

"Look," Black said. "At the end of the day, the reason we called you here was to explain the situation. It's now up to you to decide how you want to proceed. As Mr McDonald here says, Charles Sterling *is* your father, and ultimately you hold responsibility for this case." He glanced at Lindham as if also acknowledging his role. "If you feel it's impossible for you to see him, or that it wouldn't be of any value to your team, that's your decision to make." He sat back, as if expecting Sands to take time to think before responding. If so, she surprised him.

"If that's the case, it's an easy decision. I'm not seeing him."

She inclined her head to Lindham as she got up from the table. "Come on. Let's get out of here."

THREE

"We could stop somewhere if you're hungry?" Sands asked as they drove back. "I want to make up the hours we've lost by this, so we might as well eat now."

"Sure," Lindham replied. He sat checking his mobile for messages and then fell into silence. Sands accelerated down a long straight, and then leaned into a bend.

"Good," she said. There was a village up ahead, and she remembered a new delicatessen and cafe had opened there recently. It looked a bit twee, but was probably the best option. If they ate there she could work late, and she would more or less have caught up. Another bend approached and she dropped down a gear, revving the engine harder than needed.

"Ma'am." Lindham's voice surprised her a few minutes later. Sands' attention had become almost entirely absorbed by the pleasure of guiding the Alfa rather too quickly around the corners of the country lane.

"What?"

"I need to know how you see this case progressing now." He sounded glum. "Am I still looking at people with a burglary record? Am I looking at the note? I'm just not sure."

Sands glanced across, then back at the road ahead. She didn't speak.

"Because it feels like there's this black hole, and I don't know whether to look into it or just to leave it the hell alone. I don't know if it's relevant, I don't know if I'm OK to even find out."

"What are you talking about? You follow the investigation where it takes you."

"That's kind of... That's my point."

Sands didn't reply.

"Look, I know this is tough for you. It was tough when we all found out who your dad was, and this is... I can't begin to understand how hard this must be. But you're acting like you're gonna just pretend this isn't happening. And I can't run a case like that."

Sands felt his eyes on her, but didn't look away from the road. She noticed her knuckles whitening where she was gripping the wheel too hard. She forced them to relax. Lindham sighed, as if giving up already.

"So this note may, or may not," he began, "have been left by whoever killed Jane Smith, we don't know. But clearly *someone* who either put it there, or knows it was there, was able to communicate that to Charles Ster—"

"*OK*," Sands cut in sharply. "You've made your point."

For a few moments there was only the sound of the engine, the tyres, the car ripping through the air.

"Maybe *I* could try and speak to him?" Lindham suggested. "Maybe he'd speak to me instead of you?"

Sands gripped the wheel hard again. Ignoring her whitening hands this time.

"Maybe he'll think that if he speaks to me, it'll get you to change your mind."

There was a small layby a few hundred meters ahead. Sands sized it up.

"Or, like you said, maybe we should pull all the letters he's received. Try and find where he's getting the information from."

Sands checked her mirrors and assessed the surface of the layby.

"Because otherwise I can't see how... hey! What the hell?" Lindham's voice rose in panic as the car suddenly veered off the road and began to slew around. Sands had cut fast into the parking area. She spun the wheel hard, making the car skid around.

"What the hell are you doing?"

The car never quite stopped, but now it was facing the other direction. Sands controlled the power, so the wheels only spun for a moment on the gravel before the heavy car was rolling again, this time going back the way they'd come.

"I'm turning round."

"What? Why?"

Sands considered what to say. "Because I don't have any choice. The bastard isn't going to tell us anything. He'll want to play stupid games and waste all our time. But I'm the only one who knows that, so I have no option but to try. So my best play is to get it over and done with. And in that case, I'd rather get it done today, right now. So we're not wasting any more time."

She tossed her mobile to Lindham. "Black's number's in there somewhere." She watched with half an eye as he rolled the contacts, glancing anxiously out of the window as the hedgerows flew by. When he found Black's number he hit the button to dial. The call was automatically routed to the car's sound system.

"It's DCI Sands," she said as soon as the call connected. "I'll see him. But I want to do it now. I want to get this over and done with."

They both listened as Black confirmed he'd set it up. Then Sands ended the call and pushed the car faster.

FOUR

Only the top few floors of the red-brick prison building were visible over the thirty-foot high wall, topped by razor wire and CCTV cameras that sat on poles like ugly birds of prey. Sands followed the signs to an entrance gatehouse manned by two armed guards, then she lowered her window and flashed her ID. Lindham showed his too.

The guard insisted on taking the documents into his booth and inspecting them carefully before closing the window and making a call. He then opened the window again.

"You won't be able to take the vehicle inside. But if you park over there, an officer will escort you in."

He passed the IDs back then shut the window. As they left the car, a second guard was already waiting for them.

"This way." The man led them to a door where they waited as a security camera scanned them, before a buzzing sound indicated that hidden locks had been unbolted. Inside, they were blocked by a second door, and an airport-style full-body scanner manned by yet another guard. Sands and Lindham emptied their pockets and passed through, then waited again as their belongings were examined.

"Wait here. Director McDonald is on his way down."

The guard waited with them until another door opened to reveal the director. He was taller than Sands had initially thought.

"I'm very pleased you've changed your mind, Detective." He smiled the same thin smile. "Let's go to my office. We can brief you about the visit from there." He paused. "And you'll probably appreciate some coffee?"

They followed him past two more sets of heavy iron doors before they reached his office. It was large and tastefully furnished, with a bookshelf along one wall and a large antique desk. A photo stood on it, presumably the director and his family, three children standing on the basalt pillars of the Giant's Causeway in Ireland. Sands glanced at the window which looked over the prison's exercise yard, bordered by a wire fence and then the same thirty-foot-high wall they'd seen from the outside. Now they were inside it seemed more prominent, more permanent, wrapping itself around them, holding them within its solid arms.

"It does something to you," McDonald said with a smile, "seeing a view like that every day."

Sands was about to turn away from the window when an alarm sounded. On the other side of the exercise yard a light above a door began to flash red, and then the door opened. Three men came out, two in the uniform of prison guards and one man in a green and yellow jumpsuit, his hands cuffed and his ankles chained together so that he could take only short steps. As Sands watched, one of the guards removed the man's ankle chains. Slowly, the prisoner began to walk in a circle around the perimeter of the courtyard, the two guards following a few steps behind him.

The director joined them at the window. "That's Gary Hassenbach; he murdered four. His last victim was his cell mate in Broadmoor. He stole a spoon from the canteen and forced it through the man's ear into his brain."

Sands was surprised by how close to her McDonald had come. She could smell his breath: stale caffeine. She moved a step away. "He's given exercise every day?"

"No." McDonald's voice was neutral. "He ought to be. But we're way over-capacity and too understaffed to make that possible. Hassenbach is a great example of someone who poses very little danger to anyone, but who we're obliged to treat as though he were some kind of monster. On a good week he gets out like that twice a week. The rest of the time he's in a windowless underground cell. Identical to your father's."

Sands glanced at him, deciding against yet another demand that he stop referring to Sterling as her father. "You just said he killed his cell mate with a spoon. How is that not monstrous?"

"That was a mistake by the prison. Hassenbach was abused by his parents from birth. Beatings, cigarettes stubbed out on his arms. Shouted at, insulted... you name it. At the age of six he was taken into care by a Catholic orphanage. If he'd stayed there he might never have ended up here, but unfortunately his parents successfully petitioned to have him back. Then they beat him even more severely as punishment. They raped him daily. At one point he spent nine months locked in his bedroom, the windows painted black. The only human contact he had was when his father went in to abuse him." The director smiled his thin smile. "He didn't escape. Not until he was legally allowed to leave, at age eighteen. After that he fell into a life of drugs, prostitution. His first victim was a man who paid to have sex with him, but who boasted about how he liked to rape children. Hassenbach beat the man to death with his own shoe. But given Hassenbach's childhood, can we really blame him for lashing out under such circumstances?" McDonald appeared to expect a reply, but Sands stayed quiet. So the director went on.

"Every one of Hassenbach's victims were child abusers.

They all provoked him. The man he killed in his cell was a paedophile; he should never have been put in a cell with him. Hassenbach has never posed a danger to the general public. Yet he's been ordered to live out the rest of his life in segregation, almost as if he were still locked up in his bedroom."

Sands watched Hassenbach as he reached the wire fence and automatically turned the corner. His jailers followed him, looking bored.

"Tell me, Detective, does that sound like justice to you?"

Sands ignored the question. "Is Sterling allowed out like this?"

The director took a deep breath. "Actually, he's due out today but we cancelled his exercise on account of you coming to see him. I don't suppose he'll mind. Can I get you that coffee?"

Sands nodded, still watching Hassenbach from the window. A man even unluckier than her.

McDonald listed a wide choice of drinks, as if he was in charge of an artisanal coffee shop rather than the country's highest-security prison. Lindham asked for a flat white and Sands suppressed her irritation to order the same. Pressing a button on his desk phone and repeating their orders, McDonald told whoever was on the other end that he'd have his usual. "Oh, and can you please send up Barney."

McDonald released the button and smiled. "Come. Please, sit." He sat down behind his desk and smiled broadly, as if Sands' and Lindham's presence was a delightful surprise.

"You don't agree with the conditions your prisoners are kept in?" Sands asked, taking a seat.

"In some cases, yes. In some cases, no. Regarding your father, he's demonstrated to a string of psychologists that he's changed. He's followed every rule we've asked of him for over twenty years. I see no reason why he shouldn't be kept in the regular cells with other inmates. Yet he's kept in isolation due to the high-profile nature of his crimes. It's just bad luck that his crimes made the newspapers, while other, similar crimes did not." Again, the thin-lipped smile.

"What about his tricks? The illness he faked? His legal challenges?"

McDonald waved a hand, dismissing her words. "He may well have been ill, we don't know. And he has every right to appoint a lawyer, or lawyers, to protect his rights. The state has taken his liberty, and he has been denied the opportunity to ever reclaim it."

"You know why. You know what he did," Sands replied.

"Of course. But I know of many others who have done the same, or arguably worse, but who still have a life to look forward to. The opportunity of redemption, if they want to take it." This time Sands didn't reply. "Detective Sands, you must understand it was a *political* decision to keep your father where he is. His real mistake was to elevate himself to the extent that he became almost the *definition* of a murderous psychopath. The example that all other killers are measured against. It means he's now trapped here, until he dies, because no Home Secretary will ever be brave enough to risk the backlash they'd receive in the popular newspapers if they ever granted him parole." He spoke sadly, compassion written across his face. Sands watched him and considered putting him right, telling him that Sterling's mistake was choosing to murder eight women, including his wife and youngest daughter. She settled for telling him once again not to call the man her father, in her coldest voice.

McDonald raised his hands again, as if there was nothing he could do, even about this. Then there was a knock on the door. A middle-aged woman came into the room, set down a tray then left. McDonald's usual turned out to be an espresso. He took a tiny sip as he continued. "I apologise, Detective. As you can see, family is important to me." He indicated the photograph of his children. "As I believe it is important to all of us. It's my belief that it will be beneficial for Sterling to see you. It may even prove beneficial to you."

Sands sipped her coffee. She'd met people like the director before – they were surprisingly common within the correction system – but she'd never heard such an opinion from someone who actually knew her father.

"For every Category A segregation prisoner we assign a senior officer to be primarily responsible for their security and welfare," McDonald went on. "In your father's case, that's a man named Barney Atkinson. He'll brief you on the security measures which have to be followed." McDonald took another tiny sip of his espresso. "As I say, in Sterling's case the security measures are largely for show these days, but we do still have to insist they're followed to the letter."

Sands sat back, she'd heard enough. She drank the coffee but stopped listening to what the director was saying. Almost against her will her mind was reaching back in time to when she'd last seen her father. It felt dizzying, both a lifetime away – and a tough life at that – and as if it had all happened just a few weeks ago. She felt the same sense of horrifying shame that had overwhelmed her when she'd learned who he was. And then the grief, and then the free-falling terror as she came to under-stand that her life as she knew it was utterly shattered, her only remaining family literally a monster. A monster who told her she was just like him. She felt her face colour, the cup she was holding begin to clatter against the saucer. She had to fight to put it down before the director noticed.

The thoughts didn't let up. Suddenly she was twelve years old again. She felt the tension between being the smartest in her school – a place she occupied quite naturally, but also because it was the very bare minimum *he* demanded of her – and how isolated that left her from the girls who might otherwise have become her friends. She remembered the hours she spent in his office, deep into the night, listening to his teaching. On science, philosophy, politics and his favourite subject, mathematics – perhaps the only topic where she felt she disappointed him. She remembered just how much she wanted to please him, to feel worthy of the time he invested in her. Yet she remembered too the tensions in the family. She remembered how her mother worried that she wasn't making friends at school, like her sister did. She remembered how she tried to please her too. That was why, on the night it happened, she'd been excited to receive an invitation to a classmate's sleepover. She was a friendly girl, not quite a close friend yet, but the young Sands had hoped it might develop that way. She searched her mind for the girl's name, but it didn't come.

And then her mind hit play on a familiar film. A movie of what happened after that sleepover, when the girl's parents had driven her home. The car had a particular smell, and the radio had been playing. They'd stopped at the curb, and the girl's parents waited in the car as Sands thanked them and ran to the front door. She remembered her amused confusion about the front door being ajar, but then the comfort of hearing her father whistling to himself inside. Sands had turned and waved goodbye again and watched as the car drove away. Then she'd pushed her way inside, and her life had been ripped apart.

There was another knock on the door. It opened to reveal a large man with blond hair, a broad chest and huge, muscled arms that pressed against the grey of his uniform shirt. He didn't smile as McDonald introduced him. "This is Principal Prison Officer Barney Atkinson." The director waved him inside. "Come on in, Barney. Can I introduce DCI Erica Sands and DI John Lindham? Erica is here to see Charles Sterling." He smiled to acknowledge the significant look on the big man's face. "Yes *that* Erica Sands. She is also his daughter."

Atkinson stepped carefully inside, crossing the threshold as if he were entering enemy territory. He nodded a hello to Lindham, but his eyes came to rest on Sands.

"Now, if you'll excuse me," McDonald continued, "Barney will brief you on the security protocols, then take you downstairs. I'm afraid I have other matters to attend to." With that, the director drained the rest of his espresso and stood up. He held out a hand to Sands, who took it. "I'm quite sure you're making the correct choice here."

FIVE

"Call me Barney. Everyone does," the officer said.

Sands watched him a moment, trying to get a read. "OK."

"It's just you that's gonna see him, right?" Barney went on, glancing at Lindham. "That's the way he wants it."

"Just me."

Barney nodded, seemingly satisfied by this, before turning to Lindham. "You can wait with me downstairs. We'll watch on the monitors. Keep an eye on him." It didn't seem to be negotiable. Barney turned back to Sands. "It's about this murder he reckons he knows about?"

"You know about that?"

"It were me he told first. Not many other people he gets to talk to down there. He asked me to let the guvnor know." His eyes flicked to Director McDonald's now empty chair. "Kinda wish I hadn't now, though."

"Why's that?" Sands asked.

For a moment it seemed as if Atkinson thought he'd said too much. "Because *you're* here, aren't you? That's what he wants. All he's ever wanted, far as I can see. You being here is a massive victory for him. And we shouldn't be handing people like him no victories."

Sands watched him in silence for a few moments. "You don't agree with Director McDonald's assessment that Sterling has changed?"

Barney scoffed at the idea. "That's one way of puttin' it."

"Why not?"

It took a while for Barney to reply, and he glanced at Lindham as if debating whether he should say any more in front of him. "He's dangerous. That's why. Sterling might have figured out how to fool them psychologists the guvnor likes to send down. But he's never fooled me. I see him for who he really is." Barney's nostrils flared and Sands nodded. She thought he'd finished but read him wrong. "I'd cut off his food, Detective. If it were up to me. I'd let him starve away, and just be done with him." He didn't take his eyes off her. "I hope you don't mind me saying so. Given he's your dad an' all."

Sands felt her heart beating hard, as if she were facing a challenge. She was the first to look away. "He's not." She locked her eyes back on his. "My father, I mean. He gave up that right when he murdered my family."

Barney gave a half-shrug, as if he'd heard what she'd said but didn't quite believe it.

"How long have you worked with the high-security prisoners?" Lindham asked. He seemed to want to break up the tension in the room.

Barney turned to face him. "Twelve years. I was assigned to Sterling nine years ago. I bring him every meal. I'm there every time he's taken out on exercise. He never leaves his cell unless I've checked everything first."

"Do you think there's any chance he'll tell us anything useful?" Lindham asked.

It took Barney a while to answer. "I don't know the answer to that. The woman who was killed – Smith was it? I know for sure that Sterling doesn't give two shits about her. But on the other hand, he won't care about whoever killed Smith either, so it comes down to whether he can get what he wants out of this."

"And what does he want?"

Barney looked back at Sands. "I already told your boss that. He wants to speak with her."

Lindham followed the big man's gaze, now locked on Sands again. "So if she does speak to him, he might give us something?"

"I don't know," Barney replied after a while. "He's clever, and my guess is that whatever's going on here, it's something he's had planned for some time. And that should make you very cautious. Charles Sterling is dangerous."

Sands wasn't hearing anything she didn't already know, but it kept coming back to her that in no time at all she would be face to face with him again. After all this time. She realised she still hadn't eaten and she had to fight to stay fully present in the room. The edges of perception were closing in. "You think this is a trick?" she asked, just for the sake of saying something.

Barney shrugged. "I dunno. I've seen how he works. How he twists the psychologists, the guvnor. He knows exactly what to say to spin them along, but it's all an act. You spend time with him every day, you see through the bullshit, see what he's really like."

"And what's he really like?" Lindham asked unnecessarily.

Barney turned to glare at him. "He's a fucking monster."

SIX

"You've visited prisons before, I assume?" Barney asked, but looked unimpressed when Sands nodded. "Well, we do things different here. Highmoor Prison is the highest security prison in the country, but that's not enough for the most dangerous men we keep here. We have ten maximum security pens which are buried fifteen metres underground. There's only one way in and one way out. They're totally soundproofed, airtight. You'll be searched before and after you see him. You can't touch him, or pass him anything, and the entire meeting will be recorded. I'll also be watching live, along with your colleague Detective Lindham here, and if Sterling tries *anything*, I'll be in there within thirty seconds. Do you understand?"

"Yes."

"The cell walls are made from three-centimetre-thick Perspex. I dunno why they did that, because it makes it look like he could break out at any moment, but I assure you he can't." Barney's lips curled into a slight smile. "Every bastard down there's tried that. The advantage is it gives us maximum visibility on what he's up to. He has a desk and a chair made from compressed cardboard, ineffective as weapons. His bed is a solid concrete slab, his toilet and sink are bolted to the ground with plastic pipes set in concrete and I check them myself whenever he's out of the cell on exercise."

Sands listened in silence, aware of Barney measuring how closely she was taking all this in.

"There's a slit in the Perspex where we hand him his meals. I suggest you don't go anywhere near it. Or near the walls at all. I've put a chair down there you can sit on. He'll want you to move it closer. Don't."

"OK."

"I'm gonna say this again because it's important. You don't give him *anything*, or accept *anything* from him. He might try to trick you, to grab hold of you through the slit. If that happens I won't be able to get there quick enough with the stunner. He might not look strong but he exercises every day and he knows every millimetre of that cell. And we don't know why he's so keen to get you down there. It could well be for another chance to finish you off."

"I understand," Sands said. "Is there anything else?"

Barney took a deep breath. "Plenty, but nothing you need to know about right now." He looked her in the eye. "Listen, are you sure about this? I watched him crafting those letters he writes to you. The ones he says you don't reply to." He shook his head. "You going in there, that's all he's wanted for years."

Sands looked from Barney to Lindham. She thought about the note found in Smith's cottage. There really was no choice. "I'm sure."

Barney shook his head slightly, but he accepted it. "Well, you better follow me then."

They walked back down the way they'd come, and Barney searched Sands and Lindham as they entered the higher-security part of the prison. He didn't spare Sands' modesty, running his hands closely but with professionalism all over her body. There were noises now, shouts and laughter from the cells.

Barney ignored them and took a large set of keys from his pocket. "We use both electronic and physical keys. It means anyone trying to escape would need to break two entirely separate systems."

"Has anyone ever escaped?" Sands found herself asking. She didn't need to say anything: filling silences with chatter wasn't her usual behaviour. But then this wasn't a usual situation.

"Not since 1956," Barney replied. He unlocked a steel gate that blocked the corridor ahead of them, then walked forward to a lift that looked out of place in the Victorian-era building. When he pressed the call button, the door opened at once. They got in and rode a little way down. When the door opened the air felt different. Stale.

"Don't worry," Barney said. "There's no way any of them are going to escape. You want me to walk you to Sterling's cell?"

Sands was surprised. "We're here already?" But then she considered the multiple layers of security she'd had to pass to arrive here – wasn't it enough?

"He's around that corner." He pointed down the hallway where yet another set of steel bars blocked the way, and then to a small office with a bank of monitors. "That's where I'll watch from, with your man here." He glanced again at Lindham.

"No. It's fine." Sands tried to ready herself. For the moment when she would see her father after more than twenty years.

"Have it your way." Barney pulled a radio from an alcove in the wall and handed it to her. "When you want to get out, press this button. I'll be watching you anyways."

Sands nodded. Then followed as Barney unlocked the final gate.

"Just go on through. He ain't going anywhere."

SEVEN

Sands walked down the narrow corridor. The light was dim and the air felt dry. The noise from her shoes on the hard floor was deadened by soundproofing hidden in the walls and ceiling, but she could still hear the hum of an air-conditioning unit. It couldn't have been more different from her childhood home – the large house in the New Forest – and yet she was unable to stop it entering her mind. The way she would run to her father's study to tell him something she'd learned. The hope she'd feel that he'd be in one of his good moods, when he made her feel like the most special person on earth. She stopped, leant on the wall a moment and tried to stem the stream of memories. Did she *really* have to do this?

She squeezed her eyes shut, forced her breathing back under control. Too late now to change her mind. Damn it.

She turned the corner and there was his cell. It was a bizarre sight. The narrow corridor widened to a large window-less room; inside stood a rectangular box of steel beams, fitted with clear plastic walls. It was towards the back of the space, but a walkway gave access all the way around, although there was a much larger space in front of the cell. It looked as if it had been modelled on a zoo exhibit, allowing the public to view the dangerous inhabitants kept within. Inside the cell there were two sections – it was too much to call them rooms. The smaller was fitted with a toilet and sink – completely exposed – and the larger contained a slab of concrete that rose from the floor and had been made up as a bed. Opposite was a desk with neat piles of books and papers. And sitting at the desk was a figure. Somehow it was easier to look at the furnishings than at him, but that wasn't a position she would be able to sustain.

Her father looked up and smiled. He looked the same. He hadn't changed at all in twenty-five years. She recognised his expression in an instant, and somewhere deep in her brain she felt the memory of a burst of pleasure, relief. He was in one of his good moods. All would be well.

She allowed the thought to emerge fully, flower, so that it could quickly wither and die away. And she kept looking.

Sterling was dressed in the same fluorescent green and yellow jumpsuit she'd seen the other prisoner wearing in the exercise yard. And he was reading a book with the aid of a pair of glasses perched on his nose. That was different, he'd never needed glasses before. And as she looked closer, she saw there were other differences. He seemed smaller than she remembered; his face, though instantly recognisable, was now lined, and his skin was pale, with a grey tint to it. He looked up slowly as she edged towards the cell.

For a long time neither of them spoke. When he broke the silence it was with a calm smile.

"You came. My Angel."

Sands had intended to speak only about the Jane Smith case, but already she felt her reserve buckle. The name transported her back to his study, to the hours they'd spent in there, him teaching her almost any subject she cared to learn. Her father, the great polymath. And her, his *Angel*. The sheer volume of shame she now felt for the word overwhelmed her.

Such a contrast to how proud it had made her as a child. She opened her mouth to speak, but no words came out.

"Please, sit," Charles Sterling said, pointing to the chair that stood outside his cell wall. "Pull the chair closer. Barney will have told you not to, but we can safely ignore that."

Silently, clumsily, Sands sat down, leaving the chair where it was. Even so, she was furious with herself for her racing heart, the shockwaves that crashed through her body. She couldn't understand why her body was relinquishing the upper hand.

"Poor Barney, he's a good man, but he has trust issues."

When she looked up again he'd moved his own chair to the front of the cell, as close to her as he could get. She hated herself for it, but it scared her.

"I've come for the name of the Jane Smith killer," she said, trying to gain control of the situation, and herself. She tried to fix her jaw to keep it still, but still felt the shake.

Sterling utterly ignored the statement. "It's been such a time. *Such* a long, long time," he said instead. As he watched her it felt as though he were seeing *into* her, seeing the turmoil he was causing as if it were nothing less than she deserved. Eventually, he sighed.

"You don't know how I've dreamed of this moment. And it's everything I imagined." He breathed in deeply as if inhaling her scent, though Sands didn't know if that were possible from inside his cell. Then she noticed the holes drilled through the plastic. In a way they reassured her, the depth of the tunnels through the pane showed how thick the Perspex was.

"I've followed your career of course, my Angel, but it's difficult to acquire every nuance from my present surroundings." The intonation in his voice seemed to suggest his whole-life incarceration was only a temporary state of affairs. "And I'm very much looking forward to hearing about it from you first hand."

"I've come for the name. That's all."

"Of course. Of course you have." He smiled as he acknowl-edged her words for the first time. "But all in good time, yes? You're my Angel and I haven't seen you in over twenty-five years. Surely you'll allow me a few moments?"

Finally Sands felt her body was more under control. A shadow of the former anger came back. "What makes you think you deserve a few moments?"

"Aha!" The return of something resembling spirit seemed to delight Sterling. "We come at once to the question of the purpose of prison. Is it for retribution? For deterrence? To protect the public? Or to rehabilitate those who have done wrong? This is just like old times, isn't it? In my study with its views of the woods. The log fire..." He smiled, while Sands sat silently. "Tell me, do you still go to the woods?"

When Sands didn't answer Sterling raised a hand, as if apologising for pushing his luck. "You look well," he said instead. "A little thinner than your mother, but then she did like her food." He smiled again. "Tell me, are you eating properly?"

"I'm not—"

"You're not one of those ridiculous vegans, are you? I was just reading about them in the newspaper. Clearly lacking in vitamin B12."

"That's how you knew about the chess photograph in Smith's cottage?" Sands tried again. "There was an article about it in a newspaper? You saw it and guessed it'd be on display somewhere."

"For a little while I was vegan myself. A few years back. I found it amusing that the prison had to accommodate such whims."

"How did you know about the note? Tell me, who put it there?"

He paused, giving her a look that suggested he'd heard the question but it was beneath him to answer. "But ultimately I found it unsatisfying. Too bland." He smiled again, showing his teeth. "You know me, I do enjoy a nice piece of red meat."

"I don't know…" Sands replied. "I don't know you."

He was quiet for a moment; when he smiled he still looked sad. "In some ways that's true, because I have changed. But it's also false, because no one knows me better than you." The smile brightened. "And anyway, I've tried to keep the good parts." He chuckled to himself. "And I have to keep abreast of events in the real world. You never know, I may get out to see it one day."

Sands lifted her head at this to see his eyes sparkling. "You'll never get out. You're not allowed parole."

The beatific smile didn't drop from his lips. "Any sentence can be overturned, Angel."

"Not yours. You'll die in here. For what you did."

Sterling shrugged. "That's certainly a possibility. But it's only one of an infinite number of possibilities. And no one can predict which will come to pass. Life is a chaotic process, Erica, inherently unpredictable. I wonder, do you remember our trip to Cambridge?"

He gave her a look that seemed to penetrate deep into her mind. And of course she did remember, how could she forget? How could she not think of it now he'd triggered the memory? She'd been nine years old and he'd been on a panel of the European Congress of Mathematics held at Cambridge University. And afterwards she'd sat in the audience when Edward Lorenz had given a talk about his famous paper, describing how an insect flapping its wings in South America could literally change the course of a hurricane thousands of miles away. She'd been mesmerised by the man and his ideas. And then afterwards she'd been even more star-struck when her father had casually chatted with him and invited him to tea. They'd shared hot cross buns while he talked about his work.

"As Edward put it that day," Sterling went on, "'When the

present determines the future, but the approximate present does not approximately determine the future.'"

Sterling gave her a toothy smile. It was as if he could see directly into her mind, and know exactly what she was thinking.

"I didn't come for a lesson in chaos theory." Sands pulled herself together. It was a lifetime ago. "I came for the name of whoever killed Jane Smith."

The smile faded from Sterling's lips. "You know, Angel, I would never say you've disappointed me as a daughter – because you have exceeded my expectations in so many ways. But I would, respectfully, point out that you have a rather narrow set of interests these days. Is there really nothing outside of law enforcement that amuses you?"

"What's the name? And how did he contact you?"

Sterling sighed, but he seemed amused by her persistence. As the smile faded again from his lips, he let his head fall onto one side. "And why must it be a *he*, Detective Chief Inspector Sands?"

Sands took a breath. "I don't know. Is it?"

Sterling shrugged. "You tell me. You're the officer of the law. But I suppose it's a fair assumption, given that..." – he seemed to reach inside his mind – "Ninety-six percent of murderers are male. Along with seventy-six percent of victims." He grinned. "Didn't you say that once? I've collected your quotes. You're *such* a fan of data. I wonder where you picked that up?"

"Give me his name."

He lifted an eyebrow then looked away dismissively. "I suppose it must work out quite well in the mundane drudgery of your work. Mopping up the blood after a jealous husband kills his wife and her lover. Or following the money when a business partner gets greedy. But then I don't suppose those are the cases that really interest you. Am I right?"

Sands didn't answer.

"It's the edge cases you like, isn't it? Where there's no apparent motive. Where a loving husband kills his wife and one of his children but leaves the other daughter alive? They're the real puzzles don't you think? Tell me, what did you decide to call me? When you came here?"

"What?"

"At some point in our conversation you'd have to refer to me by name. You used to call me Daddy, but you'd started trying out 'Dad' when we were... forced apart. So I'm now wondering what you've decided to call me."

"I'm not going to call you anything. You're going to tell me the name of Jane Smith's killer and then I'm never going to see you again."

He went on as if she hadn't spoken. "I rather like to think we would have gotten to Charles sooner or later. Why don't we settle on that?"

Sands glared at him and then said, "Or we could go straight to *fuck you, you piece of shit*."

Sterling tipped his head back and laughed. "Do you feel better now?" he beamed. "Now you've got that off your chest? Can we speak now?"

Sands looked away. She'd anticipated the games he'd try to play with her. It was all he'd ever done. Every statement he'd ever made, everything he'd told her as a child, all carefully considered, designed to lead her somewhere. The problem was she was years out of practice. She tried to change tack. "I assume it's one of your pen pals? Some freak wrote to you telling you about the note behind the photograph?"

Sterling's smile took on a patronising air. "I definitely warned you about assuming, Angel. It makes an..."

"There's no other way anyone could have got that information to you."

"ASS out of U and ME. An ass..." His voice faded away as he drew out the sound in a lengthy hiss. Sands tried to ignore it.

"But they must have used some sort of code, otherwise the guards would have seen it when they read your letters."

"Oh, they do look at my letters, but do they really read them?" He shrugged. "Besides. There's lots of other ways of getting information in and out, even in a place like this. Information is like the damp." He glanced around at the walls beyond his Perspex prison, then shuddered. "It seeps in."

Sands ignored him, and kept up her questions. "Most of the letters you receive are too technical for the guards to understand. That's how you learned his name."

"Or her," Sterling said quietly.

"Cut the crap. We both know it's a man," Sands responded.

Sterling bit his lip to prevent himself from smiling too much and held out his hands in a shrug.

"Tell me," Sands demanded. "That's why you called me here. You got what you wanted, so just tell me."

Sterling was quiet for a moment, then suddenly stood up. "You're right. You're here, and that is what I wanted. What I've wanted for a very long time. So perhaps you'd like to take a look at one of my letters – as you call them. Perhaps I'll even give you the right one?" His tongue touched the middle of his upper lip as he smiled at the idea, then he walked to his desk and extracted a few sheets of paper from a neat pile. He took them to a rectangular gap in the Perspex, about half a metre from the ground. It was larger than Sands had anticipated, and even though there was no way Sterling himself could fit through, she remembered Barney Atkinson's warning. Sterling squatted comfortably down and held the papers so that one corner poked beyond the Perspex. Sands considered ignoring it, but there was a chance this was the game – he might be offering the actual letter with the details of Smith's killer and betting she wouldn't take it after Atkinson's warnings. She watched him, trying to weigh up the correct move, before standing up and moving towards the slot.

She had to bend down so that they were level with one another with just the Perspex between them. It was strange, being so physically close to this man after so long, but she successfully buried the thought, concentrating instead on the danger. Carefully she reached out her hand to take the paper, seeing how he pulled his own hand back very slightly as she did so. It meant she would have to put her hand a little way into the slot. Into his cell. She cautioned herself. He received his meals and post through this slot, every day. He was familiar with it. Intimately. And though she was sure this was a game, she didn't know which one. She pulled her hand back.

"I can't reach," she said, watching carefully. She ignored his eyes. He'd once taught her how to watch magicians practising sleight-of-hand. Study the muscles of their arms. Anatomy doesn't lie, not like the eyes. For a moment he held the paper a little closer to her and she snatched at it, catching it and pulling it from his hands. She rolled back on her heels, well away from the slot.

"Careful," he chuckled. "You'll tear it."

She retreated to her chair and studied the letter, barely hearing his words.

"There's no need to be so nervous, Angel," he said. "Didn't the good Director McDonald explain? I'm no longer a danger to anyone."

"Atkinson told me otherwise."

He laughed. "Ah, *Barney*. He's like a big blond bear, isn't he? Strictly between the two of us, I think he has something against me."

Sands ignored him and studied the papers. They appeared to contain a summary of a mathematical paper. She read the title: *Higher-dimensional Gray Hermitian manifolds*. It meant little to her. She scanned the equations that had been written there.

"Is this it?" She looked up. "Is this from the man who killed Jane Smith?"

He shrugged again. "It seems highly unlikely, but in an infinite universe I suppose it's possible."

Sands studied it again, trying to make sense of the equations while he went on. "As I recall, the author simply wants to submit his paper to the Society of Applied Mathematics, but has asked me to correct it for him first. It's a service I like to offer."

Sands frowned, unable to decide whether her father's studied casualness was a bluff.

"Although to be honest with you, Angel, I doubt even *I* can pull this one around. Take a look at the theorem."

She was still trying to second guess him.

"Go on. There's a most obvious error at the very root of the piece."

Reluctantly, Sands did what he said.

The aim of this paper is to classify compact, Riemannian, Hermitian conformally Kähler manifolds (M, g, J) whose Ricci tensor ϱ is J-invariant and satisfies the condition that $\varrho - (2\tau/(dim\ M + 2))g$ is a tensor, where...

She stopped.

"Well? Don't tell me you're a little rusty?"

Sands ignored him and turned the paper over. "Alexander Borokov, is that who we're looking for?"

"You could certainly check him out. I believe he lives in Moscow. Perhaps you should alert Interpol?"

Sands shook her head, suddenly certain she'd fallen for a double bluff. This wasn't the paper. She dropped it on the floor. "I didn't come here to play your games. I'm going to ask you one more time, and if you don't tell me I'm going to walk away and you'll never see me again. What's more, I'll have you charged with wasting police time and I'll negotiate with the CPS and the prison to only drop those charges if they agree to have your newspapers taken away from you and remove any other privileges you've managed to con for yourself. So no more games. Who killed Jane Smith, and how do you know about them?"

Sterling sat back on his chair, apparently appreciating the threat wasn't entirely empty. "And if I do tell you? What then? Will you promise to visit me more often?"

When Sands hesitated, Sterling pounced. "Ah! I thought not. So *if* I tell you, I'll never see you again, and if I don't tell you..." – he sighed – "I'll never see you again. You see the problem, Angel? Because the thing is, I'd so *like* to see you again. I'd like for us to get to know each other. That's what I want. Is that so wrong for a father and a daughter?"

"We're not a father and a daughter."

"You're right of course. What we had was much deeper than that. But with the passing of time our relationship has receded somewhat, so father and daughter *is* perhaps the best descriptor. At least for now."

Sands gritted her teeth. "Last chance, Sterling."

"Charles."

He said nothing more, looked her full in the eyes and didn't move.

She waited almost a full minute, her eyes locked onto his, before suddenly getting up. "OK. Here's what I think is happening. I think you don't know. Somehow you got some garbled message about chess, but that's all you've got. You won't give me his name because you don't know it. If you did know, you'd be desperate to trade it for more books or access to whatever it is you do in here while you rot your sad life away." Sands took one last look at him before turning on her heel and beginning to walk away. She got halfway down the corridor before his voice called out.

"You're wrong, Angel."

He sounded almost beatific. But she ignored him, forcing her legs to keep moving. She'd almost reached the bend in the corridor before he spoke again.

"I'll give you something."

She stopped, but didn't turn.

"I'll give you a date. The date he'll kill again. And it's soon. Whoever they are they're in a hurry."

Sands wished she didn't have to turn around, but she needed to see his face. "What date?"

He grinned. Then beckoned for her to come closer.

"What date?"

"Come here, Angel. Walls have ears."

Sands ran a hand through her hair then forced it back to her side. She sighed, then walked a few steps closer. "This is as close as I'm getting."

"OK." Sterling smiled and nearly closed his eyes. He looked sickeningly self-satisfied. When he spoke again, almost no sound came out. He mouthed the words, "It's this Friday."

The way he said it, as well as how soon it was, unsettled Sands, but she buried the feeling, trying to see past whatever trick he was pulling now. "What good is a date? What does it prove?"

"It will prove to you that I know."

"How? There's an average of two murders per day in England and Wales. You could have picked any day and claimed this killer was responsible."

"Oh no." Sterling lifted his chin, as if bathing his face in sunlight. "Oh no, there'll be no confusion. Not with this boy."

The unsettled feeling came back. The sense that she was a long way from knowing what game he was playing. "Bullshit. Give me his name. Tell me where to find him. Then I'll come back to see you. When we arrest him. I'll come back to say thank you. Otherwise, this is over. I'm never coming back.

That's my offer, and it's the only one you're going to get. But you need to tell me right now."

Sands stared at him, waiting to see his reaction, but there was none, at least nothing she could engage with. He simply lowered his head and closed his eyes, his hands laid flat on his knees. After a while she realised this was some sort of meditation, or at least the pretence of it.

"I thought not," she said to him. "Well, you lose, *Dad*. Whatever bullshit game you're trying to play here. You lose. And if you're not even going to look at me as I walk away, well that's your loss again, because this is it. The last time you ever lay eyes on me." She was furious at how calm he remained. And then she turned away.

Behind her, Charles Sterling sat perfectly still.

EIGHT

It took a while for Sands to pass through the multiple layers of security and exit the prison, collecting Lindham on the way. He had watched the encounter on Barney's monitor, so Sands was spared from recounting the details. She chose to stay silent as she drove them back towards Poole. Eventually, Lindham broke the quiet. "Do you think anything's going to happen on Friday?"

She looked at him for a while, wondering how to answer. "I don't know," she said eventually. "There's a high probability of a murder somewhere. I think it's a lot less likely we'll see one related to Jane Smith."

"Sure." Lindham nodded. "Listen, ma'am..." His face broke into an awkward half-smile. "I just wanted to say, I really appreciate that you gave it a go. And..." – he winced a little – "And if you wanted to take over the case, I wouldn't object. He's your father, and—"

"What?" Sands interrupted him so sharply he didn't seem to know what to say. "I don't know where you got that impression from. I want nothing to do with it." She stared at him.

"OK. Sure. I just wanted to..." Lindham fell back into silence.

Sands took a moment to make sense of things. "No," she said a moment later. "It's your case. You're going to need to go through the letters he's received because if he has been in communication with the killer, that's how he'll have done it. And I'll get you more manpower because there'll be a ton of mail to go through. But I don't want to be involved."

"Sure." Lindham nodded. "Thank you. And for what it's worth, ma'am, I'm sorry for what you had to go through. Growing up with that..." – he failed to find a suitable word – "And everything he put you through. It must have been..." He raised his hands in defeat. "Christ, it must have been... rough."

Sands didn't reply but turned to look at him. His hands were back in his lap, an expression she assumed was sympathy on his face. "Don't mention it." She looked away, but Lindham went on. "And if we've had our differences over the years, well, I just didn't know, and I'm sorry."

Sands watched the road for a moment, trying to clarify which emotion his words were evoking in her, but giving up. "Seriously. Don't mention it again. That's an order."

Sands worked late at the station, trying to erase the events of the day from her mind, but eventually she had no choice but to return home. She had no appetite, and just after 1 a.m. she tried to sleep, but whenever she closed her eyes her father's prison cell appeared in her mind. Would he be asleep now on his concrete plinth? Or wide awake and thinking, like her? Like it or not, she realised she'd updated her knowledge of the man and would have to spend time incorporating what she now knew – where he now existed, the way he looked and how he'd changed from her childhood memories. There was no point pretending sleep would come so she got up and paced the quiet of her flat, eventually staring out of the window onto the quiet calm of the harbour. But the view wasn't as comforting as it usually was and she soon moved away.

It took her a while, but eventually she realised where she was being drawn to.

She picked out an envelope from her bedside drawer and carefully opened it, removing an old photograph. It showed her mother – about the same age as Sands was now –with two young, smiling girls. Sands didn't know who'd taken the image but she liked to think it wasn't her father, that they weren't smiling for him. Breathing in deeply she studied her family, ignoring herself and concentrating instead on her mother and sister. As it so often did, her mind returned to the last time she'd seen them alive. The argument that had flared up with Claire over nothing more than a book her younger sister had borrowed and failed to replace on Erica's shelf, then her mother telling her they had to go. No time to tell her sister that she loved her, would always love her, whatever happened. And then in the car, her mother still angry about the argument, neither of them talking much.

There had been a few minutes at the door of her friend's house, the two mothers chatting. Then a final hug goodbye. And then her mum had driven home, never suspecting that her husband would choose that night to end her life, to slice open her neck and watch her bleeding to death before going upstairs to rape and strangle poor Claire.

The rest of the week passed slowly. Lindham ordered his officers to concentrate on the letters that had been sent to Sterling over the previous two years. But when three large document boxes of them arrived from the prison Sands assigned the rest of the team too.

It seemed Sterling had made a full-time job out of initiating and continuing correspondences with almost anyone who was willing to do so. Sands picked through a few at random, confirming in her mind just how technical and complex some of them were, and how difficult the task to search through them would be, but she still refused to get involved personally.

Instead, Sands applied herself to another case regarding a fatal stabbing just outside a Bournemouth town centre night-club. There was no difficulty in identifying the culprit, a man named Billy Kato, but the case revolved on whether he ought to face a murder or a manslaughter charge. The victim was a male in his early twenties named Ryan Spencer. Dozens of witnesses had seen Spencer rowing with Kato inside a crowded pub. And it was known that Kato was currently dating Spencer's former girlfriend. CCTV footage then showed the pair continuing the spat outside the pub, then in a nearby kebab shop, and finally coming to blows outside a nightclub. At this point the footage wasn't clear enough to see exactly what happened, but a few moments later Spencer fell to the ground. Passers-by soon realised he'd been stabbed and called for an ambulance but he died before it arrived. Kato fled the scene but was apprehended in his flat the next morning. The difficulty lay in the fact that Spencer had been carrying the knife which had killed him.

The working assumption was that they would push for a murder charge, but there was doubt over whether this could be made to stick. To progress the file to the Crown Prosecution Service, Sands had to review dozens of witness statements about the character of the two men, and rewatch hours of footage. Previously unnoticed within the witness statements had been a claim that Kato – on two separate occasions – had also carried a concealed knife on nights out. This opened up the possibility that Kato himself might have been carrying a concealed weapon on the night of the killing, even if it hadn't been used to fatally stab Spencer. By Thursday afternoon Sands had largely wrapped it up: the new evidence was enough to request the CPS to seek a murder conviction. Sands submitted the file and celebrated by sitting back in her chair and stretching her arms over her head. Then she got up.

Outside her tiny office most of the MID officers – detectives and other staff – were still working on the Sterling letters. On a whim she walked over to one of them, a detective named Luke Golding who'd joined the team permanently after shadowing her on a case in which she'd been shot twice and blown up once. He'd saved her life and yet she'd been careful to treat him no differently to anyone else on the team. He seemed to understand her reasons.

"How's it going?"

Golding looked up, apparently surprised by the interruption. "Oh, you know. Getting there." He flashed her a suppressed smile. Sands looked at what he was reading, then frowned. "Kind of getting there," Golding qualified. "We've tried to separate them into categories, but even that's a challenge."

"What are the categories?"

He leaned back in his chair and stretched out. "You've got the fan-mail stuff. There's a lot of that, including a couple of declarations of undying love." Golding's eyebrows went up at this. "Then there's the research stuff – interview requests by people wanting to write books or make films about what he did, people who want to study him. Finally, the super-weird maths stuff." Golding shrugged. "I don't get what everyone sees in him."

"During the trial the media created a narrative that he was charming. He's used it to try and stay relevant. How many of the last category?"

"The maths stuff?"

Sands nodded.

"At least a hundred. Most of it goes back and forth. He says what he thinks, and they come back with more questions. The problem is it all came from the prison all mixed in together."

She considered this. It suggested any attempt to monitor the mail had been superficial at best.

"Lindham told us about your meeting with him," Golding said. "He doesn't sound too charming to me." He shook his head thoughtfully.

"No. He's not. And you've found nothing? In any of the letters? Nothing that could relate to Jane Smith? About chess or animals?"

He hesitated. "No, but..."

"But what?"

"We're doing our best to look through it, but half of it's so damn crazy it makes no sense. The other half is so damn technical we've no idea what it means. We're just looking for references to Friday 10th November, or any mention of Jane Smith. And there's nothing."

Sands glanced at the clock up on the wall showing it was already past 6 p.m. The date Sterling had given them for the next murder was in just six hours' time. She nodded, her unsettled feeling in no way dispelled by what she was hearing. "It's probably bullshit anyway," she replied. "This whole thing is most likely just his way of wasting our time." She wasn't sure if she was trying to reassure Golding or herself. He seemed to understand this.

"That's what Lindham says," he grimaced. "Best hope he's right, I guess."

She could sense it, and she knew he could too. The anticipation that something bad was about to happen. It had been there all week, and it was becoming palpable.

NINE

When she arrived the next day just before seven, Sands was surprised to see she wasn't the first one in the office. John Lindham was already at his desk, speaking on the phone. She waited until he was done and then caught his eye, but he shook his head.

"That was McDonald from the prison. They've been trying all week to get Sterling to say more about what's supposed to happen today. But he's refusing to tell them anything."

"He's enjoying himself. This is his idea of fun."

Lindham nodded.

"Anything come in so far?"

"Nope. I've got the area control room to patch in any reports of suspicious deaths from across the whole country. The chances are there'll be something. We'll just have to work out if it's connected or not."

"Sure." Sands nodded. She went to her office and closed the door.

The day crawled by. The team checking the letters still hadn't managed to read them all, let alone analyse them in any meaningful way, but at least they were able to lose themselves in the work. For most of the morning Sands tried to distract herself, but there was little for her to do, and around lunchtime her resolve finally cracked and she joined the effort. But with so many pages of correspondence to read, and so little time, it was hopeless. Whenever the phone rang she couldn't shake the feeling it would bring news of a murder they'd been given the opportunity to prevent but had failed to do so.

Finally at around 3 p.m. a report did come in. A death in a Southampton shopping centre. On the surface it didn't appear suspicious, just a routine heart attack, but Sands ordered two of her detectives to attend anyway and paced anxiously until one of them called to say the man hadn't died after all but had been resuscitated by paramedics. Sands ordered them to take witness statements anyway from everyone they could find, in case they subsequently identified anything out of the ordinary. But it was overkill, and she knew it. By then it was nearly seven o'clock; the building was emptying around the murder unit but still nothing had happened. She checked with the area control room again. Still nothing.

"It looks like you were right, ma'am." Lindham's voice surprised her a couple of hours later as she sat at her desk. Grey-black stubble showed on his face and there were dark lines under his eyes. "We've been through all the letters, and there's nothing. No reference to any murders except the ones Sterling committed himself – he's proud of them. Chess *is* mentioned several times – Sterling appears to have several games ongoing with different people, including a Russian former grand master – but there's nothing that seems relevant. None of the letters has anything about Jane Smith, and no reference at all to Friday 10th November." Lindham gave a smile of grim satisfaction. "Looks like Sterling was gambling there'd be a murder some-where he could claim to have prior knowledge of." He checked his watch. "But it hasn't worked out for him."

Sands nodded as she read the time too. 11:20 p.m.

"I've sent the guys home. It's been a long week."

She nodded again but felt that subtle and familiar wrench inside. Couldn't they have stayed? Shouldn't they have stayed? Should she, as the senior officer in charge of the MID, have ordered them to stay, to work the same absurd hours she put in? But she knew they couldn't. They had families, partners, other priorities in their lives, and already worked many more hours than most other jobs. She looked up suddenly at Lindham, her deputy, ten years older than her. She saw again how exhausted he looked, and this time she remembered his two boys following him out of the house on their way to school. What were their names? She was sure he'd told her once.

"You should get off as well." Her voice felt awkward as she spoke, the sentiment unnatural. "Try and see your family for a while tomorrow, before you come in." She tried to force her face into an expression of apology for all the working hours of the profession they'd chosen.

"Sure. I'll do that." He gave her a half-smile. Maybe he seemed to understand. "Thanks, ma'am."

Sands nodded.

Soon it was only her left. She checked again with the area control room, but still no murders had been reported. She decided she would stay until midnight and then head home, although the thought of her empty flat was unappealing and she doubted she'd sleep. Under the circumstances there was little point not grabbing another coffee. She went out into the open-plan part of the office, where a voice surprised her.

"You still here?"

Sands spun around to find she wasn't alone after all. Luke Golding was still sat at his desk, shirt sleeves rolled up, his jacket on the chair behind him.

"Yes."

"I was just finishing up." He stretched out his arms,

yawned. "Sort of. Just don't think I can quite relax until midnight strikes, you know what I mean?"

She was silent for a moment, watching him. It was strange; in the months since he'd joined the department she couldn't remember a time when they'd been alone together. Yet they had a history. Almost. They had seemed to grow close when he was shadowing her. And when they first met, and she hadn't known he was a police officer, she'd propositioned him. Only to be turned down. She felt herself looking into his blue eyes now, reliving that moment.

"Hey, it's a bit late for coffee don't you think?" He indicated the cup in her hand. "You don't fancy going for a real drink?" His face was neutral, the eyes smiling. He was leaning back on the chair now, only its rear legs on the ground. "It beats waiting around here hoping the phone doesn't ring with news of a murder."

She blinked in surprise at the idea, but then considered. What was the harm? There was nothing more they could do on the case. And no one to witness the two of them leaving together, not that that mattered. Not that it meant anything.

"Sure." As she spoke, she nearly changed her mind. What was she doing? What even was this? Two colleagues, and nothing more? Or something else. She hesitated as he let the chair drop back on four legs and stood up.

"But—"

"But what?"

"It's nearly midnight," was all she said. "There won't be much open." She could see the endless hours of nightclub CCTV footage she'd been watching, packed full of drunk students from the town's two universities. That was the last place she wanted to be. But he smiled easily.

"Don't worry. I know a good place."

TEN

They walked towards the town centre but stopped before they got there and turned into an alleyway she'd never noticed before. Halfway along he led her down a set of steps into an underground bar. It was just the right balance between busy but not packed, the clientele older than the drunk students that mobbed most of the other nightspots.

"I didn't know this place existed," Sands said when they had their drinks.

"Best keep it that way, huh?" Golding smiled easily again. He had a broad face. The kind of handsome of a man who knew he was good looking but didn't make a big deal of it. Like Lindham he was unshaven after the long hours in the office, but unlike him his eyes shone bright and blue. "Kinda changes the atmosphere of a place when it's filled with cops."

Sands smiled, then automatically checked her watch.

"You want to phone control again? Make sure nothing's happened?"

She shook her head, then reached into her bag and pulled out a portable police radio. "We'll hear if there's anything." She put the radio on the table between them. For a few moments they both watched it without speaking.

"Kind of a weird situation." Golding broke the silence. "Like a morbid New Year's Eve."

Sands frowned. "Huh? How do you mean?"

"Here we are, doing a big countdown to midnight. Hoping we can get there without hearing that someone's been killed." He grimaced, and she wasn't sure how to respond. She couldn't tell if he was making light of the situation. "How long have we got anyway?"

She checked her watch again. "Seven minutes."

"Think we're going to make it?" When he glanced around the room it became clearer to her what he was doing. He was watching the other drinkers, as if at any moment they might start beating each other to death. And now Sands couldn't help smiling. His attitude reminded her of when the two of them had first met. It was in an art gallery, a place she'd gone simply to seek some sort of refuge at a vulnerable time. And he'd been there helping the artist to promote her work. And even though she'd turned out to be his sister, all he'd done was poke fun at the quality of her work, to try and cheer Sands up or distract her. At the time it had felt like the beginning of something. Or perhaps it hadn't. After all, the something in question was not Sands' strongest suit. The evening had ended when he'd driven her home and she'd invited him inside in the clumsiest way imaginable. He'd turned her down and the next day she'd discovered he was not only a detective, but had been assigned to shadow her. She ran a finger along her eyebrow at the memory, then looked away just as her radio crackled into life, reporting a fight outside a nightclub.

Although Sands had never become involved with anyone she worked with, it was commonplace. Indeed, she remembered the rumours that Golding was currently seeing a PC from traffic. She stopped her train of thought for a moment to register that she actually knew about this, when normally she paid no attention at all to the gossip of the department. An image formed of the woman in question, A pretty, blonde girl, younger than Golding.

"How's it going with Debra Webb?" she asked suddenly, mostly to break the silence, but also because she suddenly wanted to know. Golding's face changed, obviously surprised at the question.

"Debbie?" He frowned. "That... ended. A while back."

"Oh," Sands said. Then she frowned too, not sure whether she ought to say something more. "I'm sorry."

"It's OK. *I'm* not." He smiled again.

She considered this. Somewhere she registered that the news pleased her. She began to relax again.

"How'd you hear about Debbie?" he asked. He seemed amused.

Sands considered where she'd picked up the news. It had been two junior detectives, giggling about it in the small kitchen that served their floor. She shrugged. "I just thought I heard it somewhere. That you and she were..."

"No, no. I mean, we went out a few times. But that was all."

"Oh. OK."

They fell silent.

"It's not that I'm against seeing anyone in the force, though. It's difficult with the hours and the weekend working, you know, to make it work with anyone on the outside."

"Yes," Sands agreed. "I guess so."

"Are you seeing anyone? I mean, if that's a question I can ask my boss." He pulled a face.

Sands shook her head, trying to both indicate that it was OK to ask, and that she wasn't. He seemed to understand.

"The long hours?"

"Something like that."

Golding took a swig from his beer. "Shall we do a countdown?"

"I'm sorry?"

"Like on New Year's Eve? We're almost there." He angled his wrist so they could both see the seconds slipping away on his watch.

"Here we go. Ten, nine, eight..." He completed the countdown quietly and when the watch read midnight and absolutely nothing had happened, he picked up the radio and called the control room. Nothing. Despite the absurdity of the situation, Sands felt herself relax even more.

"No murders reported anywhere on Friday 10th November. It looks like Charles Sterling got it wrong this time." He held out his bottle again and she tapped hers against it. "Wasn't he pulling some sort of trick the night we met?"

Sands was surprised that he remembered. It was a long time ago. "Yes. It was right at the beginning of the pandemic. He tricked the prison doctors into thinking he had Covid."

"They ever find out how he did it?"

"He was on medication for a couple of other things. He pretended to take his tablets but actually stored them up. Then he took them all at once. They were treating anything unusual as likely to be Covid at the time."

"They find out *why* he did it?"

Sands shook her head. "Not really. Other than to force me to see him, I guess. He's tried a few times over the years."

He considered this, watching her closely. Then he took another swig from his beer. "Well at least you don't have to see him again now."

When Golding lowered the bottle it was empty, and he glanced at hers, which only had a little left. "Say, I actually wasn't kidding when I said I wouldn't sleep. Every time I close my eyes I just see those damn letters. You fancy another?"

Sands considered. She'd allowed herself the thought of one

drink before heading back to her empty flat. But now she was here she found herself enjoying it. The thought of staying longer with Golding made her feel noticeably better. "I do."

She watched him push his way confidently through the crowd and attract the attention of the girl behind the bar. She noticed the way the girl looked at him, obviously making eyes at him in the hope he might notice how pretty she was. But then he turned around and looked back at Sands and for a moment she let a sense of hope bloom within her. Now that the unit was aware of who her father was and what he'd done, maybe it didn't matter if there was something else for them to gossip about. Maybe it would even help? She was still pondering this thought when he came back with two more beers along with two shot glasses.

"What's that?"

"Tequila." He looked mock-innocent, playful again. "After all, we're celebrating." He walked back to the bar, then returned with a saltshaker and some chunks of lemon on a plate.

"What are we celebrating?" Sands asked.

"The future! We've solved a murder before it's happened. If we can't celebrate that I don't know the point of being in the force." He licked his hand and poured salt on it, threw the shot of tequila down his neck and finished by sucking on the lemon. He grimaced again. "Come on. Your turn, ma'am."

"Stop calling me that," Sands said a couple of hours later as they stumbled together towards the lobby of her apartment building. The bar had closed at 1:30 and they'd been among the last to leave.

"What?"

"Ma'am."

"Why not? Are you promoting me?"

"No, but I might fire you if you don't stop." She typed in the code to enter the building. But as the lock buzzed, she paused. Suddenly, this seemed serious. "You know, last time we were here you turned me down."

He stopped, his mouth open, considering what to say. "I was being honourable." He watched her closely. "It doesn't mean I didn't want to."

She looked at him, wondering if Golding coming upstairs was a good idea or not. But by then she was too drunk to really care.

ELEVEN

Sands woke to see Golding's broad back curving away from her in her bed. She blinked a few times, surprised at the sight, but then the events of the night filtered into her mind. Her normal response to such eventualities was to dismiss the memory at once, albeit with a sense of something approaching shame. She knew she was attractive to men without needing to try very hard, and from time to time she serviced her needs. But rarely with the same person twice, and always with that sense of self-reproach, disquiet. When she looked for those feelings this time, she couldn't find them. And she wasn't sure why.

She let her mind wander over her recent sexual history. She felt lucky to live in a time of dating apps, when it was relatively easy to negotiate liaisons with like-minded people. And yet she still used a false name, and gave false addresses in different towns. Eventually, unable to figure it out, she got up and walked to the shower.

When she finished, the bed was empty, Golding's clothes nowhere to be seen. She felt something else at seeing this, and again it wasn't clear what. Whatever it was, it disappeared the moment she walked in the kitchen.

"Lindham wanted us in early today. He wants to go over the Smith murder right from the beginning." He held out a coffee for her. "He thinks there's something we've missed, what with the distraction of the letters." Sands still hadn't taken the drink. "Here. I made you this."

"Thank you."

As he passed it over, their fingers touched and last night came into clear focus.

"Hey, if you wanted to keep this quiet at the station, I'd understand."

She thought a moment. "And if I didn't?"

"Well, I guess I'd understand that as well."

"OK." Sands smiled a little and took a sip of her coffee. "I have to walk in today. I left my car at the station."

"Me too. But I should go home first and change. You mind if I'm ten minutes late?"

"You better not be about to call me 'ma'am'."

He grinned.

When she arrived the atmosphere matched Sands' upbeat mood. Even though most of the detectives had been sceptical whether Sterling really did have advance knowledge of a murder, the fact that the deadline had passed still felt like a victory. When Golding arrived, fifteen minutes after Sands, the room was nearly full, but no one seemed to notice anything different about them, and they went about their work without any interaction between them. Only Lindham was yet to arrive, taking advantage of the late start Sands had promised him.

Sands still felt some residual anxiety, even after she checked with the control room whether any murders had been reported overnight. She pulled out a case that was enough of a puzzle to feel like a treat. She had a reputation of being a good person to turn to for help in difficult cases. In this one, a man's naked body had been pulled out of the water by a fishing boat off the coast near Dover. He was in his late forties or early fifties, well built, with a full beard. According to the pathologist it was possible he'd been strangled before drowning, although the marks around his neck were inconclusive and could have been caused by getting caught up in the nets. Neither the man's DNA nor fingerprints appeared on any databases they had access to, and a detailed search for his identity through dental records had proved fruitless. She was exploring the theories that had been posited – that the man had fallen or jumped from a cross-Channel ferry or been thrown off a passing container ship. Almost all scenarios meant it was pointless to investigate, since no action would need to be taken. But then Golding dropped another coffee on her desk. He'd made a round for most of the officers in the room, something she'd never noticed him doing before.

"Here you go, ma'am," he said, putting just the slightest intonation into the title.

"How's it going with Lindham?" She was alert at once, her mind back on the Smith case.

Golding shook his head. "He's not in yet." He gave her a look and moved away, taking a sip from his own drink. But Sands ignored hers. Suddenly she sensed that something wasn't right.

She got up and walked over to Lindham's desk. Still empty. She flicked open a heavily annotated count of the Sterling letters.

"Has anyone heard from Lindham this morning?" she called out suddenly.

All the officers looked up, but no one had. It wasn't unusual for someone to come in late, especially after a long day. Only Golding kept his eyes on Sands as she used Lindham's desk phone to call his mobile. It went to voicemail. Golding got up from his desk and walked over. "What is it?" He sounded concerned.

"I don't know." Sands realised she suddenly felt cold. And hot. Sweat was prickling on her back. "Come with me."

The trip to Lindham's house only took five minutes, but neither of them spoke on the way. Lindham's car was in the driveway along with his wife's people carrier. Sands exchanged a look with Golding, who seemed to share her sense of foreboding. They got out and approached the front door. Sands pressed the bell, hearing it ring inside, but no one answered. She crouched down and looked through the letterbox, then called out Lindham's name. Still there was only silence.

"Check the windows. I'll go round the back."

She left him and went around the side of the house where an unlocked gate gave her access into the back garden. There was a barbeque area on some raised decking; a child's slide was built into the wood to deposit riders onto the lawn. It looked recently built, made for parties. Sands' mouth was dry – she'd never been there. She turned and tried the kitchen door, feeling positively sick as it swung open. A quick inspection showed the lock had been forced, breaking through the frame. She called out for Golding to join her as she pulled a pair of gloves from her pocket. She went inside. As soon as she did, she recognised the smell.

Golding joined her as she took in the kitchen. There was nothing out of place, but clearly no one had eaten breakfast. Sands peered into the lounge, which also looked normal.

"Upstairs," she said. Her voice was hoarse.

She led the way, but hesitated at the entrance to the master bedroom. She knew what she was going to find and didn't want to confirm it.

The room almost looked normal. The bodies of John Lindham and his wife lay on the bed, partly covered by a duvet, and if it hadn't been for the blood-soaked pillows through which they'd been shot, they might not even have looked dead. Except when Sands stepped into the room and checked behind her, she saw the white-painted wall was horribly smeared with blood. At first it looked accidental, as if the victims or perhaps the killer had fallen against it, but then she made out shapes. A triangle – no, a second line showed it was meant to be a pyramid, and there was a number too. 1158. Suddenly the taste of tequila shot through Sands' body and she had to cover her mouth to prevent herself from throwing up. Somehow she swallowed it back down. It wasn't a number. It was a time.

11:58

Golding's face was ash grey.

"The kids. He's got two boys." Sands found she was crying as she pushed past him. She looked at the other doors that led off the upstairs landing. The next door along had the word "Danny" stencilled on the outside.

His broken little body was half-in and half-out of the bed. The bare torso white and skinny from loss of blood. Another pillow here had exploded and a gory mess of red-soaked feathers was stuck to the covers, the wall and the floor. More symbols had been crudely daubed on the wall – an eye, another pyramid. Sands squeezed her eyes shut. The second child. She had to see.

John Lindham's younger son had been called Elliot, Sands learned, from the sky-blue letters on his bedroom door. When she opened it she saw he was a fan of Everton Football Club. Or had been. He was lying face-down on the carpet, which was soaked dark with blood around where his head had fallen. When she looked more closely only half his head was there, his face was simply missing, his blond fringe giving way to a gory red and grey mulch where the bullet had ripped off the front of his skull. The sight was too much for Sands' stomach and she felt the sick explode upwards and out of her mouth. And after that, she somehow felt Golding's hands pulling her outside and back into the street.

TWELVE

"Is there any way this could be a coincidence?" Chief Superintendent Yorke paced up and down the meeting room while Sands sat in a daze, almost entirely unaware of the other officers present. A man's voice answered.

"Time of death matches all four bodies, puts them killed between 11 p.m. and 2 a.m. this morning. So the time written in blood is a reference to the murders taking place on Friday 10th November. And if that's the case, it seems almost impossible it could be a coincidence. It happened when Sterling warned us it was going to happen."

"He didn't warn *us*. He warned *me*," Sands interrupted quietly.

"There's no benefit in blaming yourself, Erica." Yorke broke the silence that had descended. "He didn't actually warn anybody. He gave an entirely useless tip that no one could have followed."

But Sands didn't hear him. The only image her brain would allow her was the sight of little Elliot, his body twisted where he had fallen, half his head blown off.

The previous hours had passed in a sort of hell-like dream.

She didn't remember leaving the house, only being outside where Golding had called for back-up. And then they had waited for what seemed like forever, in a stunned, awful silence. Finally a patrol car arrived, and then the first of their colleagues from the murder unit. But there was none of the usual order and routine that helped to normalise working at the scene of a violent death. For almost everyone attending, this crime was immensely personal, and the waves of shock, horror and disgust seemed to reverberate around everyone who came near the scene. With the victims of the attack so well known to all of them, there was confusion over which team or individuals were even eligible to initiate an investigation. Sands herself had been in no state to give instructions. It was nearly midday before Yorke ordered that a neighbouring murder unit should be summoned, at least to handle the initial scene-of-crime work. Then another hour passed before they arrived, the street by then evacuated and sealed off. Sands had sat in the back of a police car, not wanting to speak to anyone, but dumbly answering whatever questions were sent her way.

"He went home just before midnight," she said suddenly. To some extent she had recovered the capacity to operate, but it felt like she was doing so in a weird vacuum. "If whoever killed him wanted to do it on the Friday, they must have been waiting outside for him to get home. We should check if any of the neighbours noticed anyone hanging about. Anyone out of place."

"That's a good thought," Yorke agreed, but he looked around, as if unsure who to direct an order to. The other detective – Jameson, or something like that, Sands remembered now – spoke again.

"Look, this isn't my place, but I'm not sure DCI Sands should even be in the room at this point," he said. "I understand she's familiar with the background of what's happened here, but

I can't see any reason to exclude anybody on Lindham's team as potential suspects. And that includes DCI Sands."

"That's ridiculous," Yorke snapped. "There's no one here who could do something like—"

"I disagree." It was Commander Black who said this, his first words after sitting and listening for some time. They were followed by a silence. Then Black leaned forwards in his chair. "We're going to have to make some very difficult and very fast decisions on how to progress this case. Frankly I see a police department in shock, and while that's understandable, we simply cannot remain paralysed like this."

More silence. No one was prepared to disagree. And what he said was clearly true.

"I think the decision to ask DCI Jameson here to assist was the correct one. But I think we should go further and appoint him the lead investigator going forward. There's simply no way Lindham's own unit can look into what's happened here. Particularly if there is any chance, however small, that his officers could end up suspects. DCI Jameson, are you prepared to take this case on?"

All eyes turned to the outsider. He looked a serious and competent officer, older than Sands, experienced. "Yes sir."

"Good. I suggest you bring in a core team from your department, we'll discuss junior staffing later."

Jameson nodded. Commander Black drew in a deep breath. "Next. There's already enormous media interest in what's happened here today, and it's only going to get more intense. We need to work with that in mind. I want as much as possible kept out of the newspapers. Essential details only, and no one speaks to the press without my express permission. Are we all agreed on that?"

Another murmur of assent.

"Good. And I think the next step is to let DCI Sands get some rest."

Sands turned quickly to face him. "I need to stay. I need to be a part of this."

"No." He held up his hand. "No, you don't. That isn't helpful and this isn't a request." He glanced around. "Can somebody arrange for her to be taken home?" When another officer got up to follow his orders, Black looked at Sands. "You should stay there until you hear otherwise. I imagine Jameson or one of his colleagues will be wanting to speak with you very soon."

Sands blinked hard but understood there was no getting out of this. Moreover she recognised she needed a rest. She nodded and stumbled to her feet, feeling all eyes on her. She waited at her desk, trying to keep her mind blank until a female officer approached her a little nervously. "Hello, ma'am. I'm PC Deborah Watts, I've been asked to drive you home."

Sands stared at the woman through bleary eyes, then simply nodded.

THIRTEEN

Her doorbell rang on Monday morning, the intercom screen showed a man and woman standing outside. Even if she hadn't recognised Jameson, they couldn't have been anything other than police officers. She buzzed them in, then left the door of her apartment open while she made coffee. As she did so, the thought occurred to her that perhaps this was what had happened to Lindham. Perhaps whoever had killed him had got in by masquerading as police officers... But no. The door was forced. Why wasn't she thinking properly?

Both officers showed their ID when they reached the front door. "I'm DCI Steven Jameson. We met on Saturday. This is my colleague, DS Beth Chang. Thank you for seeing us."

Sands stepped back to let them in. Her head felt odd, heavier than it ought to. "I'm making coffee." She stated it as fact, not an offer.

"Thank you."

Sands led the way. This time she was able to form a clearer impression of Jameson. He was ten or fifteen years older than her, and though he reminded her of a dozen old-school detectives, he had sharp, intelligent eyes. She saw how he glanced around her flat, clearly curious how she could afford it on her salary. But more than anything else, she just felt a hollowness. An apathy. In a sense, it didn't matter how good Jameson was. He was too late. Lindham was dead. His family was dead. And for not seeing it coming, for not even getting involved, *she* was to blame. About to retch at that thought, she turned away suddenly and, when the impulse had faded, poured the coffees. Without bothering to ask how they took it, she placed a cup in front of each of them, strong and black. Without sugar.

They sat down at her kitchen table. Chang produced a notebook; Jameson didn't.

"I've been appointed as the lead investigator into the death of DCI John Lindham, and his wife, Sarah," Jameson began, "as well as their two children, Daniel and Elliot. I'd like to ask you some questions about that."

Sands nodded and sipped her coffee.

"How would you like me to refer to you? Is Erica OK?"

She nodded again. It passed through her mind that this was the reverse of how things normally happened, but the thought didn't stick. Not many thoughts were sticking.

"OK. Now, Erica. I understand you found the bodies. Is that correct?"

"Yes."

"You went to the front door of their address at about 10:30 on Saturday morning? What did you find?"

Sands described how she had found the front door locked, then gone around the side to the back of the house and noticed that the back door had been forced.

"What then?"

"I quickly checked downstairs, and it looked as though the family had gone to bed, but hadn't got up that morning. So I looked upstairs."

"And discovered they had been murdered in their rooms?"

"Yes."

Jameson waited while his colleague noted this down. Then he seemed to shift gears. "What made you check on Lindham? Did you have any reason to suspect that something like this was going to happen?"

It was a question Sands had already asked herself. "I don't know. He'd told me he was coming in, then he didn't turn up." She shook her head. "The whole week we'd been expecting something to happen. I just had a sudden sense that this was it. Even so I didn't expect..." She stopped speaking, her mind filled with those awful images.

"Expect what, Erica?" The question was crass, unnecessary.

"Didn't expect what we found."

Jameson nodded. "You just said 'we'. You weren't alone?"

"No. I was with Detective Sergeant Luke Golding."

"OK. You say you'd been expecting something to happen. Why was that?"

Sands explained how Charles Sterling had warned her there'd be a murder on 10th November, but refused to say where it would happen or who the victim would be. She assumed they already knew this but wanted to hear her say it. She tried to speak efficiently, giving them all the facts in as simple and accurate a form as possible.

"And Charles Sterling is your father? The so-called Maths Murderer?"

"Yes."

"I understand he was convicted for the murder of his wife and daughter, among others. That would be your mother and sister?"

"Correct."

Sands watched blankly as Chang wrote this down.

"I'm sure this is difficult for you, Erica. If you need a break, please just say."

"I don't need a break."

The two investigators shared a glance. "OK," Jameson said.

"We'll keep going then. I also believe you and Lindham were working on the possibility that Sterling somehow had prior knowledge that these murders were being planned?"

"*I* wasn't working on it. Sterling insisted on speaking only to me – he's been trying to get me to visit him for years and he used this to blackmail me. But all I did was speak to him. This was Lindham's case; I trusted him with it."

"OK." Jameson nodded. "But based on what Sterling told you, there was reason to believe he had some advance knowledge of what was going to happen?"

Sands considered how to answer. "We weren't sure. Sterling clearly showed he had some information regarding Jane Smith's murder, but it wasn't clear how much. He then gave us what he said was the date that Smith's killer would strike again. But just the date, nothing else. And we had no way of knowing if this was a bluff or for real."

"Jane Smith's murder was a case Lindham was working on?"

"Yes."

"OK. How exactly were you working on the warning from Sterling?"

"I told you, I wasn't. But Lindham had got hold of all of Sterling's correspondence for the last two years. Since he's kept in an isolated environment, we thought it most likely that a message was passed to him via the post."

"But he didn't find anything?"

"No."

"But even so, you thought the warning was credible?"

Sands' head felt heavy. She'd been answering questions for over two hours and Jameson's technique seemed to be to ask the same thing over and over again. She was determined to give the detective as much information as she could, but was tiring of an approach that seemed more appropriate for a suspect than a fellow officer. "Sterling appeared to have some information about the scene of Jane Smith's murder, a note placed behind a photograph. But it's unclear how much information he has. He has a history of playing tricks, for being malicious and manipulative. The whole thing could have been nonsense, designed to waste our time."

"But you don't believe that now? Now that John Lindham is dead?"

"No."

Jameson ran his tongue over his teeth. "We've spoken to a James McDonald. He's the director of the prison where your father's being held. He's tried to speak to Sterling but he's refusing to provide any more information."

Sands said nothing.

"I'd like to move on now to where you were when the murders took place. You'll understand I have to ask these questions."

Sands stiffened, but her eyes didn't waver. "Yes."

"Could you tell me where you were between the hours of 11 p.m. on Friday night and 2 a.m. Saturday morning?"

"I was at work in the unit until just prior to midnight. I sent DS Lindham home at around 11:20. Soon after, I went to a bar with DS Golding. It's called The Cellar. I'm not a regular but we bought several drinks, so they should remember us. At about 1:30 a.m. we returned here to my apartment where we both stayed until about 7:30 a.m. Saturday morning."

The two investigators were silent a moment before Jameson spoke again. "I'm sorry, to be clear, are you saying you're in a relationship with DS Golding?"

"No."

"But you spent the night with him?"

"Yes."

Chang's pen had stopped, and she glanced at her boss. He gave her a look which made her start writing again. "And you're not telling us here that he stayed over as a friend?"

"No."

"The two of you had sex?"

Sands' eyes remained fixed on Jameson. "I'm not sure that's relevant, but yes." She waited until he blinked.

"It's relevant if you don't consider that a relationship." He seemed to think for a moment. "Was this the first time you and DS Golding had spent the night together?"

"Yes, it was."

Jameson rubbed his face as he looked away. He seemed to accept it. "Alright. Thank you for being honest about that."

The questions continued for another hour before Sands provided a full statement, which ended up over three thousand words long. It was early afternoon when the two detectives finally left, and Sands felt exhausted. She was hungry too, having barely eaten since discovering the bodies. Finding her fridge nearly empty, she grabbed her coat and left the building, walking along the harbour side to a convenience store. It felt strange to be outside, unsettling, exposed. As she browsed the shelves she sensed the presence of strangers around her. She became aware she had no idea who'd murdered Lindham, no idea of their motive, no idea of their next target. That thought sent her hurrying to pay for her food and return as quickly as she could to the relative security of her locked door.

Which of course, had not helped Lindham and his family.

She put the chain on the door, filled the kitchen with the smell of microwaved food then fell into a fitful sleep.

FOURTEEN

Sands was ordered to stay at home for the rest of the week, but only made it till Wednesday. There was surely no reason to suspect her of any involvement in the Lindham murders, and her one-night stand with Golding – if that was the right term – gave her a sound alibi. When she appeared at the unit no one objected to her presence. In fact there were so many new faces around she doubted anyone even noticed her arriving.

She discovered that the entire floor below her murder unit had been transformed into a huge operations room, the investigation team far larger than anything she'd seen before. All her staff had been subsumed into it and she immediately collared one of them, a young female detective, to bring herself up to speed on what had been established so far.

It didn't make for impressive listening. The forensic investigation at the scene was still ongoing but had already fed back that the Lindham family's murderer had got in and out fast and not left much evidence along the way. No DNA or hair fibres had been recovered, and the most likely locations for fingerprints hadn't revealed anything fresh which hadn't come from the family. The evidence indicated the killer had worn gloves, and probably some sort of protective over-suit, likely putting it on once they'd gained access to the rear garden. The markings on the wall had been drawn by fingertip but had left no prints. The finger size suggested an adult male, the height of markings indicated average height, and suggested the killer was right-handed. Beyond that, the crime scene was revealing very little.

There was one possible lead. It seemed Sands had been right about the killer waiting outside the house for Lindham to return. An elderly lady who lived opposite had noticed a man sitting in his car outside her house at around 9 p.m. on the Friday night. She couldn't remember the make or model of the car, only that it had been dark-green or blue. She was unable to say much about the man – it had been dark – but also he appeared to have been wearing a mask. Due to the ongoing pandemic masks were still in common use, but it was still unusual for someone to wear one on their own in a car.

"Does the writing on the wall match the note left at Jane Smith's cottage?" Sands asked.

"It's with a handwriting expert," the woman replied. "They're gonna give us an indication on whether it's the same guy, but it looks like it."

Sands' questioning was interrupted by the arrival of a DC blowing the steam off a cardboard cup of coffee.

"Sorry to cut in, ma'am," he said, "But Commander Black is after you, right away."

It seemed someone had noticed her arrival after all.

"I need to be involved in this case," Sands began the moment she got into Black's office. The Commander was midway through replacing his desk telephone on the receiver. "I understand I can't lead it," she went on. "But I need to work on it. It makes no sense to cut me out. I supervised Lindham on the Jane Smith case, and Sterling gave *me* the warning, no one else."

Black drew in a deep breath, looking at her over his dark eyebrows. "I agree."

That surprised her.

"It's actually why I've called you here. And if you hadn't ignored my orders and stayed at home, I would have asked someone to fetch you in today anyway."

Sands blinked. "Why?"

"Perhaps we could have this conversation sitting down?" Black indicated a chair on Sands' left. She nodded and sat in it. "Go on," she said when he'd simply watched her for a while.

"We've heard from Highmoor Prison. Charles Sterling's saying he'll reveal who did this. But he'll only tell you."

FIFTEEN

There was no agonising over the decision this time. Sands agreed at once, and later that day she was driving alone back to the prison, acutely aware of the empty passenger seat beside her. She could hear Lindham's voice, his public-school vowels, now forever silent. She still saw his body every time she closed her eyes, broken and bloody next to his dead wife. And images of the children filtered in too, names she would now never forget. Each thought arrived with an agonising stab of guilt that she hadn't done enough to prevent his death, that she hadn't meant enough to him when he was alive. They hadn't been close, Sands and her deputy, and yet he was a vital part of her life, easily the closest thing she had to actual family. And yet that probably would have been news to him. Certainly it wasn't a sentiment that he would reciprocate. By the time she arrived at the prison she had allowed the guilt and the shame that Lindham's death – and life – evoked in her, and condensed the feelings into a solid black knot of anger. Aimed in only one direction.

"I'm so sorry about what happened." Director McDonald was waiting like an ambush just inside the visitor entrance to the prison. But if Sands had expected a fulsome apology for his misplaced confidence in Charles Sterling's rehabilitation, she would be disappointed. He clasped one of her hands in both of his, his lanky frame leaning forwards to do so, and that seemed to be it. After a few moments he let go and stood back, and then indicated the airport-style security scanner. Sands emptied her pockets and went through while McDonald underwent the same check behind her.

"We'll go to my office," he told her once the guard had passed his phone and keys back with a deferential nod. "I'm sure you'd like to freshen up before you see him?"

"No." Sands shook her head. "I want to get this over with."

Barney Atkinson met them at the lifts and this time McDonald accompanied them, no one speaking much as Barney unlocked the steel gates and re-secured them once they'd passed through. Eventually they cleared the security, reaching the corridor that led to Sterling's cell.

"I'll watch from here." McDonald indicated the CCTV monitors in Barney's tiny office. Sands would have preferred not to be watched at all, but knew that was impossible. When McDonald offered her a smile that was clearly designed to be encouraging, she failed to acknowledge it.

There was one more steel gate to pass through, and Barney's keys jangled as he turned the lock. "It was his fault," he spoke quietly as he stood back to let Sands through. "Sterling might not have pulled the trigger, but he's responsible for the death of that family." His eyes met Sands' and lingered there. It felt like she was staring right into him, right into the hatred for Sterling at his very core. This time she did nod back, just once. Then she turned to walk the final few metres alone. The ball of fury within her was red hot now.

"A-ha!" Charles Sterling was lying on the bed, reading some papers. He tossed them down and stood up, carefully removing a set of plastic reading glasses as he did so. "Angel, how are you?"

"Fuck you," Sands snapped. She walked right up to the transparent wall of his cell and slapped it hard with her open palm. "You knew this was going to happen and you didn't warn me." The volume of anger in her voice took her back, but it felt good to release it.

"But that's not true!" Sterling looked offended, or pretended to. "I did warn you. I told you the date."

"The date was no fucking use. And you knew it. Why didn't you give us more?"

They stared at each other, her face filled with fury, his still frozen in an expression of faux-hurt, but then very slowly a smile appeared on his lips. "There's a limit to what I can do from here, Angel. Surely you can appreciate that?"

"Don't call me that. I have no connection to you. Zero. The only reason I'm here is so you can tell me who did this. So no more fucking around. Give me his name."

She folded her arms and waited. In response, Sterling moved his chair to the front of the cell and sat, so close that the tips of his knees pressed against the Perspex.

"Please." He indicated the chair near Sands. She didn't take it, didn't even look at it.

"*His name*. And where we can find him."

Sterling was quiet, his head slightly on one side as he watched her. Then he stood again, smiling slightly. He rested his hands on his lap, studied them a moment. "I understand *you* found the bodies?" He spoke quietly.

"Name."

"That must have been... unpleasant. I'm sorry it happened like that."

"Give me the name."

"The..." He paused, as if searching for a word. "The debris left after such an incident is not pleasant." He paused. "Even for those of us who are drawn to such things." Suddenly his smile broadened and his tone reverted to that of old friends chatting casually. "It's one of the interesting facets of the whole phenomenon. While the subject is alive, or more precisely *in the process of dying*, a human being can be profoundly fascinating, and yet the very moment that life has been extinguished, it ceases to be of any interest at all."

Sands didn't reply.

"I suppose there is some interest. An opportunity for a good dissection, but I was never that keen on biology. Nor were you if I remember correctly." He laughed suddenly. "Do you remember that rat?"

She did, of course. She'd returned from school one afternoon to find his desk covered in a thick plastic sheet with a large white rat laid on top, belly up, illuminated by an Anglepoise lamp. He had given her directions to slice it open but then become confused when its bowels seemed filled with mysterious red threads which moved when placed in the petri dish.

"*Trichosomoides crassicauda*, if I remember correctly. I know you didn't believe me, but I really didn't know the animal had threadworms."

Sterling watched her while Sands did her best to crush the memory. This time if felt as if he were seeing into her mind. As clearly and easily as she was staring into his cell.

"Of course, for some, the biology is of no interest at all," he went on finally. "For some who feel driven to kill, it's all about the moments after death. Though that seems to be an uncomplicated misplacement of sexual desire, just as some unfortunates get themselves turned on by cows or sheep after making the mistake of thinking about them just at the wrong moment." This thought seemed to amuse him further, and he went on. "The association gets stuck and..." He paused, lifted his eyebrows. "A few years of eager masturbation and they can't stop themselves." He shook his head. "For me, the question was where exactly does the life *go*? And what we even mean by that. Because of course there is still life in the bodies – the trillions of bacteria inside. They're still there, only the host's life has gone." He smiled again and opened his hands to her, almost as if he were granting her his knowledge. "For the bacteria, one could say the party has only just begun."

Sands breathed heavily, hating the man who stood before her with almost every cell in her body. But she felt herself calming down. Her rage was spent and she had to concentrate. She glanced up at the camera that covered the room, imagining McDonald and Atkinson watching, her outburst recorded. She took the seat and inspected her own hands, deliberately matching Sterling as the remnants of her anger faded away. Then, when she felt more balanced, she looked up. "Do you even know his name?"

He was sitting again now, legs crossed, just watching her, his hands still folded into the lap of his vivid green and yellow jumpsuit.

"Or has he just given you a few hints, to get you excited because he knows you're such a sick fuck, and so easy to play?"

Sterling winced a little at the insult, then smiled.

"Is that what this is?" she pressed further. "You won't tell me because you don't even know yourself. It's all just a bluff."

"You know, Erica, I rather hoped you might have grown out of your outbursts of needless anger. I don't see how this can help."

Again, Sands felt pulled back to her childhood, the feelings of shame and frustration he could generate with a single critical word. She'd been so eager to please him that any slight felt like a wound. But she resisted the pull. It was a long time ago and she'd grown in ways he couldn't know.

"I don't imagine it matters if I'm nice to you or not. I don't think you know who this killer is. I don't think you knew who his victims were going to be. I think you were as surprised as I was, although perhaps not as disgusted, because you're a failure as a human being. And I think I'm wasting my time here speaking to you."

His hands moved to his lips as he considered this, and when he finally moved them away it was clear he was trying to hide a smirk. "Well in that case, my darling daughter, I'm delighted to tell you that you're wrong."

"How so?" Sands spoke through gritted teeth.

"You're correct that I did not know the identity of the last victim, poor Detective Lindham. But I do know who killed him. And his lovely family."

His sudden openness surprised Sands. She looked away, telling herself to remember. *Trust nothing this man says.* Every sentence was a game, every word a lie. "So you're going to tell me?" she asked.

"There are things I'm going to tell you, yes. But it would be quite imprudent of me to reveal everything in this meeting."

"Why?"

"You already know that. You're my daughter and I haven't seen you for twenty-five years. I want to get to know you. I'd like you to get to know *me*..."

"And yet I don't want to get to know you. Why is that so hard to understand? For a man who thinks he's so smart?"

He pretended not to hear her. "But you must be interested? Surely, if not on a personal level, then as a professional detective. Your own father – one of the most celebrated serial murderers in the world. And you have become, what? A hunter of such individuals. There's so much we can learn from each other, if you were only willing to engage."

"Is that how you view yourself? Celebrated?"

Sterling turned around to glance at his desk, paperwork piled high on it. On top of one pile was a copy of a recently published book chronicling his crimes. "It's not how I see myself."

Sands looked away. For a moment, she let herself wish she wasn't there, deep underground, facing this man. When she turned back, he'd moved his chair even closer to the glass.

"I know this is difficult to understand, Erica, but I'm really trying to help."

"Then prove it. Give me his name."

"Perhaps it's time to establish a few ground rules for what we're doing here."

"Go on."

"You've doubtless reasoned that I've been contacted by the person who committed this terrible crime. A simple enough deduction. And for the record, correct. And yes, he warned me he'd commit this murder. But while he gave me the date of the crime and told me it would shock the police into action – not his exact words, but I think I encapsulate the meaning – he didn't reveal the name of the victim. Or that there'd be more than one on this occasion. That caught me by surprise."

"So you don't know anything?"

"I said I didn't know the name of the victim. Our friend – I think we can dispense with any pretence over his gender – appears to have put his trust in me. He's given me his name. And where he lives. Rather an odd decision if you ask me."

Sands took a breath. "So give it to me."

"I will be happy to. Delighted in fact." Sterling looked away. "I have no loyalty to this imbecile, and I will gladly hand over his identity so that you can catch him. But it's only sensible for me to do so in a way that also benefits me."

Despite herself, Sands felt hope rise inside her. But it was fragile. Impossible to trust. "You want to trade it?"

He nodded gently. "I understand it sounds crude; it *is* crude. But you must see these things from my perspective." He got up suddenly. "I can pace six strides in this direction and four in this." He walked all the way round his cell as he spoke. "And I've been locked up here twenty-four hours a day for over twenty years. Except for the very infrequent exercise breaks that the director allows, I have no sunlight. No fresh air." He watched her. "I have no television. No radio. No internet. No access to music. And yet at the same time I've been examined by dozens of psychologists and psychiatrists who have written their reports confirming that I pose no threat. None whatsoever. I promise you, Angel, I'm not the same man I was all those years ago. But because of the publicity around my case, the politicians – who haven't even read those reports – have determined that I'll die in here. I'll never get an appeal hearing, I'll never get the opportunity to point out the glaring inaccuracies in my original conviction."

"What inaccuracies? You're not denying what you did?"

"Of course not." He seemed irritated by her interruption and turned away. Sands felt short of breath.

Sterling turned back, leaning close to the Perspex wall. "I don't deny anything, although the truth is I have no clear memory of committing any of those acts. But I also believe, as do the psychologists who've studied me, that it wasn't truly me who did those terrible things. It was a form of madness that overcame me. A genuine form of madness. And that simply wasn't taken into account at my sentencing."

"You explicitly refused an insanity defence."

"A symptom of the dissociative madness from which I was suffering."

Sands tried to think it all through. Was there any way he could pursue this? Even after all these years? No. The court's decision to sentence without the possibility of parole was extremely rare. She glanced at the man in front of her. The killer of her family. Sentenced to die underground. He smiled back at her.

"Is there such a thing as free will, Erica?"

"What?"

"Are we all in charge of our actions, making our own decisions, or blindly following a course that has been plotted out for us, either by accident or design?"

"What's that got to do with anything?"

"It has everything to do with everything. Many serious scientists now accept that it is simply an illusion that we are in control of our own decisions. Surely you know this? I thought I brought you up to have an enquiring mind?" His brow furrowed slightly, as if disappointed in her.

"I think it's best we don't discuss how you brought me up."

Again he went on, pretending not to hear. "Take the experiments of Benjamin Libet. Actual, measurable evidence that neurons fire inside our brains consistent with having made a decision, yet sometimes whole seconds before we *feel* any sense of having made that decision. What does that say to you?"

Sands was silent.

"If the *feeling* of making a decision is actually just the receiving of that decision in the conscious part of our brains – a decision which itself is simply a response to some infinitely interconnected set of circumstances related to the current state of the universe, a person's genetic inheritance and their life experience – none of which comes about as a result of their own choices – as Libet and many other studies have come close to proving, then where is the choice?"

Sands stayed quiet.

"You haven't been doing your reading." He offered her a smile, less triumphant now, and more genuinely disappointed. "Let me put it more simply. Where do thoughts come from? It feels like they just pop into our heads and we have no conscious control over them. Let's do an experiment. Think of an animal." He waited a moment. "Well? Do you have one?"

She didn't answer, but it didn't put him off.

"Come on. Put aside the hate and try to picture an animal in your mind. Do you have one? I know you do. Now, if you like, you can swap it for another. Any animal you like. I want *you* to choose. That's the point." He waited again, watching her, as if to ensure she did what he asked. "Now, let's suppose you're thinking of an elephant – many people do by the way – where did the idea of that elephant come from? Did it come from you, or did it just pop into your mind? And if so, where from?"

Still Sands was silent.

"But let's also flip it on its head. You most certainly didn't choose to think of a sea-lion. And not because you don't know what a sea-lion is, you're perfectly familiar with the concept of sea-lions, but when I asked you to think of an animal, you didn't think of a sea-lion. It didn't occur to you, hence it didn't appear in your brain, and therefore it simply wasn't an option for you to choose from. Ergo, you weren't free to choose it."

He chuckled gently when she didn't respond. "And if you did think of a sea-lion, then perhaps we're still more connected that either of us would be comfortable admitting."

"I didn't think of a sea-lion," Sands said after a while.

Sterling began to laugh again. "As I say, it doesn't matter. Whatever you choose, the question is where did it—"

"I thought of a rabbit." Sands cut into his words. "Benji."

Sterling was silenced.

"You remember Benji don't you?" Sands continued. "My sister's rabbit. Your own daughter's pet? I was wondering what happened to Benji, after you raped and murdered Claire." Sands stared at him, cold hatred pouring from her eyes.

He looked flustered, but just for a moment. "Yes, yes of course I remember. I expect someone took it. Or perhaps it was put down. It's of little importance." He held up one hand to dismiss the subject but took a breath before he recommenced his lecture. "The point is that thoughts appear in our heads, but there is no version of us which summons them. We must assume that they arrive out of background causes and influences. Yet they're all we have. Our genes, our experiences, the world around us, all combine in infinitely complex ways to arrive as thoughts and ideas in our heads. It might feel as if we're free to choose them, but we can only choose from the options open to us. And like a railway engine inescapably stuck on its tracks, all we can do is simply follow where these thoughts lead us."

Sands was back to watching him silently again.

"And yet we believe we're choosing which way to turn. We judge people based upon the tracks they have no choice but to follow."

"Is any of this relevant?" Sands asked.

"Yes! It's most relevant. Think of the *implications*, Angel. What is true of the micro is also true for the macro. Killers, sexual offenders – if they're only following a course pre-set for them, a course which they played no part in setting, then how can we hold them responsible for their actions?"

"You want me to not hold you responsible for killing my mother and sister?"

He stared at her, his nostrils flaring. "It's what the evidence tells us Erica. I always told you to follow the evidence." There was a silence, and for a moment he looked angry. Then he laughed suddenly. "Perhaps another example would make things clearer. Do you remember what you wanted to be as a little girl?"

Sands didn't answer, but again it didn't stop him.

"I can remember you telling me, we talked about it a lot."

"I wanted to be lots of things," Sands said in the end.

"Exactly." Sterling seemed to regard this as a small victory. "You wanted to be everything. I was so proud, even though I could barely keep up. You wanted to work for NASA. To be the Minister for Education, and reform how schools were run. And if I remember correctly you wanted to write plays, like Shakespeare."

"I was a child. What's your point?"

"Can't you see? Isn't it obvious?"

Sands skin prickled. She looked away.

"You wanted to be everything, and do everything, with perhaps one exception. I never once heard you say you wanted to join the police. To become a detective. So why choose that?"

She glanced back for a second, annoyed at the enthusiasm of his smile.

"Could there have perhaps been, Detective, some mysterious event in your childhood that triggered your interest?" His voice was heavy with mock sarcasm now. "Perhaps the unveiling of your father as a serial murderer? And yet, and yet..."

"What?" This time she snapped her head around to face him. "What is the point of this?"

"And yet..." he ignored her question. "It didn't happen right at once, did it? When I was arrested you went to live with nice Mrs Hodges in that cottage in the forest. Only that didn't work out, and you went into foster care. I was sad about that. Worried for you." He paused for a second, as if briefly reliving the compassion he claimed to have felt. "And then, after your rather volatile teenage years, then you go to university to study psychology and criminology, gaining a first-class degree and then a masters degree, before joining the police on their fast-track graduate recruitment scheme, scoring what I understand is still the highest-ever grade in the entrance exam.

"And then, your crusade's still not over. You're still following those train tracks. After all that hard work, when you could have had your pick of placements, you choose to work for the sleepy old South West Police force, where you make a name for yourself as an almost absurdly dedicated officer, digging up every unsolved case you can find and making connections that nobody has made before. Why, Erica? Do you ever ask yourself why?"

"I don't need to ask myself why."

"Because it's so obvious."

She didn't answer.

"It's obvious that it all leads back to the catastrophic event in your childhood when the path that I was on was revealed. And which set you on the course you've been following ever since. But the real question I want you to ask is this. If that's true of you, if *you* weren't the agent that picked your route through life, *if it was picked for you*, then how about me? Did I freely choose to kill my beautiful wife, my daughter, all those other women? Or did something drive me to do it? Did I really have a choice?"

Sands eventually answered, "You knew it was wrong."

"Doubtless. And at the time I doubtless behaved as if I were making my own decisions. I even believed it. But was I really? Or was I only receiving orders from the wider universe? The train driver can see the bridge is down but he's unable to choose another path."

"He could stop the train."

Sterling simply smiled sadly at this as if, by winning that specific point, she'd lost the entire argument.

Sands felt her face redden and she looked away.

"I've never told you this," Sterling continued a few moments later. "I've never told anyone this, despite being asked by dozens of psychologists, film-makers, journalists..." He sighed, made a steeple out of his fingers and rested his chin on it. Eventually he looked up.

"Your mother discovered what I was up to." He gazed at her, his eyes wide. "The day that I..." He stopped. "The day that things came to such a head."

Sands didn't reply but her heart beat fiercely in her chest.

"My plan, Angel, inasmuch as it *was* my plan, was to kill you all, then myself. The classic guilty-husband murder-suicide. And that night I disposed of Claire easily enough, your mother too. But you... You happened to be away on a sleepover, do you remember?" He smiled suddenly, as if noting his own stupidity. "Of course you remember. You were twelve years old and you discovered your father had killed your family, I'm sure the details will have stuck." He smiled again. "So when you walked in that morning, and I was whistling in the kitchen, cooking eggs, I intended to kill you. I rather fancied I'd slit your throat with that nice Japanese knife we had, and then turn it on myself. But I couldn't do it – I simply couldn't bring myself to pick up the knife. I could barely look at it. Even after you found your mother and began screaming your little head off. I couldn't touch you. And for a long time I didn't know why."

Sands swallowed, her neck feeling exposed as she remembered those minutes – hours – before the police finally arrived.

"But then I worked it out."

Sands turned away, her stomach churned and she wondered if she might throw up, but his next words stopped her dead.

"I couldn't kill you because you *are* me." He smiled. "We're connected, you and I. We're the same beast. That's the truth of it."

Sands found her head shaking and she began to speak to dispel the sensation. "So that's your excuse? You have no free will and so you're not to blame for anything you did? It's not your fault. How original."

He smiled again, shaking his head.

"You still killed those people. You should still be locked up."

"I quite agree." He leaned forward again. "I truly believe I have absolutely no intention of ever harming another person, yet on the off-chance I'm wrong, I should still be locked up for the rest of my life, to protect others in society. But nonetheless, it's simply meaningless to punish me for something over which I had no control. Don't you see that?"

"Millions wouldn't."

He grinned at her. "Oh Angel. Isn't this just like old times? Isn't this fun?"

Sands thought about her mother, her sister. She thought of John Lindham's two boys. More dead children.

"No."

Sterling pulled back from the glass wall. He seemed to deflate slightly.

Sands glanced at her watch. "So what is it you want? What exactly do you want to trade?"

"When I was arrested, it made every newspaper in the land. There I was, a world-renowned mathematician, a leading intellectual..."

"You flatter yourself."

He looked put out. "I was asked to speak at universities around the world. You might not like it, but it's true. I had it all, I really did. Two beautiful daughters, a loving wife, a brilliant career, and yet something within me impelled me to risk it all. To destroy it all just to follow some base desire. People were appalled. And they were fascinated. And why not? Isn't it the most fundamental of questions? Why would someone in my position, with all I had, do what I did? Is it any wonder my case caught the public imagination?"

He paused again, as if reliving those months on remand and on trial, as all the grisly details came out. "But once I was convicted, that media interest translated into an unfairly harsh sentence: to be held forever in a place like this." He waved his hand around the cell.

"You refused to take responsibility. You clearly posed an ongoing danger."

"I only ever harmed women, why should I be a threat in a normal prison cell? With other male inmates?"

"John Lindham was a man, his children were boys."

"And very clearly I didn't kill them." For a second he sounded exasperated.

"So that's what you want? A transfer to a normal prison." She shook her head.

But Sterling spread out his hands. "You don't have to tell
me. I understand that my notoriety means a return to a normal
prison is impossible – regardless of the fact that I pose absolutely no risk. But it doesn't have to be *this* prison. I'd like a
normal cell. I'd like a window. I'd like the opportunity to speak
with other prisoners, supervised of course. I'd like a television.
Access to the internet. I'd like to get away from Barney. I don't
think the man likes me." He smiled. "If I were treated equitably,
I'd have all those things."

Sands thought for a moment. "You didn't treat Mum or
Claire very equitably."

"No. I did not. And I regret that now. If there was any way I
could go back and make different decisions I would."

"You can make a different decision now. You can tell me
who killed John Lindham and his family."

Sterling was quiet for while. "Yes, yes, I can. And now you
know my price."

Sands stared at her father, and suddenly she was shaking
her head. "Is that it? Are we done? You've said all you're going
to say?"

He looked thoughtful. "I trust you'll pass my request on to
the appropriate authorities." He glanced towards the camera, as
if to remind her they were being watched, that the appropriate
authorities would be aware of his requests whether she reported
them or not.

"I'll tell them. But I won't be coming here to tell you they
turned you down. Someone else can do that, maybe Barney."

"Then I suppose I'd better tell you something else," he said.

"What?"

Sterling looked troubled. "I expected our little friend would
lie low for a while, but it seems I was wrong. He's in quite the
hurry." He fixed her with a meaningful look. "I have another
date, my Angel. When he will strike again."

Sands felt her stomach lurch a little. "Who?"

"Oh, come now. You know I'm not going to tell you that."

"OK. When?"

Sterling smiled. "It appears he has a penchant for Fridays. Perhaps he works in a profession where he looks forward to the weekend, I really don't know. But Friday 24th is his next deadline." He smiled icily. "And he tells me he's seeing double this time around."

He turned his back to her and lay down on the bed, placing his plastic spectacles on his nose and picking up a sheaf of papers. Then he shot a final look in Sands' direction before settling down to read.

SIXTEEN

DCI Jameson, DS Chang, Commander Black and Chief Superintendent Yorke were all present as Sands played the recording of her encounter. They watched in silence, and Sands found herself watching them as Sterling laid out his demands. Their faces were dark, troubled.

"Do you believe he actually knows anything?" Commander Black was the first to speak once the recording had ended.

Sands had asked herself the same question over and over on the drive back from the prison, each time coming to different conclusions. "I believe he's being contacted by whoever killed Lindham and his family, and Jane Smith too. I think it's less likely the killer has willingly given Sterling their identity. But if he has been able to ascertain it anyway, it must be from something in his correspondence. So we need to focus on that, and cut him out of the process."

Black considered this, but seemed unwilling to follow her logic. "If he does know, and we were able to grant his wishes, would he tell us?"

Sands hesitated. "It's highly unlikely," she replied eventually. "He'll simply toy with us until it's too late. He'll waste our time."

"With respect, sir, I disagree." Jameson intervened now, speaking across Sands, his eyes on the Commander. "This is his chance to improve his living conditions. His one shot. It makes perfect sense for him to trade what he knows."

"You don't know him." Sands shook her head.

"We could make it conditional?" Yorke suggested. "He gives us the name of the killer, we arrest them, and only then we give him what he asks for?"

"Or we don't." Jameson appeared to like this idea. "If we can do that, why not simply promise him what he wants but never give it to him?"

Yorke shook his head. "That doesn't work. Sterling is an expert on the law and has a team of lawyers. They'll insist on a contract. If we don't comply, the courts will force us to."

Jameson rubbed a hand across his face, then shrugged. "OK. So we give it to him? He'll still be in prison for life. Is it such a big deal?" He looked around the room but kept his eyes off Sands.

"He's dangerous," she said. "It's not safe to move him from the high-security cells."

"That's not what the prison director says," Jameson argued. "Or the psychologists. Why do you think you know better?"

Sands didn't reply but her face was dark.

"Is it even possible to grant what he's asking for?" Yorke asked, turning to the Commander. "How high would we have to go?"

Black pursed his lips. "Charles Sterling is very well known, and he's despised by the popular press. It would be very difficult politically for the Home Secretary to move him. I think we can rule it out, at least for now."

There was a frustrated silence in the room.

"What was all the free will stuff about?" Jameson asked suddenly, turning back to Sands. "Why'd he bring that up?"

She answered without looking at him. "It's nothing, immaterial to the case."

"It's my case. I should be the judge of that."

Sands turned slowly to face him and indicated the screen. "You saw it. It's not relevant. He just wanted to test me. It could have been any subject, anything from astronomy to artificial intelligence. He just wanted to catch me out, show that I hadn't done my reading."

"I don't understand," Jameson broke in.

Sands looked frustrated, taken down an irrelevant dead end. "When I was a child we subscribed to various scientific journals. He'd highlight articles I was expected to read, and he'd test me on them. Only his questions would be about the other articles too, the ones he *hadn't* told me to read. I was always expected to go beyond, to master knowledge like he did. Talking about free will was simply a test to see if I still remembered, if I was still reading."

"OK." Jameson paused, considering. "But I still don't understand what he was talking about. The whole free will thing?"

Sands looked to Black and Yorke, hoping they'd tell him this didn't matter. When neither did, she sighed. "Benjamin Libet was a neuroscientist. He designed experiments that suggested it was possible to predict decisions that people made before they were actively aware of making them. He put electrodes inside their heads and recorded brain activity before the subjects felt they were making a choice. He was able to read the brain activity and correctly predict which choice they were going to make. It suggests that when the subjects *thought* they were making a decision, they were actually receiving a choice that had already been made at some level beneath normal consciousness. If that's true in all cases, it follows that the sense we have of making decisions is actually an illusion. Our choices are predetermined, driven by a combination of our genes and experiences, and as a reaction to environmental stimuli."

Jameson's forehead furrowed deeply. "So what you're saying is," – he picked up his coffee mug and held it aloft – "that I didn't *choose* to pick this up? It was predetermined?"

Sands watched him. "It doesn't matter. It's immaterial to the case."

Jameson continued to hold the mug aloft, then glanced at Black, as if he'd won the point. He snorted a half-laugh. "What a load of bullshit. I never heard such a load of—"

"Then you don't understand it!" Sands snapped suddenly. "You wouldn't have picked that cup up if I hadn't just said what I did. Your action was a reaction to what you heard, and in this case your inability to understand it."

There was a silence in the room before Yorke spoke out. "OK, Erica, we're on the same team here."

Jameson slowly lowered the cup and looked to Black, as if hoping the senior officer might intervene. When he didn't, Jameson went on. "OK. So what you're saying might make sense for unimportant things, like picking up a cup, but what about real decisions? What about people who choose to commit murder? Like whoever slaughtered John Lindham and his family?"

Sands took a couple of breaths before replying. "It's a theory, apparently supported by some evidence, but not universally accepted. But yes, the theory suggests that when someone has the idea to kill, that idea is simply the latest in a long chain of thoughts or actions, each of which comes about as a result of the thoughts or actions which precede it. And it all stretches back to influences which the individual has no control over – their genes, their environment, how they were treated as a child. It's like a domino falling. It couldn't have chosen *not* to fall."

Jameson seemed baffled. "So... you're saying it's not their fault?"

"*I'm* not saying that, but it seems perverse to blame a domino for falling down if it was pushed over by its neighbour."

Jameson frowned and looked around the room again. "I don't understand."

"Evidently." Sands picked up her own cup and drained the remnants of her coffee. But then she glanced at Yorke, who was giving her a warning look. She turned back to Jameson. "OK. This isn't relevant since we live in a world where most people believe in free will, irrespective of whether it's true or not. But yes, the theory and most of the available evidence suggests our concept of fault is problematic, at best. If someone who commits a murder did so because at some level they were simply receiving a choice that had already been made deep in their subconscious, and over which they had no control, then yes, it's not really their fault, as most people would define it."

Jameson spread his hands wide. "So we should just let them all go? Every murderer in every prison? It's not their fault?"

"Of course we shouldn't. It's still necessary to lock them away. It prevents them harming anyone else. And besides," – she sounded bored now – "Plenty of people have picked holes in Libet's original experiments."

Jameson opened his mouth to say something else, but Black spoke over him. "I think what DCI Sands is saying is that we're getting a little off track here." He smiled coldly at Jameson, who nodded at once. "What about the actual case?" Black went on. "Do we have any other leads to follow up on? Can we catch this bastard without making a deal with the devil?" He lifted a hand to acknowledge the image of Sterling on the laptop. Frozen, prone on the bed in his green and yellow jumpsuit.

Jameson took a few moments to change tack. He didn't sound much happier on more familiar ground. "It's early days, but there are some promising leads. We have the man sitting in a car outside Lindham's house. We're still going house-to-house but there's a good chance someone else will have seen him. Then there's the evidence from the handwriting expert on the numbers painted on the wall. With the resources we've got we can throw a lot more at the Jane Smith murder as well. I think it's highly likely we'll be able to identify him quite soon."

"You've got nothing." Sands spoke quietly, apparently to herself.

"Excuse me?" Jameson turned to face her.

"You've got nothing," she repeated, louder this time. "The guy in the car is described as average-everything, which just means the witness never got a decent look at him in the first place. Even if she had, he was wearing a mask. You need to be focusing everything you've got on the letters."

"We're looking at the letters. As part of a balanced approach," Jameson replied. "But you have to remember that Lindham himself led a full review of Sterling's correspondence. They found nothing."

"Nothing on the surface perhaps. So it must be hidden somehow. They're using codes."

Jameson held out his hands. "Maybe they are, but if so, what hope do we have? There are hundreds and hundreds of pages of correspondence, most of it entirely incomprehensible. But we are looking. DS Chang here is leading the effort to review Lindham's work." He nodded to Chang, who so far hadn't spoken. "And we've drafted in a mathematics expert to help. Dr Paulson's from the university."

Sands didn't appear to have heard. "Let me lead the team reviewing his correspondence. I can take it over."

"No." Jameson exchanged a glance with Chang. "I prefer to rely on my own team. They're people I trust." He waited a beat for the implication to become clear. "And while I appreciate your offer, the most helpful thing you can do is continue to visit Sterling. Perhaps you'll get him to reveal something else."

Sands shook her head. "That won't work." She turned to

Black. "Sir, please. You need to put me on the letters. You need to let me see them."

The Commander considered this. "This investigation is being led by DCI Jameson," he said finally. "Therefore it's up to him to allocate his team as he sees fit. It would be the same for you if you were leading. But I'd like you to explain what you can offer over and above what's already being done. What do you hope to see that they can't?"

Sands had no answer other than to repeat what they already knew. "The letters Sterling receives are his only communication with the outside world, therefore one of them must contain this information."

"You've said that, and if I've understood correctly they fall into two broad categories. The first are from nutjobs who by definition make no sense whatsoever. The second are from scientists and mathematicians and are almost impossible for a layperson to make any sense of. Why can you do better?"

Sands wanted to reply that she knew her father. And that she knew the maths. But these days, neither was strictly true.

"Look, Detective," Black continued. "I appreciate your record, and I understand the family connection you once had means you feel you know this man better than anyone. But this is sounding dangerously like arrogance. And as Jameson says, we have no idea how far we would even need to go back to find this letter, even if it exists. The man's been in prison for decades."

"We don't need to go back years." The way Sands spoke made them all turn to her.

"What?" Black asked.

Sands moved over to the laptop, the recording from the prison still frozen on its screen. She nudged the timeline back a few moments and hit play. The scene played out again.

"Is that it? Are we done? You've said all you're going to say?"

Sands' voice rang out, tinny on the machine's inadequate speakers.

Sterling, off-centre on the image: "*I trust you'll pass my request on to the appropriate authorities?*"

"*I'll tell them. But I won't be coming here to tell you they turned you down. Someone else can do that.*"

"This next part. Listen carefully," Sands said.

The officers in the meeting room all leaned forward, watching more closely now.

"*Then I'd better tell you something else, hadn't I?*" Sterling said.

"*What?*"

"*I expected our little friend would lie low for a while, but it seems I was wrong. He's in quite the hurry. I have another date, my Angel. When he will strike again.*"

Sands paused the video and looked at them in turn.

"I don't understand, we've seen this already!" Commander Black seemed irritated, but Jameson had a different look entirely. When he spoke, his eyes were fixed on Sands.

"Expected."

She nodded.

"Damn it. Friday 24th is sooner than he *expected*. That implies the killer has only recently told him the next stage of his plans."

"Right. We don't need to be looking decades back. We don't even need to look at the last two years. We need to look at the letters he's received in the last few weeks. That's where the message will be."

SEVENTEEN

Thirty-five letters had been received by the prison and passed on to Charles Sterling over the previous two weeks. He had replied to twelve of them, writing his answers in a dense, almost calligraphic script. When Sands saw it, she remembered how she had sat as a child, desperate for her own handwriting to look half as beautiful.

She had been granted approval to go back two weeks, which gave her a total of seventy-two letters to examine. It was a manageable enough number as she was working in parallel with DS Chang and the team Jameson had put in place. And just like those who'd worked before her, Sands divided the texts into two piles, those that were broadly non-serious (ranging from fan mail to letters from people who seemed completely crazy), and the serious correspondence. The fact that the first pile was smaller gave her some encouragement. Somehow, that seemed a sign that the world wasn't quite as out of control as it might be. Or maybe she had that wrong. Either way, she focused on it first.

Most of the fan mail came from people who'd read the books, or watched the TV series about Charles Sterling and his crimes. In most cases the writers seemed unaware they were reading or watching a dramatised version of what had happened, which omitted the true depths of horror and terror that Sterling had visited on his victims and their families. The actor that played Sterling was better known for a series of popular superhero movies, which seemed to further confuse some of the letter writers – many of them questioned how Sterling could be both so good and so evil. They joked with him, they shared their favourite moments. And they begged Sterling to write back to them. Three letters made reference to Sands herself, the worst saying it was a shame he hadn't killed her as well.

She tried to keep her focus as she read the letters, trying to find something hidden beneath the text, but it wasn't easy.

Two of them had included photographs of themselves, both women: one in her late forties and taken in a photo booth. She looked unsmiling and serious. The other was much younger, her blonde hair dyed pink and green. Her photo was a selfie taken with a polaroid camera while reclining on a double bed with one of her breasts exposed, a similar pose to how Sterling had left one of his earlier victims. Sands studied the images, wondering what had driven them to believe that any sort of relationship with a convicted murderer with no chance of parole might bring them some sort of happiness. Then she moved on, studying the images more carefully, then studying both sides of the photographic paper. But she found nothing to suggest any secret message was hidden within them.

Two of the letters were utterly crazy. One ranted for three pages about devils in the ceiling and that the world was coming to an end. The other pleaded with Sterling to admit that magnetism had been invented by the government to control the population. Sands gave up and turned to the non-crazy pile.

This was immediately even more difficult. The letters began in a more conventional manner, albeit in a tone – a

grateful deference to Sterling's so-called brilliance – that stuck
in Sands' throat. But they quickly became almost incomprehen-
sibly complex. Sands was aware that her father had continued
to work from prison, but not quite how much. It seemed he had
become a go-to figure in several fields of cutting-edge mathematics. He had even co-authored academic papers, forging deep
relationships with people who seemed quite willing to hold
their noses in exchange for his personal insight into their work.

She studied the top letter. It was from someone calling
themselves Dr Fumiko Yoshida, apparently from Kyoto University. From a Google search Sands discovered Yoshida was a tiny
Japanese woman with silver glasses. Most of the text was in
Japanese, but some was in terrible English:

Dr Yoshida doing work in the sharp front side of mathematics,
she enter deeply into enigma of Langlands Program – large,
overall collection of conjecture connect diverse part of mathematics.

Yoshida's own English, on the other hand, was almost
flawless:

Dear Charles, thank you so much for your help last month, but I
wonder if I might take up more of your valuable time? I am still
having some trouble constructing a new automorphic represen-
tation using the Kasai lifting. The issue comes when I attempt
to demonstrate the Langlands functoriality principle with the
cohomological methods I'm using. As you will see, this is
proving to be a critical step, given the complexity of this lifting
in the context of Shimura varieties. Although your solution was
most ingenious, I believe it will only take us so far. However,
I'm sure your unique insights will be of immense help in finding
an alternative path...

It went on and on, interrupted now and then by complex equations.

It was inevitable that Sands' mind would go back to her childhood. She saw herself spending long, hard hours driving her way through the higher-level mathematics textbooks borrowed from her father's study. It wasn't just that he demanded it of her, she demanded it of herself in her fierce desire to please and impress him. And she had got through the books. But it always felt like walking in the mountains when the clouds were low. The ideas and formulas had a murky outline, and if she dared look away they drifted further back into the mist. Unless Sterling called her into his office to provide his own interpretation. Then, an amazing thing would happen. The mist would vanish and she'd be stunned at how the most complex idea would be laid out in front of her, as if bathed in sunlight. It was like he was able to conjure at will the very essence of beauty, paint it in the air in front of her. Sands bit her lip. She understood perfectly why Yoshida was contacting him. The obsequious tone, begging for his help in clearing the fog from her eyes.

But that hardly helped her now. She tried to drag up enough from her memory to understand the paper's meaning but she had to go online to discover what on earth Kasai lifting was, and to get a refresher on the Langlands functoriality principle. It helped her get to the end of the letter but there were still huge chunks of it she didn't understood at all, and she had no idea whether any hidden messages were buried in the subtext.

She gave it as long as she could, then went downstairs to where Chang's team was working. "You said you had a maths expert?" she asked.

Beth Chang had her head down, studying one of the fan letters. The writer had included a poem with a verse dedicated to each of the women Sterling had killed.

"Dr Paulson. Your maths expert. Where is he?"

Chang pointed across the room at a young man hunched over a desk. "Over there."

Sands nodded the briefest of thanks, then walked across. "Paulson?"

He hadn't seen her coming and gave a start. He wore glasses and had a light, patchy moustache, as if he didn't really need to shave yet.

"DCI Sands. I'm reviewing the correspondence as well."

His eyes widened, and Sands guessed he'd probably been told about her connection to the case.

"Are you getting anywhere?" Sands took a chair at Paulson's desk and leaned across, reviewing the papers spread out across it.

Implications of the Birch and Swinnerton-Dyer Conjecture in Modern Number Theory

"Erm... Yes and no, really. I'm trying to take them one at a time but it's not easy. I'm actually teaching a course in Modern Number Theory at the moment, but it's..." He stopped, looking nervous.

"It's what?"

"Well, to be quite honest, what I teach is quite basic, whereas this is... something else. Very high level, and really quite brilliant."

"We're less interested in its structural merit and more whether a means for the killer to contact Sterling is somehow hidden in it."

Paulson hesitated, then drew in a deep breath. "I'm pretty confident that's not the case. I've been able to follow it well enough, and it makes sense. More than that, it's actually quite breath-taking."

"What about the others?" Sands absently flicked through a pile of printouts.

"Well, that's where it gets a little more difficult. I was able to make sense of the paper on number theory because of my own research, but Sterling's range is astonishing. He's at the very cutting edge in dozens of different areas. My own knowledge is simply too narrow to make sense of many of them. I'm sorry."

Sands pondered. "OK. Who else can we ask? Who would understand it?"

"I've already thought about this," Paulson replied. "But the problem is, everyone's a specialist these days. We'd need a different expert for each piece of work. The only people really qualified to comment would be the people who actually wrote them. Or Sterling himself."

Sands cursed inwardly. Damn her father. Damn these people who were working with him.

When Paulson spoke again, his voice sounded more positive. "I did have one thought."

"What?"

"I had this professor, back when I was doing my doctorate, Dr Jeremiah Robbins. He's brilliant, one of the brightest minds in the world, and the thing about him is he never really did specialise. He comes from an older generation I suppose—"

"I know that name," Sands interrupted.

"I'm not surprised. He's kind of famous. He wrote the paper that all the current crypto stuff is based on. You know, Bitcoin, all the blockchains. He's a legend in that world, but then he's also highly regarded elsewhere. A bit like Sterling himself..."

"Do you know him? Would he help us?"

"I think he's retired..." Paulson began, but Sands had already taken over Paulson's computer to Google the name. A photograph appeared of an absurdly elegant black man, in his late sixties when the image was taken, and wearing a flowing purple robe which somehow added to an impression of nobility and wisdom. And not a little pride.

"University of Southampton?" Sands read from the website.

"Yeah. That's where I studied. I did my doctorate there before starting as a lecturer here..."

But Sands wasn't listening. She waved the paper in the air. "We need Robbins. He can help us."

EIGHTEEN

Within a couple of clicks, Sands found a telephone number for Southampton University's mathematics department. She grabbed Paulson's phone and dialled. "I need to speak to Dr Jeremiah Robbins. Urgently."

There was a pause from the receptionist. "I'm afraid Dr Robbins retired some years back."

"I understand that. I need his contact details. Presumably you'll have them on record."

"We wouldn't be able to give those out. I'm sorry."

"I didn't ask if you could give them out. I asked if you had them."

"Again, I wouldn't be able to say."

"OK." Sands forced herself to take a breath. "What was your name please?"

The woman replied coldly, "My name is Susan Reid. I'm the admissions clerk here. And your name is?"

"Detective Chief Inspector Erica Sands with the South West Murder Investigation Unit. Now if you have Dr Robbins' contact details I'd like them right now, otherwise I'll have you arrested for obstruction of justice in a multiple murder case."

"I'll see if I can get them for you."

"Good idea."

Sands ground her teeth while she waited.

"Hello?" The clerk read out a telephone number and an address, which Sands scrawled down. "I should warn you that Dr Robbins is no longer working with the police."

The comment surprised Sands. "What do you mean?"

"Dr Robbins is a leading expert in cryptography and code-breaking. He's assisted the police on several occasions, but as I say, he's retired now."

"Thank you." Sands hung up. Some ghost of a memory stirred, not clear enough to read, but definitely *there*. She minimised the web browser and opened the police intranet, which contained a directory of experts who'd been of assistance in the past. She typed "cryptography" into the search bar and waited while the machine whirred below the desk. When it finally spat out the results Dr Jeremiah Robbins was the first name on the list, his address not far away. But someone had added a note which read:

RETIRED. DO NOT APPROACH.

"What the hell does that mean?" Sands asked rhetorically, but Paulson replied anyway.

"I guess it means you shouldn't approach him."

Sands glowered at him. She got up, patting her pocket for her car keys. "Keep looking through the papers," she said to Paulson, "And phone me if you find anything useful."

NINETEEN

Sands called at DS Golding's desk on the way down to the parking lot. By then he'd been subsumed into the Lindham investigation. There wasn't the manpower to exclude close acquaintances of the victim.

"Are you busy?" she asked quietly. "I could use a second opinion."

"Sure." He looked up and began pulling his jacket from the back of the chair. "Do I need to clear it with Jameson?"

Sands looked over at DCI Jameson's empty desk. She didn't know where he was. "No need. Come on."

"Where are we going?" Golding asked a few minutes later in Sands' Alfa as they headed out of town.

"It's not far. A little village in the Purbeck Hills. Langton Matravers."

"I know it. Very pretty. You looking for some fresh air?"

"No."

"You mind filling me in?"

As briefly as she could, Sands did so, explaining the professor's expertise in cryptography and his previous work assisting the police in codebreaking cases. Golding listened in silence and then looked through the bundle of Sterling's correspondence that Sands had taken.

"OK. Jameson's got his own maths guru going through the papers. Guy named Paulson. Shouldn't you be taking him instead of me?"

Sands drove on a while before replying. "I could do, but then I didn't end up in bed with Dr Paulson while Lindham was being murdered." Sands turned to look at him. "I thought we should talk."

Golding looked back at her. "OK," he said.

But Sands remained silent as she steered the car around some tight bends. Either side of them were rolling hills, deep green and veined with stone walls. Up ahead the ruins of Corfe Castle appeared, sitting proudly on top of its own hill.

"I think I know what you're going to say," Golding broke the silence. "If you don't mind me going first?"

Sands stiffened, as if the pleasure of driving was about to be dispelled by something less agreeable. "No. Go ahead."

He nodded. He looked uncomfortable, she saw, but stoical too. "I was just thinking, we're kind of doomed, aren't we?"

She frowned – it wasn't a word she'd been expecting. "Doomed?"

"I mean, in light of what happened – to John and his family – it just feels kind of wrong for there to be anything between us... I don't mean working with you. I *want* to work with you – you're the best detective I've ever seen, I think the best anybody's ever seen – but with what happened, I guess it doesn't sit well with what happened between us." He fell silent and Sands made no sign to show she was going to respond. "I'm not saying we pretend it didn't happen. I just... I think we just accept it. And don't expect anything to happen again." He stopped. His head had dropped but he looked up now, his blond eyebrows raised. "Is that what you were going to say?"

Sands felt her frown deepening, but she straightened out her face, hiding it. "Yeah. It was something like that."

Langton Matravers was a one-street village with a pub that doubled as a shop and post office. Every building was built from local Purbeck stone, mostly small cottages hunkered down under thatched roofs. Sands followed the GPS down a small turn-off that led to a much larger building.

"Langton House, formerly the Langton Preparatory School," Golding read, from a slate sign fixed to the outside of the building's impressive boundary wall. "Is this the place?"

The GPS on the dashboard said it was, so Sands didn't answer. Instead she stared at the building, a look of quiet confusion on her face. For the second time that day she had the sensation of an important memory, somehow relevant, but just out of reach.

The entrance was flanked by heavy stone pillars topped with regal-looking statues of cats. Sands nosed the Alfa between them and coasted to a stop on the gravel in front of an imposing front door. They got out and Sands looked around, at the hills behind her, a copse of mature trees. She drew in a breath of sea air. The memory, if it was ever there, had faded.

There was a list of names by the door – the building had clearly been divided into flats since its teaching days. Sands tried the first apartment, leaving her finger on the buzzer when no one answered. After a while she crouched down to peer through the letterbox into the entrance hall. She felt a little foolish for coming out here without phoning ahead, but that made her think of Dr Robbins standing tall and proud in his robes. Once again she had the sensation of there being something to remember. Something she couldn't grasp. Her face settled again into a deep frown.

Golding stepped back from the door to see the building

better. "Hey, there's a light on up there." One of the upstairs windows, lined with criss-cross white leadwork, was illuminated. She went back to the bell and held it down again. Moments later the entrance hall light came on, and then Dr Robbins appeared.

In person he was huge, well over six foot, with a domed bald head. He was dressed in a purple bathrobe, hanging open to reveal a muscular and perfectly hairless chest. He wore slippers.

"I can only assume" – he stared at them, drawing himself up to his full height – "from your persistence in abusing my doorbell, that you believe whatever it is you have come to say is important enough to rouse me from my bath. So what is it?"

"Professor Jeremiah Robbins?"

He sighed impatiently. "Yes?"

Sands introduced herself and was halfway through giving Golding's name when he said "No thank you" and began to shut the door.

"I'm sorry?" Sands was quick to put out her hand to stop him. Robbins seemed surprised by how firm her grip on the door was. He sighed again.

"Whatever the question, DCI whatever-you-just-called yourself, the answer will be no. And would it be churlish to point out that such a high-ranking police officer should be capable of working that out on her own? If a man of my age is taking a bath at three o'clock in the afternoon, it's a very clear sign they are retired."

"I know that, Dr Robbins—"

"*Professor* Robbins." He smiled, his teeth standing out white against his dark skin.

"Professor... I spoke to your former university department."

"Then it was foolish of you to waste your time coming all the way out here. Not to mention irritating of you to waste mine. Now if you'll excuse me." He looked pointedly at Sands' hand, still holding the door open, but she didn't move it away.

"We're investigating five murders. I think you might be able to help."

He rolled his eyes. "You're a detective. It's your job to investigate countless murders. And yes, I could probably help with a great many of them, yet I am re-tir-ed. Would you like me to spell it?" He glanced at Golding now, as if sympathising with him for the stupidity of his boss. Sands finally moved her hand, although she wasn't sure why.

"Thank you," Robbins said, shut the door and disappeared from view. A second later the light inside clicked off, leaving Sands and Golding standing on the doorstep.

"That went well," Golding said and Sands gave him a stare before walking back to the row of buzzers and leaning on Robbins' again for over a minute until the light came back on.

When he opened the door again, he was still retying the cord around his waist. "I sincerely hope you are going to arrest me, because otherwise this is harassment and I will be—"

"We're investigating the murders of Detective Inspector John Lindham, his wife and their two young boys. They were slaughtered in their beds last week. You'll have seen it on the news."

The professor paused, breathing heavily. "Detective..."

"Sands. DCI Sands. This is DC Golding." Robbins nodded quietly.

"Detective Sands, you have my sympathy, you really do, but as my former department will have informed you, I am now retired..."

"Shut up. What the press haven't mentioned is that their killer is in contact with the serial killer Charles Sterling. He's passing Sterling information hidden within mathematics papers. I need you to look at them and decode them." Sands spoke quickly. "I don't want your sympathy, Professor Robbins. I want your help."

As she spoke the expression on the professor's face changed

several times. Shock at her rudeness and then something else, harder to read. His mouth dropped open, and for the first time he didn't look elegant, but shocked. "Charles Sterling?"

"That's correct."

Something on Robbins' face suggested that perhaps he too was chasing a memory hidden somewhere in his mind. He turned away, smiled inexplicably at Golding, then held the door open.

"Perhaps I could take a quick look. You can wait inside while I get dressed."

TWENTY

He showed them into a beautifully decorated and well-proportioned room and promised to be back soon. It was part library part office, a huge marble fireplace dominating one wall while bookshelves lined the other. The wooden sash windows framed the views out over the green hills and the blue of the sea beyond. Golding moved to examine several framed photographs on the wall, but Sands went to the window and stared out as if there were something there she needed to see. But Robbins didn't keep them waiting long.

"Might I apologise for my attitude just then, Detective Sands?" Robbins swept back into the room wearing a perfectly tailored beige suit with a handkerchief trailing from the top pocket and a cravat around his neck. Sands glanced at it and wondered how he'd had time to put it on so fast.

"I deeply enjoy bathing. I adore the feel of water against my skin." He flashed his perfect teeth again, as if this completed the explanation. But Sands didn't reply. "Would you like tea? I usually take a cup at about this time." He cocked his head to one side and looked to Golding. "Golding, wasn't it?"

Golding glanced at Sands, who gave a tiny shrug before

nodding. "Sure. Thanks." Sands scanned the bookshelf opposite the fireplace and then turned to the photographs. Eventually she realised Robbins was waiting for an answer. "Whatever."

"Excellent. I'll call Mrs Hartley." He walked over to a sideboard and picked up an ancient black telephone with gold trim, still with its circular dialling mechanism. It triggered another memory, and Sands remembered that Jane Smith had kept a similar telephone in her hallway, although that had been made of red Bakelite.

"Mrs Hartley. Could you please bring my tea a little early? And I have two guests... Yes, unexpected, that's correct. Thank you so much." He replaced the receiver and looked at them both. "Mrs Hartley is my housekeeper," he explained. "She's very efficient."

Sands continued her inspection of the room. Something about one of the photographs was familiar, and she stepped closer. It showed two men, one obviously Robbins, the other the former US President Bill Clinton. The photo had been taken on the White House lawn. Keeping her expression neutral she moved to the next photograph, of Robbins with the Microsoft founder Bill Gates.

"You mentioned that the case involves Charles Sterling?" Robbins said.

"Yes."

"Then you'll be aware I've met him?"

Sands turned to him, watching carefully. "I assumed so. You both worked for the Mathematics department at Southampton University."

He waved a hand, showing off chunky silver cufflinks. "We were not friends. I knew him only tangentially from our mutual positions in the department. I must say I recall him being a rather vulgar man, even before his arrest. A man blessed with charm, no doubt, but not possessing a particularly unusual intellect."

"Charles Sterling was also my father."

This time the surprise crashed into Robbins' face like a car wreck. He looked to Golding, as if checking whether she might be joking, but he stared back expressionlessly. Eventually Robbin's smile returned, this time wider and more genuine. He opened his huge arms.

"Then I must apologise once again, Detective Sands." He put the slightest stress on her surname, as if implying she'd somehow tricked him with it. Then he stared at her, apparently studying her features. "I had no idea. And certainly no intention to offend."

"I'm not offended. He's one of the country's most notorious serial killers. I'm hardly proud of my genetic inheritance."

"Quite. And if I may backtrack a little, I only meant to say that perhaps his reputation nowadays as a bona fide genius is a little overstated. There's no doubt he's extremely clever. And judging by your age, rather young for a Detective Chief Inspector, I infer that's a trait you must have inherited. Perhaps the only trait?"

Hearing a knock, they turned to see a woman in her fifties standing in the doorway holding a tea tray.

"Ah! Mrs Hartley, do come in," Robbins said. She placed the tray on a round mahogany table, smoothing down her woollen skirt before pouring three teas into matching teacups with saucers. She added a small amount of milk to each without being asked. As she finished, Robbins spoke again. "Detective Sands, Detective Golding, please sit."

He held out his hand, indicating two white leather sofas facing each other across a low table, the only modern furniture in the room. Mrs Hartley arranged the teas in front of Sands and Golding and retreated.

"She lives in the apartment next door," Robbins said, lifting his cup. "I had the building converted a few years ago. It used to be a schoolhouse." He took a sip.

"You own the whole building?" Golding asked.

"Yes, but it's far too large just for me. I retained about a third for my own quarters. The rest is now flats, which I rent out to local people. I charge well below the market rate. It helps a little with the problem of second-home-owners buying up all the property around here."

"Mmm." Golding gave him a look as though he sympathised with the problem. Then he glanced around at the beautiful room, the exquisite view. "It pays well being a mathematics professor?" he asked casually.

At once Robbins laughed, opening his mouth wide. "My dear boy! You're wondering how I can afford all this!" He became suddenly serious. "Unfortunately, it doesn't." He glanced at Sands. "I could explain, but I have a feeling that your boss might already know. Detective, would you like to put your colleague out of his misery, or shall I?"

Sands' gaze had fallen on a framed magazine cover which showed Robbins, apparently naked in a tin bath, with the caption *Satoshi exposed?* "The Professor here invented Bitcoin," she said.

Golding glanced at her in surprise but then waited, apparently not understanding. Robbins quickly stepped in to explain, returning his teacup to the table.

"That's not quite true, Detective Sands. In fact, it's definitely untrue. It is the case that I authored a small paper, many, many years ago, which underpins the mathematics upon with Bitcoin is built, and all other cryptocurrencies, I might add. But any rumours that I started Bitcoin itself are very much wide of the mark." He smiled, and his eyes twinkled as though he were scolding Sands for her exaggeration, but he was nonetheless pleased she'd done so. He turned again to Golding. "Would it help, Detective, if I were to explain exactly what that means, and why the suggestion I started Bitcoin is so absurd?"

Golding glanced at Sands but she ignored him, instead

calmly sipping her tea and staring out the window. He shrugged. "OK."

Robbins spread his hands wide again. "Bitcoin, Detective Golding," he smiled again, "is a currency, intended to become a type of digital gold, a store of value, if you will. It has become almost ludicrously successful. There are, and will only ever be, twenty-one million bitcoins, and at its launch you could buy one of those for 0.00008 of a dollar. If you were to buy one now it would cost around sixty *thousand* dollars. So let's play a game, Detective. Imagine for a moment you invested one dollar in Bitcoin at its launch. Could you tell me what that would be worth today?"

Golding soon gave up. "I never was that good at sums."

Robbins smiled again. "It's not the easiest of calculations. But the answer is somewhere in excess of one hundred million dollars. For *every* dollar invested. Do you see now why it is humorous to suggest I was its inventor? I am comfortably off, it's true, but if I had actually created Bitcoin, I would be living on my own island. Possibly Australia."

Golding smiled politely at the joke, but still looked confused. "So why did..." He glanced at Sands, then back at Robbin. "Why do people say you did?"

"An excellent question." He leaned forwards. "Bitcoin was introduced to the world by a man who called himself Satoshi Nakamoto – a pseudonym. But Nakamoto disappeared in 2010, never to be heard of again. Since then there have been dozens of theories as to his identity and location. And as a result of writing my origins paper, I am sometimes included in that list. But I assure you I am not he. If you are here to investigate Bitcoin's origins you'd be far better turning your attentions to the current billionaire class building their own rockets to the stars." He smiled, then put his teacup down. "But you didn't come here for a lecture on the origins of cryptocurrency. Perhaps you'd like to show me what you've got?"

Sands nodded and opened the folder of documents she'd been holding, taking out the paper on top. "Last week a man entered the house belonging to a detective named John Lindham, a colleague of ours. He shot John dead, along with his wife and their two children."

"You said. And I did see it on the television news. A terrible thing."

Sands ignored the interruption. "We were given a tip that something was going to happen on that date. The tip came from Charles Sterling, who is currently incarcerated in Highmoor Prison, and has been for twenty-five years. The only contact Sterling has with the outside world is by letter, so we assume that's how the killer's been able to contact him. But Sterling receives a huge amount of correspondence, much of it of a highly complex nature, focused on cutting-edge mathematics. We believe the information may be hidden within this correspondence. We need your help to find it."

"For what it's worth, Detective Sands," – Robbins seemed eager for Sands to give him the paper – "While I'm aware some people believe Sterling's opinion is worth seeking, it's not something *I* agree with." He held out his hand. "May I?"

Sands passed over the sheath of papers. Robbins unfolded a pair of reading glasses from his inside pocket, placed them on his nose and read silently from the top paper. It was several minutes before he turned the page and continued reading. Finally he sat back, glancing over the top of his glasses as he read the title out loud: "'Exploring Automorphic Representations: An Application of the Kasai Lifting within Shimura Varieties'."

He shrugged. "A case in point. It's extremely niche. Interesting, but hardly ground-breaking work."

"We're not concerned with its mathematical merits. We just want to know where the message is hidden."

"Well I very much doubt it's this one. I know Dr Yoshida

well, she works at the University of Kyoto and is terrified of
flying, so I don't see how she'd be running around Dorset
shooting police officers." Robbins smiled and passed it back
to her.

"OK, good. What about the next one?"

Robbins did as he was asked, reading in silence from the
second paper. Again he read out the title: "'Hodge theory and
deformations of affine cones of sub-canonical projective varieties'." He paused, as if struggling for a way to explain. "In alge-
braic geometry, a cone is a generalisation of a vector bundle..."

"And an affine cone is a geometric way to move from projective space to affine space." Sands completed his sentence for
him. "I told you, I couldn't care less about the maths. A message
was passed to Sterling in one of these papers. That's all we need
to know."

Robbins nodded. "Very good, Detective. As you wish."

Sands indicated the paper he was still holding. "Do you
know the author of that one?"

"No, but..." Robbins held his hands together in front of his
mouth, tapping his little fingers together. "I don't think there's
anything hidden here. It makes a good argument and there's
nothing that looks out of place. But again, it *is* interesting, and
I'd like to know more..."

"Then move on." Sands held out her hand to take the
second paper back, and he acquiesced with a reluctant smile.

"It this all?" he asked, looking through the remaining
papers. "Because this could take some time."

"If you don't find the message in those, there's a couple
hundred more back at the department. We'll just look at these
ones today."

Robbin's eyebrows lifted, but he said nothing.

For an hour there was little noise in the room except the
sound of Robbins turning the pages. Several times he got up
from where he was sitting and went to his desk, checking some-

thing on his computer. Another time he pulled books from the shelves, flicking through them earnestly and making notes on a pad. But each time, when Sands asked if he had something, he shook his head and handed another paper back to her. Finally, when he was almost done with the whole pile, Robbins suddenly stopped and looked up, a curious expression on his face.

"What is it?" Sands asked.

"'Irregular patterns of primes within the distribution of computationally generated pseudo-random numbers'," he read.

"And?" Sands asked.

"This is..." He stopped, frowning. "It's an odd subject for a paper, don't you think?"

"Why?"

"Well, the entire purpose of pseudo-random numbers is that they're *not* random, therefore why would you expect to see regular patterns of primes?"

"It's contradictory?" Sands narrowed her eyes.

"It's certainly..." His voice faded away as he read on, and then he gave a gruff laugh.

"What's funny?"

"This is. Whoever wrote this clearly has a good sense of humour." Robbins turned to the title page and read the name. "The entire paper is a reference to codes. Modern cryptography is built upon genuine random numbers and knowledge of extremely large primes. So the title of the work here is really a nod and a wink. It's telling the reader that this is... interesting enough on the surface, but with an invitation to look deeper. There's something hidden."

"Show me." Sands sat next to him on the sofa and followed his finger as he scanned down the lines. Stopping on one sentence, he tapped it and began to read:

Certain patterns of primes have a regular distribution, for

example 17, 23 and 57 fit perfectly within the parameters
outlined above...

He stopped and looked at Sands, his eyebrows raised.

She stared blankly for a moment before speaking. "Oh shit."

"Quite so."

"Grothendieck's prime."

"Indeed. I think that settles it, don't you?"

In silence Sands took the paper and studied it again. Golding watched them, apparently waiting for an explanation. When none came he said, "I'm, um... I'm not fully following this. Would you mind..."

Sands ignored him, but the professor turned, his eyes sparkling. "Alexander Grothendieck was a wonderful mathematician. Perhaps the finest mind of his generation. And yet he once took part in a public debate and was asked to give an example of a prime number. He chose fifty-seven." The professor chuckled again but still Golding seemed not to understand and looked to Sands for help.

"Three times nineteen is fifty-seven," said Robbins. "Therefore fifty-seven is not a prime number. Grothendieck would have known this, of course, and yet so much of his work was in the abstract realm that he made this elementary, rather embarrassing slip. As a result the number fifty-seven has acquired something of a legendary status. I'm afraid it's quite inconceivable that anyone writing a paper on primes would pick it as an example, especially by mistake. Ergo, it's a message to the reader. Don't take this at face value."

Golding turned back to Sands. "OK. So... whoever wrote this paper. He's our guy? What's his name?"

"Hendrick Tego," said Sands. She looked thoughtful, but the professor jumped up and moved to his laptop.

"It could be a false name. Does it say where he's from?"

"The Mathematics Department, University of Roma."

Sands watched as Robbins googled the name. Nothing came up, either on the Rome University website or the wider internet.

"Nothing." Robbins sat back. "What does that mean?"

Golding had taken Robbins' pad and written down the letters of the author's name:

HENDRICKTEGO

He'd then rewritten the same letters in a different order, crossing each one out as he used them. When all the original letters were gone, a new word had appeared:

GROTHENDIECK

Golding placed the pad between Sands and Robbins.

"An anagram?" Robbins's eyes widened. "A simple anagram." He lifted one eyebrow at Golding. "Very good, Detective."

Golding shrugged. "I'm no good at maths, but I do the odd crossword."

They continued searching online but found nothing to suggest anyone at the university had any links to the paper, or were working on anything similar.

"What now?" Golding asked.

TWENTY-ONE

Both Robbins and Sands seemed lost in thought. Golding watched them a moment, then turned to the professor. "OK, we don't know who the real author of this paper is, but we at least know this one contains the message. Can you tell us what the message actually is?"

Robbins took the paper back, raising his eyebrows when he came to a large number grid on the third page. "I can't tell you what the message is, but it's almost certainly hidden right here."

"How do you know?" Sands asked.

The professor took another look at the page, as if double checking his logic. "This number grid adds almost nothing to the paper – which by the way is genuinely rather interesting. It's illustrative of the general points made, but it doesn't need to be here. And that suggests it has another purpose. In the circumstances I'd say that most probably that purpose is to disguise a code or cipher."

"Can you break it?" Golding asked.

"I have absolutely no idea."

"I don't understand... again." Golding glanced at Sands but

she had walked away and was standing by the window looking distracted, lost in thought.

Robbins continued regardless. "It will depend upon the type of encryption used. If it's a simple substitution code – suppose, for the sake of argument, that the number '5' here refers to the letter 'A', while this '20' refers to 'B', then it would be simple enough to break using frequency analysis."

"OK. How long will it take?" Golding glanced at his watch.

Robbins shrugged. "An hour, maybe two. But judging from the rest of the paper, I would expect that we're actually dealing with a cipher, which is rather more sophisticated. A cipher doesn't substitute one letter or number for another, but uses an algorithm – a set of instructions for what to do with each letter or number in order to arrive at the actual message. What we call the plain text."

"OK. How long?" prompted Golding.

Robbins shrugged. "Depending on the complexity of the cipher, anywhere from several hours to..." – he looked up – "All of the time remaining until the end of the universe." He gave Golding a self-satisfied smile.

"What?" Frustration was written across Golding's face.

Robbins went on, still with the shadow of a smile. "For thousands of years the twin practices of encryption and decryption have been engaged in a race with each other; at different times one or the other has taken the lead. Unfortunately for you policemen, but perhaps fortunately for us civilians, we live in an age where encryption has become the more advanced. If there is a secret message hidden in this grid – which we still don't know for sure – then we must be realistic about our chances of decrypting it. If it was encrypted using a complex modern cipher, it will be impossible to break, the computational power required would exceed—"

"Sterling doesn't have access to a computer," Sands interrupted, turning abruptly from the window. "He hasn't had access for years. Whatever cipher he's using he's working it out by hand. That should knock out the upper end of the estimate."

Robbins considered this; he seemed disappointed, as if he'd been relishing the challenge. Finally, he nodded. "That's possible, yes. In that case we may have a chance after all. There are several computer programmes I can use to test it, applying frequency analysis attacks. Might there be more messages sent by Tego, or replies to him from Sterling?"

"We'll check. If there are, we'll have them sent over."

"So how long?" Golding pushed again.

"Two weeks? A month? A year?" Robbins held up his hands. "I'm sorry I can't be more precise." He seemed suddenly willing to concede. "In two weeks I can try the most obvious attacks. We'll know more after that."

Frustrated, Golding glanced at Sands, hoping she'd help him push the professor further. When she remained silent he said, "Is there anything else you or us can do to speed this up? Sterling has told us the killer's planning to strike again this coming Friday. Is there anyone else we can go to?"

Robbins drew himself up to his full height and looked down at Golding. "There are very few people in this world, Detective, who are capable of breaking a cipher like this. It's your very good fortune that you are right now looking at perhaps the very best of them. But I make you no promises. And I remind you that it may very well be an impossible task. Now, if you'd like me to begin, you must excuse me. Mrs Hartley will show you out."

TWENTY-TWO

Sands was in early the next morning but locked herself away, examining Sterling's other mail for more letters from the fictional Hendrick Tego, or something similar. After several hours she'd managed to identify three more with similar number grids, which she sent to Robbins. When she emerged, the investigation suite was filling up as the 10 a.m. briefing approached. But there was a more than normal buzz of expectation around the room.

"What's going on?" she asked, addressing the question to the man standing next to her, a detective named Derick Walsh, who had been particularly close to Lindham.

"DCI's brought in a ballistics guy to speak. Looks like he's got something concrete we can go on. We're going to nail this fucker," Walsh replied, making a fist.

Sands looked to the front, as Jameson began to speak. He summarised the progress that had been made in searching for the car seen outside Lindham's house. They'd spoken with all the residents on the street and most other streets within a half-mile radius, but so far only one witness claimed to have noticed the vehicle and its occupant. And the description – a dark-coloured, modern-looking car – was vague. But there was still hope, as they were waiting to speak to some of the neighbours.

Next Jameson called on Sands to provide an update on the code. As she began Beth Chang arrived in the room with a newcomer, a short man with a moustache that was just small enough to not look comical. Sands sensed the assembled detectives looking at him with interest. She finished her report and returned to her position at the back of the room. Jameson continued the meeting.

"Next up we have Dr Ian Simpson. He's a ballistic scientist and heads the lab which is running the tests on the bullets recovered from the Lindham murder scene. I believe he has a very interesting presentation for us. Let's give it a listen." A murmur went around the room.

"Thank you." Simpson was a short man but with a ramrod-straight back. As he spoke he projected slides onto a screen at the front of the room. "These are the four projectiles recovered from the scene," He used a clicker to move the slides forward. "And these are the four spent cartridge casings."

More slides showed the bullets and cartridges in closer detail and from several angles, confirming where each had been found. The sense of expectation hanging in the room was shifting with the reality that this dry presentation was failing to match what the assembled detectives had been hoping for.

"Everything I've shown you is consistent with the power and range from a semi-automatic 9mm handgun, such as a Glock 43 or SIG Saur 938. However, we're not able to precisely identify the model used." Before he could continue, Walsh called out, "You don't even know what model of gun?"

Simpson seemed reluctant to deviate from his presentation, but eventually he shook his head. "No, that's not how this works."

"I thought you guys had some sort of database that we can match the bullets to?"

Jameson stepped in. "There's a very specific reason I asked Dr Simpson here today," he began. "Crimes involving handguns of this type are very rare in the UK. For many of you this will be your first case involving this type of weapon. But it's definitely not the first time you've seen them. You've watched them every night on your TV, and you might think you're familiar with what evidence can be gathered when they're used. Most likely you'd be wrong. Dr Simpson is here so we can cut away what you think you know. Hopefully that way, we can catch the bastard who did this." He handed back to Simpson, who nodded.

"The database you're probably referring to comes from the fact that firing a gun creates rifling marks on the projectile, and the firing pin and ejector leave marks on the cartridge casing, both of which are unique to that weapon. That much is true, but it doesn't mean we can look at a bullet and simply match it to whichever gun fired it. If you're able to recover a weapon in the course of the investigation, then we'd be able to use it to test-fire a similar round into a bullet trap and then check the marks produced. We would then be able to say whether the marks were consistent with those found at the scene. But even that wouldn't be one hundred percent conclusive."

There was a silence.

"So unless we find the gun, we don't have anything. And even then, it might not help us?" Walsh sounded incredulous.

Simpson looked slightly put out. "If you recover a service-able weapon during your investigation, I could say to a high degree of likelihood if it was the one that fired these rounds."

A murmur went around the room. This was a lot less than the gathered detectives had been hoping for.

"Alright." Walsh spoke out again. "The fact that gun crime is unusual gives us something. We need to be asking where does this gun come from? Where did our guy get it?"

"There are a lot of possible answers to that," Simpson

replied. "As you're probably aware, handguns over .22 have been illegal in the UK since the 1997 Firearms Act, so it couldn't have been bought here legally in the last thirty years..."

"Could it have been bought before then?" Walsh checked. "They had 9mm guns before then. Would it still work?"

"Yes. 9mm has been the most common bore size since the Second World War. And assuming it's been well maintained, there's no reason an older gun couldn't have been used. But most handguns legally owned when the law changed were decommissioned or destroyed."

"How many were kept illegally?

Simpson hesitated. "That's a very difficult question to answer."

"Ball park figure."

Simpson drew in a deep breath, his moustache quivering as he did so. "I'd say, given the number of guns in the population before the law came in, how many were surrendered, and how rarely we've come across such weapons since 1997, we're looking at hundreds, perhaps thousands. But I don't see how that helps; we still don't know anything about this weapon or where it might be."

Walsh puffed out his cheeks. "Are there other ways to get a gun here?"

"Yes," Simpson nodded. "9mm handguns such as the Glock or SIG Sauer can be bought freely in the US, in many cases with only minimal checks, and there's a thriving trade in shipping them over here, usually hidden in shipping containers. They go mostly to Eastern Europe where they're used by organised crime. From there it's not hard to smuggle them into the UK along established contraband routes."

Another murmur went around the room, and again Walsh spoke out. "Organised crime?" He raised an eyebrow. "That'd match the MO."

Jameson cut in to answer this question. "Nothing's off the

table. We definitely need to look into any links Lindham might have had with organised crime. It could be this was a revenge killing, possibly for an arrest he made." He nodded for Simpson to go on.

"Another relatively easy way to gain access to a similar weapon is via the internet. There are sites on the dark web that are relatively easy to access, where they can be bought—"

"If it's online, there'll be records?" Walsh called out.

"Not if whoever did it was hiding behind a VPN and using encrypted messages," Jameson replied. "Which is standard for most people on the dark web."

Walsh looked frustrated. "They'd still have to pay. How would they do that?"

Simpson replied, "They typically use cryptocurrency. Several allow complete anonymity."

Walsh sighed. "So what you're saying is: it could have been organised criminals, but on the other hand, it could have been just about anyone with a computer?"

The atmosphere had changed from anticipation to frustration. The ballistics expert shrugged and the room fell silent. But Sands called out from the back, "Would it have been expensive?"

A few heads turned to look at her but Sands ignored them, keeping her eyes on Simpson. He met her gaze. "Actually, that's a good question, and I suppose the answer is, it depends on your definition of expensive. Retail price for a Glock in the States is around eight hundred dollars, but it would cost a lot more here. I've seen similar guns for sale on the dark web priced at around twenty thousand pounds. And of course you've got no guarantee you'll actually receive the weapon. It's quite possible you'd need to order several before one arrived."

As this sank in, Simpson returned to his presentation. "There's a little more where we're perhaps ahead of the Hollywood version." He clicked a new image onto the screen showing the bedroom where Lindham and his wife had been killed. The bodies still lay in the positions Sands and Golding had found them. Nothing had been done to cover them.

"We can get an idea from the spray of gunshot residue on the victims and their bedsheets, and on the carpets and walls, of where the killer was when the gun was fired." Simpson paused. "It shows he was probably less than two metres away from the two adults when he fired, slightly closer for the children. But his accuracy was good. Four shots, four dead, all head shots." He clicked again to show the children.

A silence descended on the room. Several of the detectives had to look away.

"You're saying he knew what he was doing?" Sands said a moment later.

Simpson nodded. "Certainly it could indicate some sort of firearms training, or at least an interest in guns."

"We should be looking at gun clubs, firing ranges," Jameson said. "Walsh, let's get you on that. Get a list of clubs locally and nationally."

"Can you tell if a suppressor was used?" Sands asked.

Simpson nodded at her, as if he liked this question too. "The thing with suppressors is that the bullet flies through the bore with little hindrance, so it's quite difficult to determine."

"Hang on please," Jameson said. "For the sake of ensuring everyone here has a realistic idea of what we're talking about, could you explain what a suppressor is, and what they do?"

"Sure." Simpson stood a little taller. "A suppressor – or a silencer – is a metallic cylinder containing internal sound baffles. When the weapon is fired the bullet passes through unhindered, but most of the expanding gas is forced through the baffles, which slow it and essentially convert the sound to heat."

"How silent are they?" Sands asked.

"Louder than the movies, that's for sure. They sound less like a gunshot, more like a loud crack."

"None of Lindham's neighbours have reported hearing gunshots," Sands said. "The houses are close together, your standard suburban semi. Does that suggest one was used?"

"I couldn't say for sure, but a gunshot from a 9mm is pretty loud. So if no one heard it, it's certainly likely."

"A suppressor," Walsh asked. "I assume they're available on the dark web too?"

"Yes," Simpson answered. "But they're also relatively easy to make at home. You can use an oil filter from a car and it will do a half-decent job."

There was a pause. Then Walsh decided it was up to him to sum things up. "So what we've got is a man who breaks into the house just before midnight. He's carrying a gun with a silencer fitted. He knows his guns. He comes up the stairs and he executes the whole family, one by one, using only four bullets. And unless we find that gun, we have no idea who he is?"

Simpson looked uncomfortable for a moment, but eventually half nodded.

"OK. Well I don't know about you," – Walsh was speaking to Jameson now – "But that scenario sounds a hell of a lot like a hit to me." The ballistics expert was done and already unplugging his laptop, and Jameson replaced him at the front.

"I'm inclined to agree." Jameson looked thoughtful, then gave his orders. "OK. I want us to start focusing more on the organised crime angle. Get me a list of everyone Lindham put away, and anyone connected to them. We're looking for someone who might have access to guns or any experience firing them. Ex-military. Gun-club member. Anyone with a damn computer." The room began to empty out but he wasn't quite finished.

"Detective Sands, can I have a word?"

Sands pushed off from the wall, moving against the flow of detectives going back to their workstations.

"Message for you, from James McDonald. He wants you to go by the prison."

An image formed in Sands' mind, the lanky, somewhat creepy presence of the director. "There's no point me seeing Sterling again. He's given us the next date; he won't give us anything else."

"It's not Sterling he wants you to see. It's his guard, Barney Atkinson."

TWENTY-THREE

The approach to the jail felt easier knowing she didn't have go right to the heart of the place, to where monsters like Charles Sterling were rotting away their lives. Even so, Sands was irritated to be summoned without reason. She parked the Alfa and made her way through the layers of security, then finally up towards McDonald's office where he made her wait until his secretary finally showed her inside.

"What's this about?" She didn't bother with pleasantries.

"Good morning, Detective, a moment please." McDonald continued writing on some papers on his desk. As he worked, he spoke again. "I've asked Barney to come as well, he's on his way." McDonald glanced up, offered a brief smile, then went back to his work. There was no offer of refreshments, not even to sit down, but Sands did so anyway. A few moments later there was a knock at the door.

"Come," the director called out without looking up, and Barney Atkinson entered the room. "Ah, Barney, good of you to join us." Finally McDonald put down his pen. He indicated the seat next to Sands and the big man sat.

"Thank you for coming, Detective," McDonald said,

making a steeple with his hands. "I do hope this doesn't prove a wasted trip."

Sands didn't reply.

"To be honest, I wasn't sure this was anything," he went on, "or at least not something worth bothering you about, but Barney here has convinced me otherwise. He's worked here a long time and has a nose for certain things." McDonald wrinkled his nose as he spoke. But then he fell quiet.

"Well?" Sands replied, with a half shrug.

"Let's let Barney tell you himself."

Barney Atkinson's voice was gruff; combined with his size he gave the impression of a grizzly bear. But there was an intelligence to his eyes, which he kept fixed on Sands as if McDonald wasn't even in the room.

"When Sterling's out in the yard on exercise, that's when I sweep his room. There're no hiding places exactly, but I still get a feel for what he's comfortable with me looking at, and what he'd rather I didn't see."

"How?" Sands asked.

Barney considered the question, nodding. "Little things. He likes to make notes. Mostly it's his maths stuff, and I don't pretend to understand it, but I still know when he'd rather it was kept private. Or as private as possible, given his circumstances." He paused, before coming to the point. "He was on exercise yesterday, and I found something."

"Go on."

Barney nodded again, this time glancing at McDonald, who pushed a piece of paper across the desk, a photocopy of a scrap of paper on which Sterling had scrawled a long list of numbers in his characteristic script. The dot and three letters at the end immediately identified it.

3 1 4 1 5 9 2 6 5 3 5 8 9 7 9 3 2 3 8 4 6 2 6 4 3 3 8 3 2 7 9 5 0 2
8 8 4 1 9 7 1 6 9 3 9 9 3 7 5 2 0 5 8 2 0 9 7 4 9 4 4 5 9 . c o m

Sands picked up the paper and studied it for a few moments. "It's a website?" She glanced at the director, who half-smiled and half-shrugged.

"If it is, then I have no idea what use it is. He hasn't had access to a computer in years."

"But you've tried it?" Sands insisted.

"Yes." McDonald tapped once on the keyboard of his silver, ultra-thin laptop and slid the machine round. The address bar showed the numbers from Sterling's note, but the screen itself was blank.

"Nothing comes up," McDonald said, shrugging. "It's just a random collection of numbers."

"No, it's not," Sands interrupted, irritated. Reaching for a pen and a blank sheet of paper on McDonald's desk she quickly began to rewrite the numbers, without needing to copy them from the original note. When she'd finished she held up her note against Charles Sterling's. The numbers matched.

McDonald frowned. "You did that from memory? Very impressive..."

"It might be," Sands cut in, "if I had done, but I didn't need to. It's pi. The ratio of a circle's circumference to its diameter. At least, it's pi to..." – she paused, quickly counting the number of digits she'd written – "...to sixty-two decimal places. As I'm sure you're aware, pi itself is infinite."

"Even so, you know the value of pi to sixty-two decimal places, that's quite a—"

"I can recite pi to the first five hundred decimal places," Sands replied quickly, her voice somehow different. She wasn't quite embarrassed, wasn't quite angry. Perhaps for a moment she wasn't quite there at all. "Sterling made me learn it on my tenth birthday. I wasn't allowed to open any of my presents until I could do it perfectly. It took me a week." She blinked. "I'm sorry, that's not your... issue. It's mine." She picked up Sterling's list of numbers again, before either of them could respond. "Sixty-three characters is the maximum allowed for a website address," she said. "It's the closest to pi you can have."

When neither McDonald nor Barney answered her, Sands changed tack. "This is a photocopy. Where's the original?"

It was Barney who answered. "I put it back into the cell, same place he left it. So he wouldn't know we'd found it."

"That's good. Where was that?"

"He has a Bible. Sterling isn't religious, but every prisoner gets one. I reckon he only keeps it because he thinks I don't check through it properly. But he likes to hide stuff in there."

"Where was it in the Bible?" McDonald asked suddenly, his voice hopeful. "Perhaps that might be relevant?"

But Sands ignored the suggestion. "It doesn't match," she said quietly.

"Excuse me?" McDonald went on.

"They *don't* match, my list and Sterling's. There's a digit different. Look here. The forty-ninth decimal should be a '1', like I've put, but Sterling has a 'two'." She held out the sheets for McDonald to check, pointing to the difference.

"Maybe he made a mistake?" McDonald suggested, but Sands shook her head.

"Sterling has an eidetic memory. He wouldn't get that wrong." She continued to stare at the paper, deep in thought, but McDonald scoffed at her.

"I've been through this with his psychologists. They assure me there's no such thing as a photographic memory."

"I didn't say a photographic memory, I said an *eidetic* memory. If he's studied a piece of text closely enough, he's able to remember it in perfect detail. And he's studied pi. He knows it to at least a thousand decimal places."

"Well could *you* perhaps have made an error?" McDonald suggested. "You've told us you learned this when you were ten, so—"

Sands cut him off. "I also learned to sing 'Happy Birthday'

when I was three years old, you think I'd get that wrong too?"
Brusquely she grabbed his laptop and drew it closer, replaced
her father's '2' with a '1' and ran the search. At once the screen
went dark before gradually lightening again, as if they'd arrived
at a website running a crude animation.

A line appeared towards the bottom; it became clear it was
meant to represent the ground as a structure started to push
upwards from it, a pyramid. Finally a man – a stick figure, but
apparently in ancient Egyptian dress – walked along the line
carrying a sign and a hammer. When it arrived at the pyramid it
seemed to be fixing the sign there, banging in a nail here and
there. Eventually it looked out towards the viewers with a
beaming smile. As the cartoon figure stepped away, Sands and
the two prison officers were able to see what had been written
on the sign:

Stay Tuned!

And then the screen faded back to black.

TWENTY-FOUR

Sixty-three miles from Highmoor Prison, back in the ordinary world – far removed from the underground dungeon of Charles Sterling – it was pick-up time at St Joseph's Primary School. Several hundred children, released from their confinement, were scootering, running and in some cases skipping down the pavement beside the busy main road that led to the school. And a steady stream of parents followed, some hurrying, some slow walking to lengthen the time available to chat to friends. All were adjusting in their own way to the everyday transition from when the kids were at school to the afternoon parenting duties. It was a perfectly ordinary afternoon, the end of a perfectly ordinary day, and none of them would have any reason to connect the far-away prison to their school. To their lives. And yet the thread of a line had been drawn. It was about to be pulled tight.

Leon Webb was one of the parents strolling down that road. A father of twins, he was a well-built man who ran his own small building firm, successful enough that he was able to take an afternoon off once a week to pick up his girls up from school, walking from a large, conspicuously well-maintained house in a side-road near the school. So close to the school, in fact, that many of the other parents parked their cars near there at drop-off and pick-up times. This was a source of some frustration for Leon's neighbours, but since he'd converted the front garden to a driveway large enough to park his work van, and he was well enough known to the school community that no one dared block it, it wasn't something that particularly concerned him.

Nevertheless, when the car bumped up onto the pavement in front of him, his first thought was that it must be one of the pushy mums the neighbours often complained about. It was always the mums, Leon had noticed, and they'd sometimes block the pavement completely with their ridiculous 4x4s. (His own wife did drive a Range Rover, but that was easier to justify as she sometimes needed to drive onto the sites where he worked.) But then there was something wrong with the explanation too. The car was moving unusually fast, and it wasn't a 4x4, but a BMW 5 Series. The M5 he noticed now. A nice motor.

The wide, low-profile tyres ripped at the turf on the strip of grass that separated the pavement from the road itself. Then the wheels locked, and the big car part-skidded on the mud as it came to a halt.

Leon kept walking, moving closer to the car.

It wasn't a middle-aged woman who emerged, but a man. Young, probably in his twenties, but pale and slightly built. He wore a bright-yellow North Face jacket, a face mask. And again, there was something about him that was wrong. He was moving too fast, he seemed... he seemed overdosed on adrenalin. On drugs maybe? Leon didn't have time to make sense of much more before the man opened his jacket and pulled out something metallic. Heavy. Astonishingly, ridiculously – cutting into the ordinariness of the day so it seemed almost offensive – it was a gun. Then the man pointed it directly towards Leon.

"Don't fucking move."

Leon took two more steps. His brain spun like a suddenly

unconnected cog. He did weights. He ran his own company, employing a dozen people. People respected him, maybe even feared him. No one told Leon what to do. Certainly not with guns.

The twins had been ahead of him on their scooters; the gunman was now between him and the children. Sky, the younger of the two by fifteen minutes, had stopped, looking behind her to see what was happening. Some part of Leon's brain realised she couldn't see the gun, which perhaps explained why she began wheeling back towards them. Automatically Leon took another step forward, meaning to stop her. At once the gun came up higher, now it was pointing at Leon's face. He was no more than five metres away, close enough that he could see down the barrel.

"I said, don't fucking move." The man's eyes were wide, they looked insane. "Unless you want to die right now."

"What do you want?" Leon heard himself ask. He was simultaneously amazed by how calm he sounded, but also almost fascinated at how it felt to have the weapon pointed at him. It seemed to lock him in place with its promise of instant death. Would he even see the bullet coming? He felt a surge of adrenalin now, tunnelling in on the man in front of him, his children beyond. Everything else dropped away as if it had never been there at all.

The gunman moved to the middle of the pavement. He suddenly seemed nervous, changing his grip on the weapon but still keeping it aimed at Leon. Sky now seemed to sense something was wrong, but she hadn't connected it with the man since she still couldn't see the gun or his masked face. The gunman moved again, this time towards the back passenger door of the BMW, which he yanked open. Then he glanced around. Saw Sky, waved the gun towards her.

"Get in the car."

"What?" This time Leon reacted at once. "What are you

doing?" He took two quick steps forward, nearly halving the gap between him and the gunman, who wheeled back round. He aimed the gun at Leon's head again but now he was screaming, suddenly at the edge of control.

"I told you not to move! Do you know who I am?"

The question threw Leon, and for a moment he actually ran through the people it might be – the business had done well, but not because he'd shafted suppliers or contractors. It was simply that the housing stock in the town was old, and pretty much every home could benefit from extending or renovating. He had no enemies. Or did he? He'd been quite aggressive in some land deals; had he trodden on toes without even realising?

The gunman moved again, reaching into the car and pulling out a newspaper. Had Leon been quicker he might have had time to charge at him, but the opportunity was gone before Leon saw it for what it was. The man levelled the gun again, his breathing fast and shallow. Their eyes met for a moment, then the gunman tossed the paper towards Leon. He caught it with both hands and looked at it, totally confused now, wondering how he was supposed to find whatever it was the gunman expected him to see. But then he saw the main headline on the front page:

POLICE OFFICER AND FAMILY SLAIN IN THEIR BEDS

"Yeah? You get it now? You know who I am?"

Leon did. Of course he did. But it made no sense. The terrible murders, just a few miles from the school, had made national news. He'd discussed it with his wife, with the lads on site, about how terrible it was. But he hadn't considered for a moment that it might affect him in any way. He let the newspaper fall to the ground and stared at the gunman.

"Tell 'em to get in the fucking car." The man gestured to

Sky with the gun but she didn't move. Worse, her sister Ocean had joined her now, so that both of them were closer to the gunman than Leon was. And they seemed both to have realised that whatever was happening here was something to be frightened of. Very frightened.

"You can't—" Leon began, but the gunman cut him off.

"I need your kids. If you want 'em to live, tell them to get in. Otherwise, I shoot you and put 'em in myself. You got it?" His nostrils were flaring wide. A vein was standing out on the side of his neck.

It was the immovable object and the irresistible force. Every instinct pushed him forward to protect his daughters, but the gun pointed at his face stopped him with equal strength. The man he should have been – the kind of guy who never took shit from anyone, a guy who could take care of himself and his family – was suddenly gone, and he didn't know how to react. The worst of it was, he believed this man. A man who had shot a police officer and his whole family would just as easily shoot him and his twin daughters. And he was powerless, utterly impotent to stop him.

"Get 'em in, if you don't want 'em to die."

The man was sounding increasingly agitated, and now Leon sensed why. With an almost audible whoop he became aware of the scene around him: a busy street with cars streaming by in both directions; the face of a kid from the nearby secondary school, curious as he cruised past the unusual scene on his bike; parents walking their kids home on the other side of the road. This whole thing was surreal.

"Fucking hell." The man suddenly wheeled away, taking the gun with him so that it pointed instead at Ocean. And then he grabbed her, holding the weapon against the side of her head. Leon felt immediate and immense fear. Ocean screamed and Leon let out a yell too, no words, just a howl of terror. Perhaps it stopped the man from firing. Perhaps not.

"Let her go. Please let her go." He managed the words, just. He held his hands up, begging, as if they might stop the bullet.

The man glanced at him but continued to drag Ocean towards the open car door. She was too scared to resist, the man too strong. The panic was vivid in her eyes, but she did what he said. She got in the car.

"No!" Leon roared, and this time he moved.

The gunman had the advantage. The exact order of what happened next didn't make sense. He swung his arm, then Leon's head spun around. Then came a horrible whizzing sound, and finally the explosion of the gun firing.

"I fucking warned you, man." Somewhere within the shock and adrenalin, Leon understood that the man who had just shot him was upset about it. Leon's legs buckled and he dropped to his knees, his vision filled with red on one side. Through it he saw Ocean disappear into the car, and then the man reached back for Sky, who could perhaps have run, but didn't. Her scooter clattered to the ground. She almost seemed to wait for the gunman to push her in.

His head hurt now but Leon didn't care. His only thought was the twins, and despite being on his knees he tried to move forward. When the gunman saw what he was doing, Leon thought he was going to fire again and braced for the impact of the bullet, knowing this one would kill him. But the man didn't fire. Instead he slammed the door shut and then ran round to the driver's door and pulled it open, glancing once more at Leon before disappearing inside. The rear lights flicked on, the engine burst into life and the wheels spun on the grass verge. The horn blared as the car pulled away, forcing its way into the afternoon traffic of the school run.

TWENTY-FIVE

The journey back from Highmoor Prison was plagued with traffic, but Sands was grateful for the distraction. Before she left she'd managed to get into an argument with Jameson. She'd phoned to give him the web address found in Sterling's cell, and to order him to arrange for the department's tech team to look into it right away. He'd agreed to that, but not to her subsequent idea of going down to Sterling's cell and demanding to know what the hell it meant. Jameson insisted on letting the tech team do their thing first, arguing it might give them an advantage if Sterling wasn't aware they knew about this website. It pissed Sands off, mostly because, beneath her anger, she actually agreed with him.

It was early afternoon as she approached Poole, and Sands wanted a break from thinking. Out of habit she switched on the police radio scanner, not expecting to hear much of interest, but just checking in to whatever was going on. But she got quite a shock.

It was hard to follow as so many people were trying to use the radio at once, but she quickly understood the fundamentals. An active-shooter incident had taken place moments before on

Middlebrook Road, near the primary school. One man had been shot, apparently in the head, and two children had been taken at gunpoint, in front of dozens of witnesses. The suspect was in a green or possibly blue BMW, the reports varied. What was certain was that the car was now travelling north. It took Sands a moment longer to register that she had just turned onto Middlebrook Road, to the north of the school. Then she saw a car heading towards her travelling far too fast, its colour a pearlescent blue-green.

As it flashed by she caught a snapshot of the driver: young male, late twenties, yellow jacket, ponytail. She snapped her head around to watch it flash past, grabbing her radio to report the licence plate before realising that shouldn't be her priority. There were two children in the car and the news had just come through that their abductor had identified himself as Lindham's killer. Glancing around, Sands saw there was space to manoeuvre and swung the wheel. The Alfa skidded around across the carriageway, almost coming to a stop when pointing in the other direction. For a second she sat there, still wondering if this was some crazy dream. Then she floored it.

The Alfa could do zero to sixty in just under five seconds, but there wasn't room to do that now. She got up to fifty before a car pulled out ahead of her and she had to jump onto the brakes to prevent herself rear-ending it. She let out a stream of expletives as she fought to overtake, squeezing between the flow of vehicles coming the other way. Only then did she remember to turn on the blue emergency lights fitted inside the Alfa's radiator grille. She still hadn't reported her pursuit, and she took a moment to do so. Then there was another car in front of her, and it took an age to react to her angrily flashing headlights. Finally it pulled over into a bus stop and let her flash by.

Now she was back out of town and into the countryside. But the BMW hadn't taken the dual carriageway – she'd seen it fly by the junction, blasting through a red light before disappearing out of view. She gave pursuit, barrelling down the old road leading into the forest. Fully alert now she pressed the accelerator to the floor, waiting until the turbo kicked in and punched the powerful car forwards, dabbing the brakes to skim off speed before the corners. Although Sands had taken an advanced driving course, it had felt very different from this: on a track with wide run-offs in case anyone misjudged a bend. Here the road was narrow and the trees – heavy trunks that might as well have been concrete – were just a few feet away on either side. As she'd been taught she forced her vision wider to take in more information while continuing to press the car forward. There was still no sign of the car ahead. Had it turned off? Could it have stopped somewhere and was perhaps hidden by the trees? Sands glanced at the speedometer – ninety-six mph, on a road designed for half that. Either side of her the trees flashed by. She pushed the Alfa faster.

There! Ahead she saw a glimmer of brake lights. *There!* The BMW. She was catching him. Guessing he perhaps didn't even know she was following him she killed the blue lights and hit the brakes hard. Then, with the cars separated by a bend, she accelerated again, so that when she saw the BMW again they were closer. It wasn't travelling much above the speed limit now so she slowed down to trail him, reporting her position on the radio as well as the make, model and licence plate of the BMW, noting it was an M5 Sport model, and therefore even quicker than her Alfa. She thought she could see the two children on the back seat. Although the suspect was still presumably armed, Sands wasn't. Very few UK police officers were. She radioed that she would attempt to follow at a distance, while directing the firearms squad to closely follow their progress.

They were approaching a major junction now and Sands watched carefully to see which direction the BMW would take. But then suddenly she heard sirens and saw blue flashing lights on her left-hand side. A marked police car was coming through the junction, fast. The BMW reacted at once, changing lanes to turn right, and then streaking across the road to go left instead towards the other police car, which tried to follow but was going far too fast to make the turn and spun sideways, narrowly missing another vehicle coming the other way.

Sands swore again, dropping the radio handset. She concentrated on the wheel and the car's controls and just managed to get on the road after the BMW again. But this time instead of keeping to the speed limit, it was travelling at what felt like the very edge of control. Twice it made terrifying overtakes, sweeping across to the wrong side of the road directly into the path of oncoming vehicles. Both times the cars coming the other way had to swerve out of the way onto the verge, horns blaring. Sands flicked on her blue lights again, making her own overtaking a little easier, but still she waited until there was more of a gap. She was reminded, as she worked the wheel, of what her police driving instructor had warned her about, how the kind of toe-rags she might end up chasing had their own instructors these days – the driving games on their PlayStations. All the time the BMW lengthened its lead.

"Where's the damn chopper?" She found a moment to yell into the radio, but the reply dismayed her.

"It's being refuelled. It'll be half an hour."

"That's too late!"

The operator didn't respond and Sands watched as the BMW made another near-suicidal overtake, this time screaming towards a supermarket home-delivery van. For a second it looked like there was no way the rushing metal could avoid a collision, but at the last possible moment the van swerved left, slamming into a tree. Somehow the BMW squeaked through the gap it left. Sands was there ten seconds later. It felt like an age. As she flew past the stricken van she quickly assessed whether the driver was injured, and, guessing not seriously, kept up the pace as she reported the accident. But by then the BMW had already disappeared around the corner ahead. Sands pushed the Alfa now as hard as she dared.

The road ahead straightened. She saw the BMW again, all her attention focused onto it.

They were still in the countryside but up ahead was a small village, a parade of shops, a pub. Sands had driven through it many times before; she thought there might be a school there as well. As she approached the outskirts, the road still straight, she knew she had to slow down, but the driver of the BMW was determined not to. She glanced again at her speedometer – 1 1 2 mph this time. In a thirty limit. *Fuck.* As the first houses blasted by – so fast it felt she was in an aircraft – she saw pavements. Village life. A woman pushing a pram flew by. Somehow Sands saw how she raised her hand to her mouth as the Alfa smashed by. Still Sands kept her foot down.

Brake lights came on up ahead as the BMW slowed hard to take the roundabout. Then they flicked off. The road was busy with cars, but they seemed to slew out the way in slow motion as the BMW skidded and slipped its way around, its tyres screaming. This time a white builder's van was left with nowhere to go, and smashed hard into the side of another car. There was no chance of Sands reporting it this time; as she approached the roundabout she knew she had to slow down. If she didn't, there'd be another crash. She hammered the brakes, shedding speed enough to make the turn. Even so the Alfa flew into the roundabout, drifting sideways for a second before squirrelling straight as she barrelled out the other side. Up ahead the BMW was almost out of sight again. She visualised the road in front of her – up a slight rise, a flat section on the top of the hill and then a long descent where, she realised now, there was another school. She blinked angrily, pressing the Alfa hard up the hill as the BMW dropped out of sight ahead, back up to well over a hundred miles per hour. Sands flashed past more pedestrians. Two girls stepped into the road ahead of her, deep in

conversation. She had time to make only the slightest adjust-
ment to her track, and it was only just enough. Another step
forward and she would have struck them both. At the speed she
was going she was seconds away from the school.

Sands suddenly leaned onto the brakes and the Alfa
juddered as it shed speed. "I can't pursue." She breathed hard,
then continued into the radio: "I can't keep after him. Someone's gonna die." She felt the long pull of the seatbelt against
her chest as the heavy Alfa slowed to what felt like nothing,
though when she glanced at the speedometer it still read sixty
miles per hour. She took another ten off, hoping that when she
crested the hill the BMW would still be in sight.

But when she got there it had completely disappeared.

TWENTY-SIX

By the time the fire service extinguished the blaze there was little left of the BMW for forensics to pick over. A little more had been discovered about its previous whereabouts, but nothing that appeared to add much to the story. It had been stolen two months earlier from the driveway of a house just outside Portsmouth, and the owner admitted to leaving his front door open, allowing the thief or thieves to simply walk in and pick up the keys. Needless to say, there was no CCTV. It had been assumed that the car would likely end up somewhere in Eastern Europe, probably Albania or Hungary, whose motor-ways were chock-a-block with high-powered UK-registered cars. The plates on the burned-out wreck didn't match the BMW, however. These were quickly traced to a 2004 Renault Clio which had spent the last two years sitting in an old-fash-ioned scrapyard which still allowed visitors to wander around, unwatched by CCTV.

"What do we know? Talk to me, what *do* we know?"

Sands' hope for a rest were dashed when she found herself in the operations room with an almost-hyperactive Area Commander Richard Black pacing up and down. Alongside her were the senior members of the investigation team. Beth Chang began reading from her notebook.

"The twins' names are Sky and Ocean Webb. They're eight years old. They were taken at gunpoint from their father just after he'd picked them up from school. He's a forty-two-year-old builder, name of Leon Webb. He was shot in the ear, but the doctors say he's gonna be OK. We have several witnesses who saw the gunman, but..." – Chang paused – "they don't agree on a description. The father claims he was tall, with blond hair tied in a ponytail, and a narrow face. Yet a lady waiting at a nearby bus stop describes him as quite short, with brown hair and possibly a beard and moustache. Another eyewitness claims he might be Asian. They do all agree he was wearing a bright yellow jacket."

"For Christ's sake." Black stopped pacing. "We have multiple eyewitnesses to an abduction in broad daylight, and that's the best we've got?"

"It's likely the brightness of the jacket interfered with their ability to recall any other features," Sands interrupted. "I'm confident I saw a ponytail too. Blond, but not super-light, more like straw-coloured. I didn't see a beard or moustache. I'd guess white European, but I only saw him for a second."

"OK." Black took a deep breath as if attempting to control his frustration. "There must be something else. I can't accept this guy can fire a gun on a crowded street, abduct *two* children and we don't have anything in the way of leads?"

Sands finally broke the ensuing silence. "The way he took the kids, the way he was driving, it was all extremely high risk. That tells us something, like he's not fully in control of things. Why not? Is he desperate? If so, why? Or is he just insanely reckless? It also matches the other evidence we have. The note left in Jane Smith's cottage was hurried and careless."

"The execution of Lindham and his family wasn't careless. It was professional. Planned."

"Maybe, but if he was sitting in his car outside Lindham's house waiting for him to get home from work, he could have been seen. We're really unlucky he wasn't. It was still a substantial risk."

"So he's a risk-taker?"

"Sometimes. But today he used a car that had been stolen two months ago, with fake plates that might have been stolen much earlier. And we have to assume he had another vehicle waiting where he dumped the BMW. That's a lot of careful preparation. There's a tension there we need to understand. We need to develop a theory that fits that contradiction."

Black listened, seemingly unimpressed. "Go on. How would you do that?"

Sands felt the eyes of everyone in the room on her. This was supposed to be Jameson's investigation, but he'd barely said a word. "He stole the BMW two months ago. It's a distinctive car, in a showy colour. It has to have been stored somewhere. We need a public appeal to find out where. Then we should get identikit images from anyone who saw him during the abduction or afterwards, me included. Between them we might be able to piece together what he looks like. Then we put them out. Perhaps someone out there will put a name to him, or place the car."

There was silence while the assembled officers considered this.

"OK. Good." Black glanced at Jameson, seeming to remember he was supposed to be leading. "What else?"

Jameson breathed in deeply. "We have a preliminary report from ballistics. They haven't been able to recover the bullet yet but the casing is the same type as those used in the Lindham murders, and the marks left suggest it was fired from the same gun. So we're looking to see whether there's any connection between the twins' family and John Lindham."

"You're still thinking organised crime?"

Jameson hesitated. "It was our most likely scenario. Now, I'm not so sure."

Black rubbed a hand over his face, roughly scratching at the skin. He turned back to Sands. "Where are we with this maths professor? Has he got anywhere with this code supposedly sent to Charles Sterling?"

Sands shook her head. "Nothing yet."

"Chase him up. Whatever deadline you gave him, it just got significantly shortened."

Sands considered whether to pass on Robbins' warning that the cipher, if it existed, might be unbeatable. "Yes sir." She paused a moment. "There's one thing I don't understand."

"What?"

"The date's wrong."

Black's eyes narrowed. "Wrong?"

"According to the warning Charles Sterling gave, the next crime should be this Friday. Sterling told us he'd be 'seeing double'. We didn't see it at the time, but clearly that can now be taken as a reference to twins. Yet our man took them *today*, Tuesday. He's planned this for months, maybe longer, and yet he's either got it wrong or he's speeding up his timeline? Why?"

"Maybe not?" said Jameson, a little dismissively.

"What?" Sands was irritated by his tone. "Explain."

"Maybe Sterling got it wrong. Maybe the guy's feeding him lies, knowing we'll eventually figure out how they're communicating. Maybe the whole thing's just a huge diversion designed to waste our time. And God knows, we've wasted enough time and resources going through Sterling's damn letters."

"Maybe." Sands looked doubtful. Abruptly she rose from her seat and clicked on the laptop in the meeting room.

"What are you doing?" Black snapped.

"I'm checking something," she said while the computer booted. "I got a message from Highmoor Prison. They found a reference to a website hidden in Sterling's cell. He had it stashed in a Bible, but he must have known it'd be found. Which perhaps means he meant for us to find it..."

Sands began typing Sterling's numbers into the address bar. "There was nothing there except this weird animation," she said. "A message to 'stay tuned'. There." She pressed search.

It was different this time. Instead of the animation she saw what appeared to be the feed from a video camera on the left-hand side of the screen. Only Sands was close enough to the laptop to see it clearly and she yanked down the projector screen on the far wall. It showed two almost identical girls lying on a bed. Their hands were bound behind their backs and their mouths taped over. Thick black straps held them down on the bed, yet every now and then one or the other moved slightly.

"Oh God," Black murmured. "Please no."

Next to the image a digital clock counted down from forty hours and thirty-five minutes. The seconds were also displayed, ticking down one by one.

"Forty hours until what?" Black asked.

There was one more item on the page, a small question mark, underlined as if it were a link. Sands hovered the mouse pointer over it and cautiously pressed the button. The question mark disappeared, and five lines of text appeared in its place:

Here you may spy
On the twins as they lie
But the time is the king
When it's gone the wrong twin
*Will be first up **to die**.*

"Forty hours from now is midday Friday," Sands said grimly. "He's not speeding up his timeline, that's when he's going to kill them."

TWENTY-SEVEN

The department was suddenly alive with activity. But to Sands it felt frantic, as if the new direction the investigative team was taking was movement for the sake of movement, a panicked response that had no chance of identifying the twins' kidnapper before the timer ran out. She locked herself in her office, trying to make sense of the rhyme, to understand the website, Lindham's death, how it all fitted together. Her only hope was that Robbins might be able to break the killer's code in time. They might then have a name which could lead them straight to the twins. But though she kept trying to call him, the phone went unanswered. Eventually she realised it was past 10 p.m., the department finally quiet.

She rang again several times the next morning but there was still no answer. At nine o'clock she decided to drive out there herself, again grabbing Golding on her way to the car park. They arrived at the old school yard just after ten, and once again Sands leaned on the bell to Robbins' apartment. Again no one came to the door, only this time, when Golding stepped back to see if any lights were on, he shook his head.

"Where the hell is he?" Sands grumbled out loud, more to

herself than anyone else. She was surprised when a voice answered. It came from the next front door along, which had opened slightly.

"If you're after Dr Robbins, he's taking his daily bath." It was the housekeeper, Mrs Hartley, who'd served them tea on their previous visit. Sands glanced up again at the upstairs windows, where she assumed the bathroom must be.

"Oh no, not there. Dr Robbins bathes outside every morning. Down in the pool. You've just missed him."

It took Sands a moment to make any sense of this. "What pool?"

The housekeeper pointed towards the sea, a half mile away across the fields. "Down by the sea. If you follow that path it takes you to Dancing Ledge. There's a bathing pool there, cut into the rock. Dr Robbins visits it daily."

Golding sighed. "You know how long he'll be?" he asked, unimpressed. But Sands didn't give the woman time to answer. "That's OK. We'll catch him up."

Turning to zap the car locked she set off, assuming Golding would fall into step beside her. Which he did, but he looked a little confused.

"I've been here before," she explained.

"Sure. We came last week."

"No. I mean I came here as a child. We used to park right there." They were passing a small National Trust car park just beyond the old schoolhouse. Beyond that a pathway cut through a field towards the sea. "I didn't properly recognise it until she mentioned the pool."

They passed through one field to an ancient stone farmhouse, and then another field, and then the vista opened out in front of them. The route ahead dropped steeply down a lush green hill towards the sea, so that it appeared they were making their way down the inside of a huge half bowl. At the bottom, when they just about to climb over a stile across a dry-stone wall, they spotted the tall figure of Dr Robbins. Too far away to shout, although Golding tried.

Sands was better dressed for the slippery path down, her boots having some grip, and she was unconcerned at the mud getting onto her jeans. Golding, however, looked out of place in his suit. She arrived at the bottom of the hill first, where she stopped and took a few moments to study the view. On the route down, Dancing Ledge itself had been hidden, but now it was revealed. A natural steppe of platform of rock, the very bottom of which was being washed by the waves. Above it, quarrying work – long since abandoned – had cut into the hillside. It formed the perfect playground for a half-dozen rock climbers who were working their way up routes marked by chalk. The only sound that came was the wash of the waves and the metallic clink of the carabiners.

Sands stood rigid, pressing her hands to the sides of her head.

"You OK?" Golding asked, puffing a little.

She didn't answer him at first, instead looking around, frowning deeply. "I'm fine."

Her eyes were resting now on the pool, on the lowest step of the rock ledges. It was roughly rectangular, and not large, but the water inside – perfectly still – was a beautiful emerald green. As they watched, Dr Robbins arrived at the edge and put down his bag. When Golding seemed about to shout, Sands held out a hand to stop him. "No. We'll go down."

He looked at her, clearly irritated with this change in character, but she was already leading the way, stepping down the loose, rocky path that led down onto the upper part of the platform. This was where the climbers were, working their way up routes in the semi-circle of cliffs. Sands seemed to know exactly where to go and led them to where it was possible to scramble down more rocks onto the lower platform. By the time they got to the pool, Dr Robbins had removed his clothes except for a tight-fitting pair of trunks. For a man north of sixty he was in good shape. His black skin shone in the weak sunlight, and his limbs were lightly muscled and loose. He noticed them now, and paused before entering the water.

"Detective Sands. Golding. What brings you down here?"

Golding opened his hands expectantly. "You're not returning our calls. We need to know if you've made any progress with the code."

Robbins seemed disappointed with this. "So you're not here to drink in the beauty of this place then?" he smiled.

Golding looked to Sands, apparently expecting to share a frustrated look, but she was gazing around, as if listening to Robbins.

"We don't really have time for beauty, sir," he said with a clear streak of sarcasm. "We're searching for a murderer, who as you've probably seen on TV has now kidnapped two children."

"Mmm. I did see that. But you should always make time for beauty. I come down here every day. Rain or shine. It keeps my head clear." He looked at Sands. "Won't you swim? Now that you're here?" He held out a hand to indicate the water. In places it looked shallow enough to stand; elsewhere it was deeper, but so clear that the bottom was perfectly visible, streaks of seaweed adding colour to the rocks.

"I don't think so." Golding's voice cut in again, clearly angry now. "And maybe you could skip it, given the circumstances, because we could really—"

"I'll swim," Sands interrupted, her eyes on Dr Robbins. Golding was stunned.

"Ma'am?"

"I said I'll swim." She slipped off her coat and laid it down on the rock floor, pockmarked like the surface of the moon. When Golding looked closer he gave a double take.

"They're ammonites," Dr Robbins said smiling, tracing his toe around one of the dimples in the rock floor. "Two hundred million years ago these seas were teeming with them. It rather puts a different perspective on our day-to-day concerns, doesn't it?"

Golding lowered his voice as he turned to Sands, who was now taking off her boots. "Ma'am do you have... anything to wear?"

"No," she replied, unbuttoning her jeans and pushing them down over her hips.

Golding moved back, a look of incomprehension on his face. But while he made some effort to avert his eyes, the professor didn't. Nearly naked himself he watched Sands undress to her underwear, and then neatly fold her clothes.

"What's that?" He pointed to a white scar cut into the side of her waist.

"Gunshot wound," she replied. "Shall we?"

"Be careful, this part's slippery," Robbins said. She refused the hand he offered her as they stepped into the water. He pretended not to notice.

"I've swum here for years. Mostly alone," he said. "But it's become more popular in recent years. Less so this time of the year of course." Robbins smiled ironically. "The trick with the cold is to keep breathing." With that, he closed his eyes for a moment and then pushed himself off the ledge and into the deeper part of the pool. He didn't gasp; his breaths were deep initially but he was soon breathing normally again, apparently impervious to the temperature. He turned and trod water while he watched Sands.

She stood in knee-deep water feeling the cold bite at her skin. The wind was light but enough to chill her shoulders and back. She took a breath and quietly rolled forwards into a shallow dive. Immediately the water felt icy against her, but she made herself stay underwater, opening her eyes and swimming past Robbins' kicking legs. She watched the rocks glide past, felt the slippery ribbons of seaweed touch her. She reached out and took hold of a rounded outcrop of rock, using it to prevent her buoyancy from pulling her towards the surface. The cold was still clawing at her but its grip was loosening a little, replaced by a strange numbness. She looked about her, noticing the shafts of sunlight that danced on the steep rock sides of the pool, feeling how the cold paradoxically was beginning to feel warm, to almost burn her skin. Finally, her lungs protesting from the lack of air, she surfaced at the far end of the pool.

Robbins was swimming lengths when she came up, an elegant breaststroke. He went on as if his unrequested narrative hadn't been interrupted. "You might think it's natural, but this pool here has a very interesting history." He parted the water with his hands almost reverentially. "The headmaster of the school that is now my house had the place blasted out of the rock by dynamite. It was a quarry then. The stone that was once here is now St Paul's Cathedral."

Sands looked around her and glanced at Robbins as they passed halfway across the pool. When she reached the shallower end she felt for the bottom with her feet, then turned and did another length.

"James Bond was a pupil." Robbins smiled. "Well, the author Ian Fleming at least. Apparently he didn't much enjoy it, it had a rather spartan ethos, but I think I'd have liked it." Robbins ducked under the water and there was silence for a while, just his shape kicking like a large black frog as he swam one length after another under the clear water. When he surfaced at the shallow end he began to climb out, breathing more heavily now. Sands followed him.

"It's dangerous to stay in too long this time of year," he explained. He dried himself with a towel before passing it to Sands. "Though the walk back up does tend to warm one up."

They dressed, and then the professor led the way back, his hands and feet going easily to well-worn footholds in the rock until they reached the upper platform, where he pointed out

where climbers had fixed metal bolts into the rock of the man-
made cliffs around them. Sands looked around with interest
while Golding watched her, still somewhat confused by events.
The climbers worked slowly in pairs, one steadily inching their
way up the sheer face of the rock while the other rappelled with
the ropes below.

"But we can't stay here all day," Robbins said at last. "You'll
want to know about your cipher."

TWENTY-EIGHT

When they arrived at the house Robbins asked Mrs Hartley to make hot tea, which they took in the library. When Sands declined the offer of a hot shower a little too demurely, Golding glanced nervously across at her, apparently still expecting her to finally lose patience. But she seemed to have summoned an almost preternatural calm since the mention of the pool and Dancing Ledge, content to sip from her cup while the professor talked more about the village, how it had once been the base for the quarrymen who'd cut the stones from the ledge below and shipped it out on calm days by boat. Only when they'd finished their tea did Robbins suggest they visit his study.

It was up a flight of stairs, another beautifully decorated room with a stunning view out over the fields and down to the sea. There were shelves lined with leather-bound books, and more photographs of Robbins alongside the great and the good. And yet there was evidence of disorder too. On top of the antique desk was a dated desktop computer, and books and papers were piled all over.

"Please, sit." He indicated two wooden chairs in front of the desk, and took the leather one behind it for himself, swivelling to face them. "Now. Your cipher."

He had the papers ready in front of him, studying them for a moment before pointing towards the grid on the second page. "What you see, if we take the paper at face value, is a list of pseudo-random numbers. That is to say, *apparently* random numbers, but generated by an algorithm. However, we suspect that these numbers are actually a ciphertext, and therefore not random at all. Yet we need to decrypt them to produce the plaintext. All with me so far?" He glanced at Sands, but she didn't appear to be listening, her eyes softly focused on the view outside the window, frowning as if lost in thought. The professor gave her a curious look, then turned his attention to Golding.

"I'm with you," he said. "Keep going."

"OK. So, when I took this on, I imagined this would be something relatively simple. We know that Sterling has no access to a computer. That drastically narrows down the potential cipher techniques that could have been used here. We're likely dealing with a pen-and-paper cipher, something the coder can implement manually. So, no asymmetric encryption or anything that requires significant computational power. And, I have to admit, it was rather fun going old-school. I started by looking for patterns in the code – repeating groups of numbers. These repetitions are known as 'cribs', and they could give us a clue about the length of the key, like in the Vigenère cipher."

He pointed to the number grid and showed Golding two instances where the digits ran sequentially 4, 5, 6, and another 12, 13, 14. "These could indicate a repeating keyword used for encoding. But," – he held up his hands – "Nothing.

"Next, I looked at frequency analysis. Even in complex codes, the frequency of symbols often aligns with the frequency of letters in the language of the plaintext. In English, for instance, 'E' is the most common letter, followed by 'T', and then 'A', and so on. This method can be incredibly effective against simple substitution ciphers. But again, nothing. Which led me into the world of transposition ciphers. These jumble up the order of the plaintext without altering the characters themselves..." He shook his head. "No dice. So I spent some time exploring whether this might be a null cipher of some sort. That's where the actual message is hidden in the plaintext and the rest of the text serves as a kind of smokescreen."

He paused, again seemingly confused by Sands' apparent lack of attention. "Are you alright, Detective?" he asked.

When she didn't answer, Golding glanced across at her before replying, "Please, go on. Is it a null cipher?"

"No." Robbins chuckled. "Of course, this is only a very high-level overview, there are a wealth of manual ciphers out there, but I think I can say with some certainty that this isn't one of them." He stopped, sitting back in his chair and waiting.

"So what are you saying? It's just numbers? There is no secret message?"

"Oh no. The contents of the accompanying article make it abundantly clear there is something to be found."

"But you can't find it?"

"The message does not appear to be protected by any traditional, manual cipher, and even Charles Sterling would be unable to perform the calculations required to unscramble an RSA or elliptical-curve protocol by hand. So for a while I must admit I was confused. Clearly there's something here, and it's something that does not require a computer to decipher. So what could it be?"

Robbins' eyes gleamed. His attention was fixed on Golding now, his audience, and he was enjoying himself.

"I give up. We were rather hoping you could tell us."

"It's a book cipher," Sands said suddenly. Robbins and Golding turned to look at her.

"A what?" Golding asked.

"The message is protected by a book cipher."

Robbins seemed disappointed, but he tipped his head in acknowledgement. "Very good, Detective Sands. I assume you showed this puzzle to other cryptographic experts, besides myself?"

"No. I realised when you showed us in here."

It was Robbins turn to look confused. He opened his mouth to reply but Sands cut in. Her attention was back. "Your desk is littered with books. What else could it be?"

There was a brief silence before Robbins began laughing, a loud, booming sound.

"Hang on, hold it please," Golding interrupted. "I appreciate this makes perfect sense to both of you, but can one of you please tell me what a book cipher is?"

With Sands lapsing back into thoughtful silence, Robbins seemed delighted to provide an explanation. "A book cipher is a cryptographic system where the key to decoding the message is a specific book or piece of text held by the sender and receiver. The coded message consists of a series of numbers, each of which refers to a word or a letter in the key text. It could be anything from a book, a poem, even a newspaper article." Robbins smiled broadly.

"OK..." Golding seemed none the wiser. "Is that good or..."

Robbins shrugged. "It has no intrinsic value, Detective. It simply describes how the numbers in a coded message don't relate to the frequency of letters or words in the plaintext at all. Instead they relate to their position in the key text. This makes frequency analysis, or any other common crypto-analytic method, almost completely ineffective."

When Golding remained silent, Robbins held up the number grid again.

"This first number here, 27281. If this is a book cipher, it might be an instruction to look on page 27, line 28 and word 1. Of course, there are variations. You might need to reverse the order, so page 18, line 27, word 2. But you understand the essence of it?"

"I think so." Golding nodded. "So is this good news? Or not?"

Robbins was silent a moment, considering. "That depends. Historically speaking, book codes have been some of the most difficult to break, and in several instances have never been broken at all, even with the help of modern computers. They are protected by the sheer number of possible key texts – there are billions of books, texts, articles, poems, published and unpublished. But, they have one notorious weakness." He waved a hand over the piles of books on the desk. "If you can discover the text used, you can break them quite easily."

"So what have you tried?" asked Golding.

"Take your pick. Certain types of texts are traditionally associated with book ciphers. You might have heard of the Beale cipher? The location of a huge treasure hoard was hidden within the text of the United States Declaration of Independence. Given we're dealing with Charles Sterling, I've also tried various mathematical papers." He pointed to a pile of texts next to Sands. "But no luck yet. However, what might seem a hopeless case looks slightly more optimistic, I believe, in view of the fact that Sterling is in prison. He will have access to only a very limited subset of texts, and we should be able to check them all. What I need from you now is a list of all the texts in his cell, and any others he might have had access to. If you can get me that, then I'm confident of success." Robbins smiled broadly and Sands picked up the top few sheets from the pile of mathematical papers. The first, she noticed, was the paper Robbins himself had authored, laying the groundwork for the development of cryptocurrencies, and making his fortune. She tossed it back on the desk, then went back to staring out the window.

"OK. We'll put you in touch with the prison director." She inclined her head to Golding. "We need to go."

TWENTY-NINE

Golding waited until they were nearly back at the station before speaking. "Is everything OK? You seem a bit out of it."

She didn't answer, as if proving him right.

"That was good news, wasn't it? There's a good chance we can find the text, and then we can decipher whatever information Sterling's being sent?"

Sands finally opened up. "There's something I don't like about Robbins."

Golding's eyebrows rose a fraction. "Really? Well he likes you."

Sands turned sharply. "Why do you say that?"

"Because it's true. He likes you, or you *interest* him, or something like that."

She said nothing, just frowned at him.

"I don't know. Maybe smart people just like smart people. Why don't you like him?"

"I'm not sure. Maybe I'm reading more into it than I ought to."

"Into what?"

They were at the station now, but instead of turning into

the car park they stayed outside, half blocking the road. "There's something I need to do. Will you come with me?"

"Sure."

She took off again. Faster this time. Golding didn't ask where they were going, he just waited.

Sands drove the short distance to her apartment. Inside, she opened a filing cabinet in one of the spare bedrooms she used as an office. Rooting through the folders, she eventually found what she was looking for, an unmarked brown envelope. She shook the contents out into her hand, an old, heavy key. She stared at it for a while, then put it into her bag.

"Come on."

It was a longer drive this time, first towards Southampton, and then out into the New Forest. Although it had been many years since she'd been there, there was no danger of getting lost, even as she wound the car down smaller and smaller country lanes, past stands of old trees, their leaves turning red and gold. Eventually she turned into what was little more than a muddy track and bumped the Alfa through potholes filled with milky-brown water. She pulled up in front of a long, stone building. One end of it was clearly lived in, though it had the pretty-yet-basic look of a holiday property, or one used for short-term lets. The other end had the tall, wide doors of a barn. The building stood alone in the forest. On one side were trees: tall, mature oaks, sycamores and beeches. On the other was a wide grassy clearing where a few of the Forest's famous ponies grazed.

"I used to live here," she said after a while. "After my mother and sister died, a woman named Dorothy Hodges – she was a friend of my mother – she took me in."

There were no other vehicles in the cottage's parking bay and Sands walked up to a downstairs window and peered in, shielding her eyes. There was no one inside but the place was spotless, presumably awaiting a new set of guests.

"She didn't have any children of her own, and she didn't...

she didn't know how to cope. I wasn't exactly easy." Sands let her mind wander back to the years after her father's arrest, the months of the trial. She remembered the mood swings, the depression. The raw aggression. She had lurked in her new bedroom, sometimes for days on end, refusing to come out to eat, so that Dorothy had left food outside her door, begging her to eat it. And then, when she did finally emerge, she would fly into an animal rage at the slightest provocation, smashing plates and glasses in the kitchen, roaring and sobbing without end. There were better times too. She was eventually enrolled in the local school, but there were fights. And she began setting fires, declaring that she wanted the world to burn. Eventually Dorothy Hodges had admitted that her murdered friend's daughter was too much, too difficult. Sands had been sent away a second time. And soon after that Hodges had died from a hith-erto-unnoticed cancer. Sands had blamed herself for that too. At the funeral she felt how others there blamed her as well.

She turned away from Golding, not wanting him to see how much just being there was affecting her. She led the way to the other end of the building, which looked almost derelict, although the barn doors, made of heavy, solid wood, had clearly been maintained at a basic level. She felt in her pocket for the key and slipped it into the lock.

She had to tug hard on the door to open it; the grass and soil had grown too high to allow the bottom of the door to slide over it and she hacked it away with the side of her boot. With Gold-ing's help she was able to pull the door open as far it would go. She flicked on a torch and shone the light around. Inside, loosely piled up and covered in places with dust sheets, the space was filled with furniture, boxes and old chests.

"When Sterling was arrested, they pretty much tore the house apart looking for evidence of other murders. But after his conviction it all got returned. I was living here then, and Dorothy had the space, so it just got piled up here in the barn."

Sands touched a dark wooden dresser. It had once stood in her old hallway, and for a second she was back there, following her mother in from school, squabbling about everything and nothing with her sister.

"When Sterling was sentenced to life in prison, the judge ordered all his assets to pass to me. The house, his investments – which had done well. I wasn't allowed to spend any of it without agreement from a lawyer until I was eighteen, but when Dorothy died they thought it would be good for me to buy this place. It meant none of this had to be disturbed. I guess it was easier that way for everyone." She took in the dirt and the dust and the decay.

"Someone manages it for me now. They rent out next door, and it all... It all kinda pays for itself. I haven't been here for years."

Golding was quiet.

"I don't know why. I don't know why I still keep it. I should have it cleaned out. The place would probably be worth a fortune if it was done up." She tried a smile, but it faded as she shone the torch around again. The light fell on a painting that had been only half-covered by a dust sheet. It had once hung over the fireplace in the Sterlings' living room. It looked damaged by damp, possibly insects. "I can't quite bring myself to let it go."

With that, Sands seemed to shift into another mood. She flicked the light from the torch off the painting and back around the space. She led the way, picking a route carefully through the barn.

Boxes were piled from the floor right up to the ceiling. There were beds, a sofa; long ago it had been used as a nest, but was now covered with dried guano, sticks and moss. She saw her mother's dressing table, the curved mirror now cracked. A tea chest sat next to it. A memory connected in Sands' brain.

"Help me move this."

They heaved the chest up and carried it onto a table close enough to the door that they no longer needed the torch. Sands opened the lid, the hinges protesting for lack of use.

There were yellowing newspapers inside. Sands burrowed into them and pulled out a dining plate. It was of a reasonable quality; someone must have decided an older Erica might want to keep the set. For a second she saw her teenage self, throwing plates at the window in the cottage next door. Perhaps Mrs Hodges might have appreciated them more. She put the plate gently on the table and then checked the rest of the box, finding only more dishes.

She shook her head and then looked around again, this time noticing a dark green rucksack. She remembered it at once and unclipped the top, to find it loosely packed with a jumble of ropes – her father's old climbing gear. And now she was moving quickly, suddenly familiar with the space and its contents, through which she'd roamed many times as a teenager. Next to the rucksack were two suitcases containing his clothes, the jackets and shoes he'd worn in his academic life. She passed them by and moved on. Deeper in the room there was a bicycle, then another – hers and her sister's. More tables and chairs. Another sofa, and then the two armchairs that matched it. And then another stack of boxes. These she approached more cautiously, knowing she was close this time.

The first box contained nothing but books. For a few moments she lifted a few out – novels her mother had liked. Travelogues, true stories of adventure that her father had read – expeditions in the Himalayas or sailing adventures across oceans. Some kids' books too. She remembered Robbins' describing the book code, but there was no real reason to suspect that any of these, amongst the tens of millions of books out there, would have been used by the killer. She slipped them back and moved onto the next box.

Finally, she found what she was looking for.

Both her parents had been keen photographers in their own way. It was the days before cameras were digital, when films had to be developed or sent off to labs, packets of photographs coming back in the post a week later. Her mother had then arranged them into albums, one or two for each year. Sands remembered looking through them before it all happened. She opened the topmost album which contained baby pictures; her mother, looking younger than she remembered her, smiling as she held the infant Erica. She turned the pages to see Sterling, smiling and laughing while she learned to walk. She swallowed and kept going.

She dug deeper into the box, knowing she needed to skip forward only a few years. Her mother had written the year on the albums' spines and she was able to skip right to the time period she wanted: 1991. When she had been four years old. Her baby sister two years younger.

She took the album outside and sat on a picnic bench in the pretty garden, ignoring the dampness of the seat.

The first photographs showed a party she had no memory of: she'd probably been asleep upstairs. From the decorations she guessed it was a Christmas party, perhaps New Year's Eve. She studied the images one by one, staring at the people holding glasses and dancing. She didn't see what she was looking for. She skipped forwards, past a skiing holiday that sent a jarring memory into her mind, of driving to the Alps, her head resting against the same fabric seats in which they'd soon discover blood, hair and fibres from Sterling's victims. More pages forward. More photographs of her and her sister. And then, suddenly, an image that almost leapt out of the page.

The photograph itself was a little faded, but the location had been so recently fixed in her mind that it seemed almost more vivid than reality. It had been taken at the same stone platform and quarry she'd visited just hours earlier with Golding and Robbins. In the foreground, however, a girl aged about four

– Erica – a beaming smile on her innocent face, had been caught mid-air as she leapt off the rock platform into the calm green water of the Dancing Ledge pool.

She remembered it now. The splash, the wonder of the underwater world of the pool, cold but so compelling that she'd wished she could stay there forever. The other people swimming with her. Her mother and father, their legs, weird, magnified by the refraction of the water. Pale, where they hadn't seen much sun. And then another man whose legs *weren't* pale.

This wasn't quite the image she was after. She turned the page to see more swimming shots, and then a few of her being taught to climb, roped-up and halfway up one of the smaller, easier sections of the cliff. Then more climbing shots of her father, on much higher, harder routes, her mother belaying him from below. Then her mother climbing as well, top-roped so that if she slipped her fall would be arrested at once. And then, there it was.

The next image showed two men smiling at the camera. One of them was her father, his face relaxed and handsome. He was laughing at something. The other man she blinked at in half-remembered confusion. He was taller than Sterling, and as a younger man somehow had even more of an appearance of African nobility. The man next to her father, with his arm draped casually around his shoulders, was Jeremiah Robbins.

THIRTY

"I don't think I fully understand what's going on here."

Golding spoke from the passenger seat of the Alfa – it had started to rain, and they'd taken shelter in the car, still parked outside the barn. Raindrops pattered softly on the windscreen. The photo album lay on the dashboard between them.

"I didn't recognise his name when he came up as a mathematics expert, but when we turned up at his house... I don't know."

Golding waited.

"There was something. Some part of a memory. But it felt... buried. Like it was too deep to access, but then I couldn't shake it either. Then when we went down to the pool..." She stopped.

"That's why you swam? You remembered something? I thought you'd gone crazy."

She nodded. "In a way. Once I was under the water the feeling was stronger. I knew I'd been there. But I didn't know when."

Golding picked up the album and studied it. "So how old are you here?"

"Three." Sands considered the date written by the photograph. "Nearly four."

"Shit." He shook his head. "I'm pretty sure I don't remember a thing from when I was four years old." He turned the page and stared the photograph showing Sterling and Robbins arm-in-arm.

"Maybe I don't remember it exactly." Sands spoke carefully. "I've read about memory. For most people, what they think of as early childhood memories are actually what they've been told about, or seen photographs of, later on in their lives. I definitely remember looking at these photographs with my sister, and maybe that's all I have. It's complicated. After my family died I had no one to share memories with; no one showed me these photographs."

"So you're saying Robbins lied about knowing your dad? You think it might be relevant?"

"He didn't exactly lie. He admitted to knowing him."

"Yeah. But he said he didn't know him well."

"Maybe he didn't. Maybe this was a one-off."

"It doesn't look like a one-off. They've got their arms around each other. You wouldn't classify that as not knowing someone well, would you?"

"I might. If that person went on to be revealed as a multiple murderer."

The rain grew heavier now, the view of the cottage and the forest blurring with the water.

"OK, but he should have mentioned that he knew *you*. As a child. Why's he hiding that?"

Sands sighed and shook her head.

"And is it relevant to our case?" Golding added. "Or just a coincidence?"

Sands flicked on the wipers to reveal the cottage, looking sad and cold in the rain. She flicked them off again. "I don't know."

"OK." Golding seemed to sense she needed his help through this. He picked up the album again. "Do you know who took the pictures?"

Sands was still lost in reverie. "Dad... Sterling was into photography, he had his own dark room in the house. But Mum took photos too, only she sent them away. You remember those envelopes people used to use?" She half-smiled. "Or are you too young for that?"

"I kinda remember."

Sands watched as Golding turned the page to show the image of her mother climbing.

"So I guess whoever was there that day passed the camera around." She flicked the ignition again, but this time the wipers squeaked when they swished across. The rain was easing.

"How about later on?" Golding asked suddenly. "In these pictures you're just a little kid. Do you have any memories of Robbins being around when you were older?"

She shook her head. "No. Nothing."

"We should check."

She shook her head, convinced she wasn't mistaken about this. Golding went on carefully.

"OK, but Sterling was arrested when you were twelve, right?"

Sands nodded.

"So Robbins and Sterling go climbing together, like buddies, when you're three years old, but then he never comes around anymore. But their break-up happens ten years before he gets caught."

"If it was a break-up. We don't exactly know."

"We could go ask him," Golding suggested. "Robbins, I mean."

"We could ask either of them," Sands replied. "But we'd be giving up any advantage we might have. They don't know we've seen this photo."

Golding stroked his chin. "When we first turned up there, at Robbins' house, he didn't want to help, said he was retired. Then when you mentioned Sterling, that's when he agreed."

Sands worked the wipers again, this time leaving the ignition on.

"How about family members. Grandparents? Uncles? Other friends? Anyone you can ask?"

"My grandparents were dead long before Sterling was arrested." She turned to Golding with a wry smile. "Natural causes. And both he and my mother were only children so..." Sands shrugged. "As for friends of the family, I don't know. I wasn't exactly popular as a child, and my parents' friends – I guess they all kind of melted away."

Golding sat back in his seat. "Jesus. You know I haven't really said this before, but I'm genuinely sorry for everything you went through."

Sands stiffened but said nothing.

"It's... I had the most easy, normal upbringing you could ask for. I just... I have no frame of reference for what it must have been like for you."

Sands looked away until she'd brought a wave of emotion under control. She hadn't been expecting it. When she looked back at Golding, he was staring closely at another image. There was something about the look on his face. "What is it?"

He looked up, handing the album across to her. "Who's *that*?"

He'd given Sands another photograph of her, from the same day, beaming at the camera in her bathing suit, standing on the edge of the pool, its translucent waters sparkling in the sunlight. She gave him a look. "I told you, that's me."

"No, not you, *there*." His voice had changed and he stabbed a finger at the album, then looked up and stared at Sands. She peered at the figure of a woman in bikini top and shorts, perhaps twenty-five years old.

"It's just a woman in the background."

"No, it's not. You don't recognise her?"

Sands looked again. "No. Do you?"

"I think so. I can't be sure, because she's younger here. And I've only seen her dead, after someone pushed her down the stairs. But Lindham had me working on the case, and I found a load of her photos while looking through her things." He was excited, and now Sands saw it too.

"How did this whole case start? What was Lindham working on? I'd swear that this is a picture of a young Jane Smith."

THIRTY-ONE

"So where do we begin?" Golding asked, finishing the first of the sandwiches he'd grabbed from the canteen on the way upstairs, one for him, the other for Sands.

The two of them were in her office, the photographs from the pool laid out next to images of a much older Jane Smith. It wasn't possible to say for sure whether they were the same person. When she saw Golding eyeing the second sandwich, Sands pushed it over to him.

"You sure?"

"I don't eat sandwiches from the canteen."

Golding shrugged and pulled open the wrapper. He extracted a limp cheese and ham sandwich on white bread. "What we need to do," he said taking a large bite out of the middle of the triangle, "is confirm whether this really is Jane Smith."

"OK. How?" Sands asked.

"How did Robbins know Sterling? At the university? Were they colleagues? Perhaps someone there can tell us whether they were close or not. Phone the university."

Sands weighed the idea for a few moments. Then picked up the phone.

It turned out the mathematics department at the University of Southampton was rather poor at record keeping. Sands' call was passed to the human resources department and eventually produced a list of six former lecturers and professors who'd worked there around the time the pool photograph had been taken. All were retired. A bit more digging established that three had passed away, none under suspicious circumstances. The others had moved away – one to her native Norway, another to Texas. Only one, David Bell, still lived in the UK, in York. A Google search told Sands it was just over five hours drive away. She began to gather up the photos from her desk.

Golding glanced at his watch. "We should phone first, make sure he's there."

"I'll call. Can you get some more of those sandwiches and meet me in the car?"

Sands drove fast, keeping the Alfa in the fast lane all the way up the M1 and stopping only once for fuel. When they arrived, around 9 p.m., Bell was already at the door.

"Detective Sands? Over here."

He wore brown corduroy trousers, a check shirt and black-rimmed glasses. It wouldn't have been hard to pick him from a line-up as a former mathematics lecturer. He invited them inside and led them to a small kitchen where he'd set out three mugs next to a chipped brown tea pot. He gestured for them to sit and clicked the kettle onto boil.

"This is all very dramatic," he said. He looked a little excited. "I don't usually have visitors this late. In fact, not usually at all. Certainly not the police!" He laughed nervously. When the kettle had finished boiling he filled the pot. "What exactly is it about?"

Sands made a point of identifying herself properly, showing her warrant card and waiting until Golding did the same. She glanced around the room, taking in the single plate drying by the sink. One knife, one fork. Only a few medical appointments were written on a calendar on the wall.

"We're investigating the murder of a police officer and his family, which may be linked to the kidnapping of two young children."

"I saw it on the news. A terrible thing. If there's anything I can do to help I will, but I don't see..."

"There may be another link," Sands interrupted, "to Charles Sterling, the serial killer caught in 1999." She paused. "I believe you worked with him at Southampton University?"

It took Bell some time to answer. "Yes. But I don't see the link. Surely he's still in prison?"

"He is. And we're not sure it *is* linked. We're just trying to establish some background facts."

Bell seemed satisfied with this. He checked the tea, and that was apparently OK too as he then poured, added a splash of milk and passed the mugs around before sitting opposite them. He took a slurp from his cup and waited.

"Did you know him well?" Sands began.

"Sterling? Thankfully not."

"But you remember him?"

"Of course. It's not the sort of thing you easily forget, a colleague being uncovered as a killer, especially in a case like that. I remember the sense of shock and outrage. How he could have done that and then just waltz around the department, calm as you like. He was arrogant. A nasty man."

Sands nodded. "We're interested in what happened before he was uncovered. Do you have any recollection of that time?"

"I suppose so. Yes."

"Did he have any friends in the department?"

Bell looked confused. "I... I mean, I suppose he must have

done, but I don't recall anybody in particular. I think most people felt like I did. That he was rather unpleasant. He liked to think he was one of the world's great thinkers, if you know what I mean? And he acted accordingly." Bell smiled and Sands nodded back.

"Uh huh. Did you do anything socially with him? Go out for drinks? Departmental meals?"

"I... Not that I remember."

"Why not?"

He seemed surprised. "How do you mean?"

"You were both staff, I'm sure there would have been some sort of social scene? Did you all go out for drinks?"

He seemed taken aback. "I suppose so. Yes. Yes we did, on occasion."

"But you never went out with Sterling?"

"Look Detective, what is this about?"

"Please just answer the question. Did you ever socialise with Sterling?"

"I might have done. I don't remember. But I wasn't a big socialiser to be honest."

Sands felt frustrated, unusually unsure of herself, and she was pleased when Golding took over. "Did you know Jeremiah Robbins?" he asked.

Bell gave a surprised smile. "Of course."

"How?"

"I worked with him for a decade or more. A great man, first-class mind."

"Did Jeremiah Robbins know Sterling?"

Bell paused, thinking, then shrugged. "I don't know. Robbins is something of an institution at Southampton. He was there for... decades, I'm pretty sure he overlapped with Sterling. In fact I know he did." He nodded to himself. "I remember his reaction when Sterling was arrested."

"What was his reaction?"

"He was profoundly shocked. We all were."

"Was he especially shocked? More so than other people?"

"No. I mean, not unusually so, if that's what you're imply-ing. He was like everybody else, stunned. It's just that the two of them worked much more closely together."

Sands took over again, suddenly interested. "How so?"

"They both worked on cryptography. The mathematics behind it."

"I thought that was Robbins?"

"It was. At least, he authored a very famous paper on it. Many claim it was the foundation for all modern cryptography, cryptocurrencies – almost everything that modern money move-ment relies upon. But I believe Sterling worked in a similar field for a while."

Sands frowned, thinking hard.

"So they were friends, working together?" Golding cut in.

"I... I don't know. I wouldn't quite put it that way. Sterling was much more junior than Jeremiah."

"How would *you* put it?"

"I wouldn't... I wouldn't like to say."

"We *would* like you to say," Golding pressed, staring hard at Bell. "We've driven five hours to ask you."

"I'm sorry, Detective. I really don't remember. It was a long time ago and – what happened afterwards rather dominates the memory, do you know what I mean?"

"I do." Sands interrupted again. "I know exactly what you mean, but this is important. Is there anything you can remember about the relationship between Sterling and Robbins?"

Bell seemed to take a sudden interest in the inside of his tea mug. "I don't know why this would be important, but I don't want to get Professor Robbins into any trouble, he's a great man."

"Why would it get him into trouble?" Golding said, but Sands held up her hand.

"Just tell us what you remember."

There was a long pause before Bell eventually continued. "Robbins tutored Sterling when Charles was doing his PhD. They seemed close then, but afterwards, when Sterling came onto the staff full-time, things changed."

"And you don't know why?"

When Bell hesitated, Sands let the silence grow.

"I know there was some sort of a disagreement."

"What about?"

Bell shook his head. "Some aspect of their work?" He shrugged. "A girl? Professor Robbins had a string of girlfriends, and Sterling was married, but he had a bit of a reputation too. That was before it came out what he was really up to."

"Do you have a particular girl in mind? Do you remember her name?"

"I... don't. I'm speculating."

Sands tried another tack. "Do you remember a woman named Jane Smith? She might have had some sort of connection with Robbins. Or perhaps with Sterling. Maybe both."

Bell seemed to search his memory, but in the end just shook his head.

"Are you sure? It's a common name, quite easy to forget," Sands prompted. If he'd never heard of her, they'd come all this way for nothing. She watched his face carefully as he replied, searching for clues that he might be concealing something.

"No." His eyes looked directly into hers.

Disappointed, Sands glanced at Golding.

"I do remember a *Caroline* Smith," Bell said suddenly.

Sands snapped her head back to look at him. He looked earnest, as if trying to be helpful. And Golding was already replying. "Thank you, Mr Bell. As DCI Sands says, 'Smith' is a very common name, so—"

"What did Caroline Smith look like?" Sands interrupted.

"She was... It was a long time ago." He shrugged. "Brown

hair. Medium height. Quite..." – he looked embarrassed for a moment, unsure where to look – "Quite pretty, as I remember."

"What did she do?"

"She worked at the university. Something in the administrative department."

"Was she connected to Robbins in any way? Or Sterling?"

"I..." Bell stopped. "As I say, I have nothing but respect for Professor Robbins, and I hope this isn't anything he wouldn't want me to reveal. But it..." – he hesitated – "It wouldn't have been out of character if he'd had an affair with Caroline. She was very pretty, and he was always interested in pretty girls. When he was younger, I mean."

"And you're quite sure this woman's name was Caroline?" Sands asked. "It couldn't have been Jane?"

"Absolutely. I was... I was friends with Caroline myself." The way he said the word left little doubt of his own feelings for the woman.

"And is this her?" Sands had pulled out the photograph taken by the edge of the pool.

"Oh yes." Bell seemed to drink in the image of the woman in her bikini. "That's Caroline."

"Thank you," Sands said. "You've been a big help."

THIRTY-TWO

By the time Bell showed them out it was raining again. They hurried to the Alfa and shut the doors. The clock glowed red in the darkness: 22:15.

"Now what?" Golding asked.

"It's late. I don't feel like driving back tonight. Do you want to see if you can find a cheap hotel somewhere? There must be a Travelodge or something?"

Golding hesitated.

"Separate rooms," Sands went on. "Obviously. We'll charge it to the department."

"Sure." He pulled out his phone and began to search.

"I've got a couple of calls to make too," Sands said. "I'll be outside." She pointed to a large tree with enough leaves to offer shelter.

Five minutes later she pulled open the door and slipped back in.

"Well I don't know about you, but I'm hungry and thirsty." Suddenly, her mood seemed to have improved.

. . .

She followed the signs into the city centre and before long spotted what she'd been looking for: an open Indian Restaurant. She expertly manoeuvred the car into a small parking space and jumped out, Golding trailing behind her. The restaurant wasn't busy, and the staff seemed happy to give them a table, despite the hour. It smelt good, aromatic and sweet. Sands ordered beers, then studied the menu.

"What's good here?" she asked the waiter, a young Indian man in a starched white shirt. At first he seemed unwilling to answer, telling her that everything was good, but she pressed the point. "What would *you* have?"

Still a little reluctant, he told her, his accent a melodic blend of Black Yorkshire and south India. "I'm vegetarian, so I usually take the lentil dhal and the aloo baingan, that's a potato and aub—"

"That's great, I'll have that. And do you do a chana masala too? Chickpeas always go well with aubergines."

"Sure."

"And a couple of naans. And poppadoms." She handed back the menu and looked expectantly at Golding.

"You know, I think I'll have the same," he said, handing his own menu back. The waiter shrugged and returned languidly to the kitchen.

"You sound a little like you're celebrating," Golding said a few moments later as he watched Sands take a deep gulp from her lager.

"I am. Partly. We're beginning to figure out what's going on in this case."

He waited, hoping she might go on, before replying, "Yeah, I agree."

The waiter returned with a plate of fresh popadoms and a tray of pickles. Sands dug in, cracking the huge crisps and piling a shard high with lime pickle.

"OK, I give up," Golding said. "Tell me."

Sands took her time crunching into the poppadom and savouring the pickle before answering, still looking satisfied. "OK. We have Jane Smith, murdered in her home two months ago. We thought it was a burglary gone wrong before a tip-off from Charles Sterling suggested otherwise. But how did Sterling know anything about her death, and why does he care?"

"We don't know..." Golding began, before correcting himself. "*I* don't know."

"Nor do I." Sands bit off another mouthful and chewed it before continuing. "But we do know he's somehow communicating with whoever killed Smith. Mmm, these are good."

When she broke off again to refill her plate Golding gave up and joined her. Eventually, Sands was ready to continue.

"We also know that Charles Sterling worked in the same department and conducted similar research to Professor Jeremiah Robbins at Southampton University in the years before Sterling was arrested."

"Uh huh."

"We also know that a Caroline Smith also worked there, and may or may not have had an affair with Professor Robbins, and/or Charles Sterling. In fact, we can be fairly confident that if she was having an affair, it was with Robbins, since she's in that photograph at Dancing Ledge with him. Sterling was also there that day, but he was there with his wife, my mother. Finally, we know that you recognised Smith in the same photograph."

The waiter came back and placed a silver tray on a side table, their food sizzling on hot plates. Carefully, he lifted them onto the table.

"I thought I saw *Jane* Smith," Golding replied when the waiter had backed away. "The woman who was murdered."

"You did." Sands began spooning rice onto her plate, then topped it with the curry. She tore off some naan.

"No. Bell just identified her as Caroline Smith."

"Caroline... Jane... what's the difference?" Sands waved a hand airily as she carried on eating.

Golding blinked carefully. "Caroline Smith *is* Jane Smith? She changed her name? Is that it?"

Sands paused, looking at him strangely. "No," she said through a mouthful of curry. "Why are we here?"

Golding looked around the restaurant.

"Not here. *Here.* Why did we come to York?"

"To speak with Bell. To identify Jane Smith in the photo. Only we didn't, because he said it was actually Caroline..."

"Wider, think wider."

"Because the killer's going to strike again, he's kidnapped the..." Golding stopped.

Sands looked at him now.

"Twins."

"Uh huh. Jane Smith had a sister. She lives in Canada. That's why her house was in such a state. There was no one left here in the UK to sort it out." Sands lifted another forkful of curry to her mouth, still smiling.

"OK." Golding seemed to be thinking quickly now. "The rhyme on the website, it mentioned something about the wrong twin dying. So if Caroline Smith is alive, could that somehow be a reference to that? Whoever killed Jane Smith got the wrong twin?"

"I have no idea," Sands replied. She still looked uncharacteristically pleased.

Golding finally shrugged. "I don't get it. Even if it is Caroline Smith she's in Canada, we'd have to fly over there, and there's zero chance of that happening. Even less by Friday. So we're stuck."

"We certainly would be, *if* she was in Canada. But she isn't. Her phone number's in the file for the Jane Smith case and I just called her. She's here. She's in the UK arranging the sale of her sister's house. So we're meeting her at eleven o'clock tomorrow morning."

She forked a large portion of the curry onto the rice already resting on her plate.

"This case is coming together." Sands smiled.

THIRTY-THREE

Even though they left at 6 a.m. the following morning, Sands still had to push to make the meeting. But by 11:30 the Alfa was nosing between the gateposts of Jane Smith's country cottage and crunching to a halt on the gravel. Another car was already there, a small Ford that looked like a rental. The cottage seemed a little more cared for this time, the police tape was gone, the smashed window replaced. A gardener had been at work too, the lawn freshly cut and the hedge trimmed. Angled so it could be seen from the road, an estate agent's board announced the cottage was for sale. In the sunshine, it might even have looked pretty.

Sands' good humour hadn't survived the night and much of the drive had been spent in silence. Now she seemed impatient, marching quickly to the door and rapping sharply with her knuckles.

"Caroline Smith? I'm DCI Sands. We spoke last night." Sands held out her ID while Golding also introduced himself.

Smith led the way through to the lounge and invited them to sit. Sands glanced around, remembering when she'd last seen the place, before focusing on Smith. The family resemblance was clear, but as adults they were far from identical.

"Can I offer you a tea?" Smith asked. Her voice had acquired a Canadian twang.

"No thank you," Sands answered quickly, not giving Golding the chance. "We had coffee on the M1."

"We want to talk to you about your sister's death," she continued, dispensing with small talk. "You were told it was probably a burglary that went wrong. That theory may well be incorrect."

"I see." Smith looked guarded.

"We think it might be connected to a series of other crimes. Including the kidnapping of two eight-year-old girls last week."

Smith looked uncomprehending.

"And before that, the death of a serving police officer and his family. Detective John Lindham."

Smith waited a beat, then held out her hands. "I'm sorry, that's horrible, all of it. But I don't see how I can help. I've been living abroad for many years. I only came back to the UK last week."

"We know." Sands nodded carefully. "There may also be a historical element to this case. It may involve Professor Jeremiah Robbins... and Charles Sterling."

Smith's eyes darted up from the floor at the first name, and then quickly back down at the second.

"Do either of those names mean anything to you?"

"I worked with Sterling. And with Jerry." Smith seemed to force her eyes onto Sands, as if she knew that was expected of her.

"We've spoken to someone who knew you back then. They told us you didn't just work with Robbins. You dated him too. At least for a while."

A range of emotions seemed to cross Smith's face. In the end, she nodded. "Briefly. But why would the police be interested in that? And why now? Surely you don't..." Her voice tailed off.

"Don't what, Caroline?"

"Surely you don't think Jerry has anything to do with my sister's death?"

"Do *you*?"

"*No.* Of course not."

Sands watched her, seeing the flash of irritation.

"And not Sterling..." She stopped, and Sands simply stared at her. Eventually Smith went on. "I presume you're aware that Charles Sterling's still in prison?"

Sands nodded. "We're interested in the relationship between Sterling and Robbins. When you knew them."

Smith took a moment to answer, and used the time to try and improve her appearance. She smoothed an eyebrow, shifted in her chair so her back was straighter. "They were... friends. For a while."

"Go on."

"I think Sterling..." Smith stopped and stared at the carpet. "You know, don't you?"

"I have an idea," said Sands. "I'd like to hear it from you."

Smith's eyes dropped.

"You know, maybe I would like a tea," Sands said after a while. "Detective Golding, would you mind?" Sands didn't take her eyes off Smith as Golding got to his feet.

"There's tea bags in—"

"He'll figure it out," Sands interrupted her. She waited until Golding had gone, then reached out and took one of Smith's hands. "Before you say any more, there's something I need to tell you. It will come as a shock." She kept her eyes on Smith. "Charles Sterling was my father. He killed my mother and sister when I was twelve. And of course there were other victims before that."

"Oh my gosh." The shock on Smith's face was palpable. Her

hand came up to cover her mouth. And then her eyes grew even wider. "*I remember you*. When the trial happened, I remember there was a daughter he left alive." She had to look away now. "That's... oh my gosh."

"I'm sorry I wasn't clear at first. We're – I suppose *estranged* is the best word for it – I hadn't seen him until this case came along. But I wanted you to know. I want you to know that if there's anything you need to tell me about Sterling, I *will* believe you. And I *will* understand."

Smith seemed to be in shock, but did manage a small nod. A few minutes later Golding came back carrying three mugs of tea. He placed them on the coffee table and sat back down. Smith watched blankly, but then seemed to take the ensuing silence as a sign she was expected to continue. She seemed ready to talk.

"I was young..." Her voice was changed, faltering, but grew in confidence as she spoke. "And Jerry was this brilliant man who everyone looked up to. And he was completely beautiful. I mean, I couldn't believe my luck when he showed an interest in me."

"What happened?" Sands pressed gently.

"We started dating. Sort of, it was on a very casual basis. I suppose I thought it was more serious than he did. With Jerry, his work always came first, and he was a very confident man. He had other girlfriends, if you know what I mean."

"We understand you visited a place called Dancing Ledge, a rock platform on the Dorset coast, with Robbins?"

For a second Smith looked perplexed, but then the memory must have come back. "Yes!" But then her eyes widened dramatically. "*You!* Sterling was there too, and he took his daughters. One was just a baby, but one was... you?"

Sands nodded. "I was three, nearly four. I have no real memory of it. Which is why I need you to tell us what you know."

Smith nodded. "Well it *was* a long time ago. But I do remember it was hot, it must have been summer. Robbins and Sterling liked to go climbing together. And there was a pool you could swim in."

"So Robbins and Sterling were friends? As well as colleagues?"

"Oh yes, they were then. Not afterwards."

"After what, Caroline? What happened?"

Looking anxious, Smith managed a sip of her tea. "Detective Sands, I don't want you to get the wrong idea. I was young, I was naive, and I didn't know what I was getting into, not with Jerry, nor Charles."

Sands waited, not saying a word.

"Jerry was beautiful, physically I mean, but Charles..." She paused. "Before anyone knew who he really was, he was incredibly charming. He was handsome too, in his own way, but more than that – he had this ability to make you feel incredibly special." She put her mug down and began tapping the table top repetitively with her thumb. "I don't know what I expected. I knew Jerry was seeing other girls, he never promised me otherwise, so when Charles asked me to go for a drink with him, I said yes." She looked up, guilty.

"I shouldn't have. I knew he was married, I'd met his children, but maybe I didn't really expect anything to happen. Maybe I thought it really was just a drink. We were colleagues after all. He'd been a doctorate student at the university, but by then he'd joined the staff as a lecturer."

"What happened?"

Smith scratched at her head. "We had a drink. Just the two of us, in this little pub, but I got cold feet. It just felt wrong to me – it turned out I wasn't the unfaithful type. He told me he understood, and he'd give me a lift home. He had this car, with lots of space in the back. An estate car you call it here. In Canada they call them station wagons." She flashed a smile.

"Anyway, on the way home he took a detour, to this piece of waste ground, where no one would go after dark. I knew what he wanted – he was still charming, even then. I wasn't scared at all, but I was insistent. I didn't want to do it."

"But then?"

Smith gave a sudden, bitter laugh. "But then he just changed." The laugh stopped. "He attacked me. He grabbed my throat and he covered my mouth, and he told me he'd break my neck if I didn't do what he wanted."

The ensuing silence in the little sitting room was broken by the buzzing of Sands' phone. She pulled it out to stop it, noting the caller: DCI Jameson.

"What happened next?"

"He forced me into the back of the car. The seats were down already, I think he'd explained it before, something about having moved a sofa earlier that day. But he had rope too, so it was more like he'd been planning it. The whole thing." She stopped, took another sip of tea then looked Sands full in the face. "He raped me, and while he was doing it he strangled me."

When Smith covered her eyes and fell silent, Sands gently placed her hand on her knee. "What happened next, Caroline? You can take your time."

Smith began anxiously scratching her hair. "I must have passed out, because when I came too he'd finished, and he was acting as if nothing had happened. He was whistling. He just drove me home, as if it hadn't happened."

"Did you go to the police?" Golding asked, very carefully, very gently.

Smith shook her head. "I didn't... I was scared. I went to see Jerry. I told *him*. I thought he could handle it. I thought he'd get Sterling fired."

Neither Sands nor Golding replied.

"Would there have been any point?" Smith's eyes were wide, pleading for them to tell her she'd done the right thing.

"Who would they have believed? Sterling was a married man. He was writing articles for magazines. Everyone thought he was a genius. I was just a secretary."

"There might have been other accusations against him," Golding insisted.

"I thought Jerry would handle it. I trusted him to handle it."

"And did he?" Sands asked.

Smith froze, but then she shook her head. "No. He didn't do anything. He told me he'd spoken with him, but I don't know if he did. Nothing changed. That's the reason I left. I was scared to be anywhere near Sterling, and I realised that Jerry – he valued what he had with Sterling more than whatever the two of us ever had. Ten years later Sterling was arrested. I knew I should have gone to the police then, when he was arrested for killing all those women, but I felt guilty. If I'd done the right thing, when he attacked me, maybe they'd still be alive?" Smith was on the verge of tears now.

"Nothing changed? That's why you moved to Canada?" Sands asked gently.

Smith nodded. She went back to her tea, slurping noisily now. A tear slid down her face. Sands seemed to look right through her, staring into space.

THIRTY-FOUR

"Now what?" Golding asked. Sands had driven a quarter mile down the road before pulling over. "Do we go back to Robbins? He knew what Sterling was, and he did nothing?"

Sands tipped her head back against the headrest, but didn't reply.

"Do we confront him? If he'd gone to the police Sterling might have been put away. All those murders might never have happened." He stopped suddenly, then shook his head in apology. "I'm sorry. You have more right than me to be angry, but this pisses me off. If Robbins had gone to the police, Sterling probably wouldn't have been free to kill your family."

"We can't change it," Sands said. "Sterling did what he did. Nothing we do now changes that." Sands started the engine and headed back towards Poole and the MID.

"Nothing changed," she went on thoughtfully. "We heard from Bell that Robbins and Sterling were close. And then they had some sort of falling out. But Smith just told us it *wasn't* Sterling raping his girlfriend that pushed them apart. It was something else. So what was it?"

"Maybe we ask him? Robbins, I mean."

"We could, but will he tell us? And would he still help us try to decipher the code? That's still our best chance of catching the killer before his next deadline." It was 3 p.m. and Sands realised with a jolt it was already Thursday. They'd made real progress on the case, perhaps for the first time since Jane Smith's body had been discovered. But time was running out. Now there was less than twenty-four hours to go before the killer murdered the twin girls. And he'd made good on every one of his previous promises. Sands drove on for a while.

"Call him." She tossed Golding her phone. "He's had that list of books from the prison for more than twenty-four hours now. Let's see if he has anything. Let's see if he's even working on it, or if he's wild swimming up some river somewhere. That'll tell us something." She grimaced, then waited, listening in as Golding did what she'd asked. To her surprise Robbins answered quickly. Sounding as calm and imperious as ever, he explained that he was working through the list of books as fast as possible. Golding glanced across at Sands to see if she wanted anything else, but she shook her head silently.

"Keep working on it and let me know the moment you find anything." Golding ended the call, then held up the screen for her to see: four missed calls and two voicemails from DCI Jameson. And finally, a text message. He opened it:

Where the hell are you? You need to get back here now.

Back at the MID Sands and Golding headed straight to Jameson's office at the back of the incident room to find him with Commander Black.

"What's happened?" Sands interrupted, leaning both hands on his desk.

"What the...?" Jameson held up his hands questioningly. "Where have you been? I've been calling, leaving messages."

"I've been following leads. What is it? What's happened?"

He stared at her. "Well, I'll tell you one thing that's happened. I'm up against a serial murderer who is going to kill two children tomorrow, and you've disappeared with one of my officers without informing me where you are and have then refused to answer my calls. What lead were you following?"

Sands went back to the door and closed it. She took a seat, waiting until Jameson did the same. "Professor Robbins, the man we've got trying to break the code. Somehow, he's connected to this. He knew Sterling before he was arrested, they were close friends until they had some sort of falling out."

Jameson looked confused. "And you knew this? When you insisted on sending all Sterling's mail to him?"

"No. Yes... I had a vague memory of it, but not really. I think I was about four when they had their falling out. But I found some old photos that showed the two of them together. And in the background was a woman that looked like a younger Jane Smith."

Jameson breathed heavily, his anger fading as he tried to make sense of what she was saying. "The woman who was pushed down the stairs? The woman with the cats?"

"Yes and no. It *looked* like her because it was her twin sister, Caroline Smith. She worked with both Sterling and Robbins back in the nineties. We think it fits somehow with the message on the website. *The wrong twin.*"

Sands looked towards Commander Black, whose face was dark, listening carefully.

"Is there a chance that this Robbins is our man?" Jameson asked. Sands swung back to face him and shook her head.

"The man who kidnapped the twins was white, average height, and in his twenties. Robbins is nearly seventy years old, six-foot-four and he's black. And the only possible suspect we have for the Lindham killings is that man in the dark car. We don't have a good description, but it does more closely match the kidnapper."

"We don't have anything for the Smith murder. That could have been Robbins."

Sands shrugged. "It's possible," she conceded. "But why?"

Jameson looked away; clearly he had no answer.

"How is it exactly that Robbins has ended up trying to crack the code sent to Sterling?" asked Black. Sands turned again to face him and drew in a deep breath.

"He was listed on our directory as an expert on anything to do with cryptography. He's retired now, but he agreed to take this case when he knew Sterling was involved. On the other hand, it's not *so* much of a coincidence. It's unlikely we could have gone to a mathematics expert who *didn't* have some connection to Sterling."

"And he's still trying to break the code? Is that wise? If he might be involved?"

"He's the best chance we've got. And unless something's changed, that's the *only* chance we've got before the deadline." Sands glanced back at Jameson. "Unless there's something else? Why did you need me so urgently?"

Sands noticed Jameson's glance towards Commander Black. "What is it? What's happened?"

"Charles Sterling has made us an offer," the Commander explained.

Sands felt a chill of alarm. "What offer?"

"He's said he'll tell us the name of the killer, and where he's keeping the children."

"In return for?"

Black hesitated. "Not a lot actually. A few small improvements to his living conditions. And two hours access to the internet."

"Tell me you're not considering it." Sands' face was white.

"I haven't made a decision yet. I told DCI Jameson I needed to discuss it with you first."

Sands stared.

"Sterling wants the computer tomorrow at 9 a.m. So we have time to get to the killer before the midday deadline."

Sands shook her head. "You have to refuse. It's a trick. A trap."

"I don't doubt it. But what sort of trick? What can he do on the internet?"

"I've no idea, but you can't trust him. You can't let him online."

"He'll be completely secure. I've already spoken to Director McDonald and they'll arrange things so we can monitor exactly what he sees. If anything he does causes a problem, we just pull the plug." He paused. "There's a kicker. Sterling has also prepared a press statement that his lawyer will put out if we decline his 'reasonable offer'. It'll make him look worse than us, but if the twins are killed, we'll look pretty bad as well." He paused and shook his head. "Unless you have any other suggestions, I don't see what choice we have."

Sands searched her mind for a way to stop this, but knew there was none. She closed her eyes and looked away.

Black watched her for a while, then turned to Jameson.

"Get it set up."

THIRTY-FIVE

Sands spent the rest of the afternoon, the evening and then late into the night examining the number grid that had been sent to Sterling. Robbins had made no further progress but had directed Sands to a website that might speed up the process by combining number codes and possible source texts. If the result was a series of random letters, it meant the text was incorrect; on the other hand, if a message was revealed... But with billions of possible texts to choose from, the effort felt futile. She gave up at midnight and set her alarm for 6 a.m. She tried to get some sleep.

She collected Golding on the way to Highmoor and they arrived at the same time as Jameson and Chang. All four passed through the security cordon together and were met by McDonald. He led them upstairs to a small meeting room close to his office where two laptops had been set up; a young man was working in front of one of them.

"This is Steven Daniels," said McDonald, "our head of IT; he's highly experienced in this sort of thing. I've asked him to set up a second computer mirroring Sterling's screen, so we can see exactly what he gets up to."

Sands looked closely at the screen Daniels was working on. The command prompt was open, the long list of commands he'd typed in still visible on the history logs. She ran her eye over them, trying to follow what he'd done. "What if we need to stop him?" she asked.

"We'll be able to," McDonald replied. "Steven, would you...?" He nodded at Daniels, who pressed a few keys and cleared his throat.

"OK, sure. So," – he pointed – "that machine over there is the one Sterling's going to use. If one of you wants to grab it and just go online, you'll see what happens." Being the closest, Jameson sat down in front of it.

"I'll be Sterling," he said and clicked onto the internet. It was slow to react.

"It's slow because everything's being routed through this second machine here." Daniels indicated his own computer, but a few seconds later the app opened on Jameson's machine. "Now go to a page, any page."

Jameson navigated to a page discussing the latest football results. The second laptop changed too, showing the same website in a small window.

"We can see everything he's doing, and if you want to stop it," Daniels explained, "you can just kill it from here." Sands leaned down and clicked on an icon showing a glowing green chain. The chain immediately broke and turned red. At the same time Jameson's screen turned black and displayed the words *Content Blocked*.

"And there's no way around this?" Sands asked.

"Absolutely not," said McDonald confidently, but Sands ignored him, looking at Daniels.

"It's pretty secure." Daniels glanced at the director as he spoke.

"But not *completely* secure?"

Daniels hesitated. "There's always theoretical weaknesses

in any system, but the two devices have been lined up sequentially. All the packets of data come to our computer first, and then flow to Sterling's device through a gateway. And only *we* control the gate."

"Could he hack the gate? Gain access to the controls?"

"It's... never going to be impossible, but pretty technical," Daniels replied, before adding hurriedly, "And we'd see him do it. We could stop him long before he'd get anywhere close. Even then the sequential nature means we just pull the plug here and there's no data flow at all. He could play around with the bios of this system all he likes, but he'd be offline."

When it looked as if Sands was going to protest further, McDonald stepped in. "Detective Sands, I understand the concerns you have about your father, I really do, but in this instance they're misplaced. He hasn't had access to a computer for so many years, so even if he was once the master hacker you seem to think he was, anything he knows will be decades out of date."

Sands turned to look at the director who was smiling confidently, patronisingly.

"Did you review the list of books Sterling loaned from the prison library?" she asked.

The smile wavered. "Yes, I saw it."

"Then you'll be aware it contained a book called *Network Defence and Countermeasures: Principles and Practices*. That was published two years ago. And there was another called *Network Intrusion Detection and Prevention: Concepts and Techniques*. An updated edition which was republished earlier this year. There were several others." Her nostrils flared with contempt as she stared McDonald down.

"Your father reads books on all manner of subjects, and if our library facilitates that, I don't see it as a bad thing. Many of our inmates learn skills that are critical to them starting lives and careers on the outside."

"Charles Sterling isn't supposed to have a life on the outside," Sands replied. She moved Daniels' hand off the keyboard and scrolled up to see what he'd done. The fact that she couldn't follow it only added to her frustration and grumpiness.

"It's safe," said Daniels after a while. "If there's anything untoward, we can just pull the plug."

Sands felt her stomach churn. She hadn't bothered with breakfast. Hadn't felt like it. "He's going to have access in his cell?" She turned back to McDonald.

"No, that's not possible. There's no possible way to bring the internet to the underground cells. He'll be in a secure room above ground."

Sands' hands clenched. She closed her eyes.

"Detective, Highmoor Prison is the highest-security institution this country has ever built. Sterling will be in a room with a four-inch-thick steel door and concrete walls. There's no telephone reception, no wi-fi. We'll be able to see Sterling's screen and watch him on a full-colour CCTV system. Finally, Senior Prison Officer Barney Atkinson will be in the room with him at all times. There's really no risk at all."

"I've seen enough," Jameson cut in before Sands could respond. "DCI Sands, your concerns about this have already been discussed in detail. The twins and their parents do not have the luxury of rehashing these same discussions over and over. Let's get on with this and see what he gives us."

A few minutes later Daniels was ready, and McDonald summoned Barney Atkinson to take the laptop. He was deferential and respectful to his boss, but it was clear from his demeanour that he shared some of Sands' concerns, or at least her distaste at Sterling getting what he wanted. As Daniels talked him through the set-up, Sands moved closer to him.

"You're going to stay with him the whole time?"

"Yeah," he replied in a low growl. "Don't worry. I'm gonna

watch that bastard like a hawk. I don't care what the director says. Sterling's up to something."

She nodded, but wasn't reassured. Atkinson said, to McDonald, "He gets the computer for two hours, right?" He took the laptop in his huge hands and walked out of the room.

A woman in a grey prison uniform appeared with a tray of coffee while Daniels set up a third computer, this one carrying the feed from what looked like a police-station interview room. Sterling was already seated at the table wearing his green and yellow jumpsuit, his legs shackled together.

Daniels glanced at McDonald. "You want me to stick around while this all goes down?"

"Definitely."

The technician nodded smartly, then fetched himself a coffee. Jameson, Chang and Golding all did the same, but Sands just stared at her father on the screen, wondering what the hell he was planning.

The image on the CCTV wasn't perfect, but Sands could see his eyes were closed, as if he were meditating again. But then they sprang open. He got to his feet.

"What's happening? Is Atkinson there already?"

When no one answered Sands rounded on the technician, suddenly angry. "Why is there no volume? Why can't we hear him?" On the screen it was clear that Sterling was talking, and Daniels hurriedly put down his coffee. He moved quickly to his laptop, adjusted something and suddenly the sound from Sterling's cell was fed into the meeting room.

"Take a step back, then kneel down, facing the wall with your hands on your head. Don't turn around." Atkinson's voice was raspy through the speakers. "I'm going to approach the table."

"*Oh*, Barney, you still think I can't be trusted." Sterling sounded playful but did what was asked. There seemed to be a slight delay between the sound and the image. Sands moved closer to the screen, wishing that doing so would improve the resolution. As she watched, Sterling twisted his head around, presumably to watch Atkinson.

"I said *don't* turn around. You do that again, I take this computer and rip the cable out. This'll be over, you understand?"

Sterling turned back. "I think I can follow your logic, Barney," he said.

Atkinson's voice sounded annoyed when he spoke again. "OK. Here it is. Come and get it."

Because of how the cell's CCTV camera was positioned, it only captured what was happening in Sterling's side of the room. Atkinson wasn't visible. Sands watched as Sterling got awkwardly back to his feet and shuffled to the table where the laptop she'd examined earlier was now placed. An ethernet cable trailed from the back. Sterling sat down, his eyes alighting on the security camera before settling on the computer screen. His hand rested on the mousepad.

At once the computer screen in front of Sands flickered, as it mirrored what Sterling was seeing. Sands could see his mouse pointer roaming around, but glancing back at the CCTV screen she realised suddenly that Sterling had angled his laptop so the screen wasn't visible on the CCTV camera.

"Radio to Atkinson, get him to turn Sterling's screen so we can see it."

McDonald answered her. "Actually, we can't at the moment. The transmitters are being replaced, there's no reception in that room at the moment."

Sands whirled to face him. "Why didn't you tell us that earlier?"

"Relax, Detective, we can see it all right here. Everything is under control."

Sands felt her stomach clench. She almost didn't notice

Golding coming to stand next to her. He had two coffees in his hand and held out one for her. After a beat, she took it.

"Here we go," he said.

They watched as Sterling clicked the icon to open the internet. It loaded slowly to the Google homepage. He typed a search: *waterfalls*. Then he clicked *image search*. The screen filled with images of waterfalls from around the world. Slowly, he clicked through them one after another. He spent around thirty seconds on each image before moving to the next. Sometimes he missed one out. Other times he stayed longer on one image. In the monitoring room the detectives frowned, but no one spoke. Sterling opened a new tab and began a second search. Sands was surprised how quickly he was able to type, not rusty at all after ten years. This time the search was *beaches*. He spent a few moments looking through the normal search results before clicking on the image results. Again, he pulled up photograph after photograph – white sands and turquoise water from the northwest coast of Scotland, palm-fringed beaches from the Caribbean – before closing it and moving onto the next. Then he opened a new tab. This time it was *forests*.

"Do we have any idea what he's doing?" Jameson asked eventually, squinting at the screen. "Anybody?"

Sands shook her head. Golding took a slug of coffee, shrugging as he did so.

"Maybe he's just trying to drink in something completely different to what he sees every day?" Beth Chang suggested. "You know, like filling his memory banks?"

"He could have asked for books if he wanted that," Golding replied, then glanced at McDonald. "Or used the prison library."

"Well, maybe it doesn't matter," said Jameson. He checked his watch. "Twenty-six minutes gone already. Just over an hour and a half left, and then he tells us where this bastard is, or we're pulling the plug."

Sterling barely moved at his desk, slightly hunched over the laptop. After he spent nearly half his allotted time simply looking at images, he clicked away a couple of the tabs, opened a new one and typed into the YouTube search bar. He was so quick Sands could barely catch what he'd typed, but she caught the words *music for meditation.*

Sands frowned, but Jameson gave a muted laugh. He was starting to relax.

A new sound emerged from the speakers, music, the introduction to the video Sterling had selected. It sounded eastern, the twang of a sitar.

"He hasn't heard music for over a decade." McDonald had joined them now, watching the laptop closely. "Can you imagine what that must be like?"

"And this is what he wants to hear?" Jameson replied. "He really is fucked up."

Sands ignored both of them, studying Sterling's posture. Something about it looked unnatural to her, but she couldn't quite identify why. She turned to Daniels, who was watching from a chair behind the detectives. "Everything look OK?"

He glanced over the computers he'd set up. "It looks fine."

The mouse pointer moved on the mirror screen. Sterling seemed to be browsing the other videos available on the right of the screen. He hovered on one and then, making it look like a random decision, selected another below it. The video window filled with a kaleidoscope of colour and they heard a man's voice on the speakers. Sterling paused the video and fast forwarded, apparently adjusting the time slider at random. He hit play again.

...Where does your next thought come from? Can you know what it is, before it appears? And if not, do you have any control over what that thought will be? Tell me, my friends, where is the free will in that?

"This again. He really gets off on this shit," Jameson

muttered, next to Sands. She glanced at him, irritated, then looked back to the laptop.

Thoughts simply appear in our minds, as if from nowhere. We have no freedom to choose them before they appear. And when we consider our thoughts, after they appear, when we choose whether to act on a thought, where does that thought come from? Do we choose that, or is it somehow chosen for us?

"This is the same bullshit he was saying to you." Jameson's gruff voice rang out, louder now.

Every decision you think you're making, you're not. Every step you take through life is determined by steps that came before, steps you made, and steps that were made for you, by your parents, by their parents, right back up the infinite river of time.

"Maybe we should turn the volume down?" said Jameson jokingly, but Sands wheeled on him at once.

"Will you shut your mouth? This is important. This matters."

There was a shocked silence in the meeting room, but slowly attention settled back onto the screen, the speaker's voice drawling through the laptop.

Eventually Sterling clicked away before the video had finished. And then he seemed to browse at random. He played more music, an Irish fiddle band. He read the *Guardian* newspaper. He browsed the menu of a two-Michelin-star restaurant in London, but beyond letting the minutes tick away, he seemed to be doing nothing useful at all. Ten minutes before his hour was up, Commander Black called Jameson's mobile. Sands listened as Jameson filled him in, overhearing Black saying the armed response unit was ready, and simply waiting for an address.

"If he's going to tell us anything, it'll be in the next ten minutes. If he doesn't, it's over, but at least we haven't lost anything," Jameson said, chuckling grimly.

When he'd hung up he turned to Sands. "Sterling's

promised to give you the killer's whereabouts several times, right? If you agreed to see him regularly, stuff like that? You reckon he might just be doing this to make a point? Making us wait right to the end before he tells us? His way of saying we should have just believed him from the beginning."

At that moment, surprising them both, a message box popped up in the shape of an envelope that jiggled comically on the screen. A name was written on it. *Detective Chief Inspector Steven Jameson.*

"Hey!" Jameson called back to Daniels. "How do I open this?"

"He's sent a message," Sands said. "How's he done that?"

Daniels didn't seem to know which of the questions to answer, but Jameson was already holding the mouse, moving the pointer onto the envelope. "I just click here right? This is it," he added to himself. "This has to be the location of the killer."

For a second Sands' eyes stayed on Daniels, but then Jameson clicked the envelope. A graphic played out, the envelope opened and a letter slid out. It unfolded itself, revealing the message:

The twins are being held by a man named Ian King, a paranoid schizophrenic who believes that he has been ordered to sacrifice them by the Egyptian Sun God Ra. You'll find him at 32, Bridge Road, Salisbury. Be careful, he's armed, but then you already know that.

If you'd like to verify the truth of this message, I suggest you check his Facebook page: IanKingRA

Good luck!

"How's he done this?" Sands asked Daniels, but Jameson interrupted.

"You can look at that all you want once the twins are safe. Right now, get me the goddamned internet," he demanded. Daniels opened Google Chrome on the second computer.

"Here." He slid the laptop to Jameson.

Clumsily, Jameson brought up the Facebook home screen, but there was no account logged in.

"*Shit*. Anyone know their Facebook password?"

Again it was Daniels who rescued the situation, but valuable seconds were lost. Finally Jameson navigated to IanKingRA.

For a second, Sands couldn't see what was wrong. It looked like standard conspiracy-theory nonsense. A video began claiming to show how the pyramids were built, by a giant sun lens that melted graphite into moulds. Another image simply showed a huge hieroglyphic eye.

"I don't get it, what are we supposed to be looking at?" Jameson asked.

"Oh shit. There." Chang was the first to spot it. It was another image that had been posted that morning, a still of the twins tied up on the bed.

Jameson whistled. "It's him."

He was already dialling on his mobile while Sands reread the message. "Sir, we have a name and an address. One Ian King, 32, Bridge Road, Salisbury... We're not far away, we'll meet the armed response unit there." He snapped the phone off.

"He came good," Jameson said to Sands, shaking his fist in triumph. "The bastard actually came good." He was already walking towards the door.

"Hang on." Sands stopped him, pointing upwards with one finger, as if trying to point out what was wrong, but not quite able to grasp it.

"*What?* He's dicked around with us for two whole hours. You want to waste any more time? It's less than an hour before the deadline."

"How did he do that? We're supposed to see a mirror of his screen, and we didn't see him set up that message, it just appeared. *How?*" She turned to Daniels, whose anxious expression clearly showed he didn't have an answer to give her.

Jameson seemed to change his mind. "OK, you're right. It's a concern. But we have to prioritise. He's given us what he promised. We have a name for this arsehole, and an address where the twins are being held. There's still a chance we can get there before his fucking death-timer runs out, so we need to be there. We need to check it out."

Sands said nothing for a second, trying to keep her head clear. She read the message to herself, a third time.

"Look, if you want to stay and check out how he sent it," Jameson conceded, "that's probably a good idea."

Sands nodded.

"Good." Jameson got up. "Chang, let's get the hell out of here."

THIRTY-SIX

There was a sudden silence. Sands turned to Daniels. "Well?"

For a second the young man looked lost, but then he leaned into his keyboard. He pulled up the command prompt again and typed quickly, opening screen after screen, too fast for Sands to follow. After a while she gave up trying, instead turning to the spare laptop which was still showing Ian King's Facebook page. The twins were still there. Still tied up on the bed. The cryptic rhyme hadn't changed. The counter had less than fifty minutes left. Sands turned back to Daniels who was sitting back in his chair staring at the screen.

"How did he do it?"

The IT specialist spoke through gritted teeth. "I'm not exactly sure, but somehow he had a second window open. I don't know how he did it, if he just had the one screen—"

"What did he do? In the other window?"

"I don't know... unless..." The man's eyes lit up. "He split his screen. He divided his screen into two halves, and he sent the feed from one half to the mirroring software, so we couldn't see what he was doing on the other side. I don't have a clue *how* he did it..."

"Can you see what he did? On the second screen?"

"We can check the key logs, see what he typed. I wasn't monitoring it because he was doing almost everything with the mouse."

"Open it up. Now." Sands crouched down behind him as he opened a file that contained every key press Sterling had made. They scanned through it together, but it didn't appear to show anything they hadn't already seen Sterling do.

"There's nothing here," Sands said, but Daniels looked confused. He pointed to a short line of code that was different. He copied it to the clipboard, pulled up a web browser, pasted it in and hit search. A website loaded, showing a keyboard.

"What's this?" Sands demanded. She was impatient now.

"I... don't..." Daniels studied it. "I think it's a website where you can type letters through the mouse. The key log only records inputs made through the keyboard. If you type a message through this we won't be able to see it. That's why he seemed to be clicking things at random. He was typing on this."

Sands hit the table with her fist. She looked back at the live feed but Sterling was no longer there. Atkinson must have moved him back to his underground cell. She turned back to Daniels, seemingly about to take out her frustration on him, when his machine made a pinging sound.

"What's that?"

"I'm not... it's..."

"*What is it?*"

"It's another message."

Sands almost wrenched the computer from him, but settled for pulling it across so that it was in front of both of them. But she didn't see anything. "What other message?"

"No, it's not a message, it's... an email. He was using an online email server to compose an email. That noise was it sending; now it's gone we can't see what it was."

"Christ!" Sands lost what was left of her cool. Frustrated,

she turned to McDonald. "I thought you said you had this under control?" McDonald didn't answer, but his face was white.

"There might be a way," Daniels interrupted her. "Just let me..." He typed frantically, his tongue poking from the corner of his mouth. As he worked, he explained. "This browser makes a cache of every page you load in case you want to reload it again later; it makes it quicker. I'm checking the cache to see if it caught whatever it was he sent..." He pressed a few keys, then sat back, triumphant.

"There."

The webpage displayed an almost complete message. The problem was, it made absolutely no sense. It was just a long list of numbers.

"What's that?" Daniels asked, frowning. "Why's he sending a load of numbers?"

Sands felt her brain screaming in frustration inside her head. It was all she could do not to punch the computer, but she settled for making a fist and slamming it onto the table top. "It's not a list of numbers," she said. "It's a book cipher." She got up and paced the room, before going on to explain, more for herself than Daniels.

"The messages the killer has sent to Sterling have all been encrypted with a book cipher, which we can't read because we don't know what the book is."

"I saw something about book codes on TV the other week," Daniels said. "It was numbers, like what you've got there. And it gave the location of ancient pirate treasure, only it was encoded by some book."

Sands looked at him, shocked he thought the anecdote worth sharing at such a moment.

"Only it wasn't a book, but some academic paper or some-thing, I can't remember what exactly, and they only cracked one of the codes. There're still two left, and no one's found the treasure—"

"Stop," Sands interrupted. "Stop talking."

For a second, Daniels misunderstood. "I'm sorry, it's just that I talk when I'm stressed..."

"No, what did you just say?"

He hesitated. "I have this thing about talking when—"

"You were talking about the Beale ciphers. You said something was used to decipher them? On the show?"

"Oh, I think it was the Constitution of the USA, or something."

"That's not what you said. You said academic papers." She fell silent, her forehead deeply furrowed. Suddenly she swung around to Golding, almost grasping something.

"What if we're not looking for a message to the killer, but to someone else?"

"What do you mean?" Golding asked.

"We've been assuming it's been the killer and Sterling exchanging messages with each other. But what if that's wrong? What if it's not a message to the killer, but to someone else?"

Golding was quiet for a moment. He looked troubled. "Who?" he said eventually.

"The person we've trusted to try and decode them."

Sands moved into action. "Get out the way," she snapped at Daniels, waving him out of his seat and then sitting in it herself. Her fingers were already moving on the keys.

Golding sat down beside her as she logged onto the online portal of the *Journal of Advanced Mathematics*. She began to scan through its archive, rolling back the years until she reached 1991. The library was poorly filed and it was Golding who first spotted the link to Robbin's famous paper that had formed the basis for modern cryptocurrencies.

"There." He pointed at the screen and she clicked to open

it. After a few moments a poor-quality PDF copy opened of the actual paper journal.

She glanced at him, checking to see if he understood, but it was clear from his face that he didn't. "This is the paper Robbins wrote," Sands explained. "He had it printed out on his desk when we went to see him, meaning he'd checked to see if it was being used for the cipher. Given the context of what we were looking at, it was an obvious text to try, but he told us he hadn't been able to read the message, which meant it wasn't the right one. I never double-checked it, because at that point we had no reason to doubt him. But what if Robbins was lying?"

Golding hesitated before replying. "He's already lied about how well he knew Sterling. Can you check it?"

"Yeah. I can."

She opened another window and quickly loaded a website.

"This is a book-code cracker," she explained as she worked. "It lets you upload a suspected book code, and then the texts you want to check against it." The site had two spaces where users could input text. In the first she quickly copied and pasted the numbers from Sterling's message. In the second box she directed the computer to upload Robbins' paper.

"What exactly are you doing?" McDonald had moved closer now but Sands ignored him, tapping her fingers while the website did its work.

"OK, it takes a few seconds." The website had generated a dozen or so different texts automatically, each representing a different method of interpreting how the numbers applied to the text. But none of them made any sense. Each one appeared to be a random collection of unintelligible gibberish.

"Damn it." This time Sands whacked the table with her hand.

McDonald spoke out. "It doesn't appear to matter now anyway. Detective Jameson has the name and address he needs. Let's just hope and pray he gets there in time... Anyway, I think

I'll monitor things from my office. If you'll excuse me." He got up awkwardly and left the room. Sands' only reaction was to minimise the code-cracker website and pull up Robbins' original paper again.

She stared at it on the screen, reading the abstract and trying to second-guess the maths Robbins had used. Somehow this paper was the key, yet it wasn't the *actual* key. But what did that mean? She moved onto the paper itself, trying her best to follow the logic, but it was frustratingly difficult. It wasn't just a lack of practice either, it was the same issue she'd faced all those years before in her damn father's office. He'd give her some assignment, to understand some concept or another, and she'd work away at it, trying to batter her way towards clarity. And when she'd go to him, ready for her test, he'd show her that she hadn't *quite* got it, had somehow missed the essence of the thing. And then he would go on to explain it to her in such a way that its inner beauty would finally emerge. And for a few moments it would be almost visible, written in the air in letters borrowed from the crackling fire. A truth as wide and deep as the very universe. But it wouldn't last. Once her father stopped speaking the apparition would fade, and the mists of her own inadequacy would drift in to cloud her understanding once more.

"How can *you* do it and I can't?" she'd asked him once, and his reply was both supremely arrogant yet somehow generous.

"I have the gift of insight, Angel, but you are more gifted than I. You possess the gift of struggle."

"But you don't have to struggle!"

She still remembered the sad smile that had appeared on his lips. "I keep my struggles hidden, my Angel. But I have them all the same."

She blinked the memory away, not knowing why it had appeared but irritated that it had, stealing valuable seconds from her. But she went back to what had indeed become her strength, to ploughing on, no matter how hard it was, to battering her way forwards. So what if much of Robbins' work was beyond her? So what if underneath her extraordinary drive to succeed, there lurked an ordinary mind? A little problem like this wasn't going to stop her. And ordinary was a relative term. Plenty of successful mathematicians' work was built upon the brilliance of greater minds.

She kept going, following what she could and leaving space in her mind where she couldn't. And then she came to a set of brackets, and the names of other papers that Robbins' work was based on, the citation:

Robbins, et al 1989.

Et al. *Et Alia.* Latin for 'And others'. She paused, unsure what had stopped her. Her thought repeated. *Plenty of successful mathematicians' work was built upon the brilliance of greater minds.* Suddenly she jumped to the back of the papers, where the citations were listed out as full references. And then she stopped in shock.

Robbins et al: *The peculiar persuasion of primes, Cincinnati Journal of Advanced Mathematics,* Jeremiah Robbins, Korai Hakamoto and Charles Sterling, 1989.

It was no surprise that Robbins' famous paper was itself based on earlier work, but to see her father's name listed there made Sands' blood chill. She glanced at Golding, seeing the surprise on his face too, and then ran a search on the journal's website. It no longer existed. Sands clicked her tongue in frustration, but it didn't take long to find a cached copy. Mathematicians and academics had been some of the first people to adopt the internet, and some of its most careful archivists. As Sands read the opening paragraph, she recognised the light tone of her father's words.

Anxiously, she copied the text from the new article and went back to the book-code-cracking website, still open on another tab. She found herself holding her breath as the pages of the paper uploaded one by one, and then were processed into a digital format compatible with the website. When it was finally finished, she was presented with a text box in which to input the code from the message. Again, she copied and pasted the text from the email that Sterling had sent. Then hit the button to run the search.

With the paper already uploaded, it was quicker this time. Almost at once a dozen results were displayed on the screen. The first three were clearly nonsensical, but as her eye scanned the fourth, she stopped cold. Instead of random letters, there were the words: *Ian, have sent you some visitors...*

She clicked it, her heart thudding in her chest.

Ian, have sent you some visitors. I trust you will make them feel at home, in your own unique way. But I wanted to give you time to finish your work, so I've sent them to the flat, not the farm. Take care, And give my regards to Ra.

"Oh shit," Golding said.

Sands knew that back at the department's incident room a handful of detectives would already be investigating Ian King's background, even as two minibuses filled with armed-response officers were on their way to raid his property. But where were they going? She scrambled for the first message – 32, Bridge Road, Salisbury – was that the flat? If so, where the hell was the farm?

"Get the incident room on the phone," she ordered Golding, her voice ice-cold. Moments later she took the phone from him. "Has anybody there found anything about a farm?"

The detective who answered, a young female DC, not senior enough to hitch a ride with the raiding party, said she hadn't, but she was working with several others and it was just too early to say.

"Stand up. *Right now,* get everyone there to listen. Ask if anyone has come up with any reference to a farm."

Sands listened as the young officer did as instructed. Then another voice.

"I've got something."

The phone was transferred, and Sands found herself speaking to a young man this time.

"Hello, ma'am. The address for Ian King's parents is listed as a farm, and also a former abattoir. It's not in use anymore."

"Give me the address."

Sands lodged her phone behind her ear as she listened, then typed the address into Google maps. It was less than half-an-hour's drive from the prison, yet a good hour from the location in Salisbury the armed response team were raiding. She hung up and turned to Golding.

"Get this to Jameson," she said as she sent the route to the GPS in her Alfa. "Give him this address and convince him the ARU is going to the wrong damn place. And then get the rest of the messages decrypted. We need to know what they've been saying to each other."

"You're not thinking of going there alone?" Golding asked.

Sands glanced at her watch. Forty-five minutes till the killer's deadline. She shook her head. "Course not. Just tell me what those messages say."

THIRTY-SEVEN

The man who saw himself – in his preferred timeline of the multi-universe theory – as Sekhmut the Great, but was known in the more-accepted twenty-first century as Ian Robert King, checked his watch. He still wore it, despite the fact that it clashed with the otherwise rather convincing Egyptian stoneworker uniform he'd pieced together. He'd laced a pair of leather sandals on his feet. His legs were bare, and around his waist he wore a grass skirt held in place by a hemp and copper belt, with a buckle showing an image of the sun. A leather tunic completed the outfit, all of which had been sourced from Amazon. The watch wasn't as much of a problem as some might have thought – Sekhmut was quite sure the ancient Egyptians had a wide range of technologies that had been denied and hidden by modern archaeologists. While they might not have worn watches *exactly* like his third-generation Apple iWatch, they certainly had similar items, probably significantly more advanced than this.

Besides, he needed to know the time very precisely. Because in just under one hour, the world, as the people who lived in this version experienced it, was going to instantaneously cease to exist. More than that, in the flash of less than one second it would cease to have *ever existed*. And yet he – assuming he had correctly completed the series of sacrifices required of him – would escape this final reckoning. He would be transported back through time to the most wonderful moment in the history of the planet – the opening ceremony of the Grand Pyramid at Giza. He was giddy with excitement and struck with sheer awe that this moment was at last approaching.

It hardly seemed real, and yet the delusion and madness which had settled upon King years before completely prevented him from even considering the possibility it wasn't real.

He opened the back door of the property and went outside. There was no need to be careful. The yard wasn't overlooked; a wood had been planted long ago to shield walkers on a public footpath that traversed a nearby hill from the difficult sights, smells and sounds that had once emanated from the largest of the farm's stone buildings.

When King was born, in the farmhouse itself, it had worked both as a place of life and death. His parents owned around two hundred sheep which grazed on the surrounding hills, but the greater part of their business was operating a small, local abattoir for the other farms in the Purbeck Hills. It supplied speciality butchers, supermarkets and restaurants, allowing them to offer premium, locally sourced lamb. So his childhood had ticked by to the idyllic sounds of braying sheep, but also the noise they made as they were herded off the pasture and down towards the killing pens. At first irritation, then alarm and then sheer terror as they were pressed forwards by the weight of the sheep behind them and witnessed what was happening to those who reached the front.

Those days were gone now. King stepped carefully around the mud towards the chicken coops – one of the few remaining sections of the farm where the animals were still alive – and here he was careful to shut the door behind him.

Inside, the birds ran about – they had come to treat King as a threat – but he quickly and expertly caught one and then cradled it in his hands. The bird flapped its wings trying to escape him, but he moved his head close to it, talking soothingly, explaining carefully that it had been chosen – not by him – but by an entity far more powerful than them. It was unclear whether this information quietened it or it was simply accepting its fate. Either way, King turned around and left the coop. He began to secure the door before the futility of such an act struck him. It didn't matter if a fox got in. It didn't matter if the birds escaped. None of it mattered anymore. Their world – this world – would simply no longer exist in... he checked his watch again.

Forty minutes.

He swallowed, shivered. Looked around himself in total disbelief. *All of it would disappear.* The trees, the sky, everything. Where would it go? He had asked himself the same question many times, but never came up with an answer that made sense. But then of course it *couldn't* make sense. The very concept of sense was human, and even the tiny role he was to play in that day's events dwarfed everything that humans had ever achieved. There would be no answers, not in this world. He hurried back to the farmhouse.

There was a familiar excitement taking over now. He'd been here before. The thrill of action. Yet this time it was different. His actions before had been important, but they had only been tests. This time, he would reap the reward. And what a reward! It was amazing – incredible, in the literal sense of the word – to think what was about to happen. What *was* happening. Even now, separated from this life by a river of time exactly twenty thousand years wide, he was simultaneously carrying a chicken into his kitchen, *and* jostling his way through an excited crowd on the Egyptian river plains. There, in his Sekhmut guise, he was readying himself for the moment the gods would declare the Great Pyramid Project complete. And not as a tomb – for a second he scoffed at the ridiculous notion that the pyramids were built as burial monuments. They were engines. They were machines. Creators of energy powerful enough to birth stars. They were portals, calling the chosen few to that moment in time.

King knew he was special, but not unique. There were others like him. People born outside of the chosen time of ancient Egypt, who were nonetheless called to be there. Others like him who needed to demonstrate their worthiness via a series of tests, and who, throughout history, were doing just that at this very moment, thousands of years in the past and across a thousand different futures. The archaeologists who lived in this sad, damaged world had no idea, but this was what the Great Pyramid Project was *really* about. An incredible machine capable of pulling the chosen people through time to place them there, at the scene. Fusing their bodies with ancient Egyptians. Thus, Ian King would finally shed the last few remains of his twenty-first-century body. He would finally become, for all of time, Sekhmut the Great.

But there was still work to do. He had to pass the tests to complete his end of the portal. The sacrificial lambs had to be slain at the allotted hour.

King had long accepted that the details involved were, and would always be, beyond his comprehension. On a superficial level he understood why he'd been told to kidnap a pair of twins – the fusing of Ian King with Sekhmut the Great could only be achieved through the simultaneous death of those-who-were-already-joined – the twins. But he neither knew nor cared how it all worked. The practical reality of their deaths meant very little to him. As a young child he'd played around the sheep as they shuffled forwards to their noisy deaths. As a teenager he'd worked in the holding pen, pushing the sheep forwards, pressing the bolt gun against their skulls and feeling that satisfying thud as it punched through the bone. And then hoisting the animals by their rear legs before slitting their throats and shoving the still twitching carcasses forwards on the ceiling track as their blood gushed like a vivid crimson stream over the concrete floor.

But none of that mattered. None of that meant a thing. The whole point was that *everyone* would die. Not only the twins, but *every other living thing*. In this version of reality in which Ian King had been unfortunate enough to be born, everyone would simply cease to be the moment he travelled back to become his true, Egyptian self. So yes, the twins had to die, but in taking their blood he would only be hastening their death by a matter of seconds. It was entirely justifiable. There'd be nobody left to blame him here, and where he was going there'd be no blame either. He would be welcomed as a traveller from the future. One of the chosen people, able to take a seat on the council to guide Egypt in a new direction, so different from the old, failed version people were taught about in this reality. Armed with the knowledge of Sekhmut, and others like him, the great kingdom of Egypt would never fall. Instead they would colonise the stars, immortal travellers of the network of Great Pyramids built on planets around every sun in every galaxy in every dimension of every universe.

He felt giddy at the sheer scale of it all but needed to return to the cold focus that normally marked his work. He drew in a few breaths, then glanced around the kitchen for a knife. He didn't see the filth, the empty tins of half-eaten food, the plates covered in green mould. He pulled open the cutlery drawer and took it as a powerful omen that the one remaining piece of silverware was a steak knife.

He held the knife in one hand like a dagger, while with the other he pinned the chicken against the filthy work surface. It flapped again, sensing the end, but his grip was firm. He began mumbling what he truly believed to be sacred Egyptian incantations, but which in fact were closer to his half-remembered schoolboy French. Then he stabbed the bird, bursting through its breast feathers, seeking out its heart. Blood spurted out over his hands as the chicken flapped its wings in death while King closed his eyes, drinking in the moment. When the bird was still he pushed his thumbs inside the body and tore it open, before pressing the corpse to his face and breathing in the coppery smell of sudden death.

It calmed him somewhat, but still his heart fluttered. He checked his watch again. Half an hour to go.

It was time to see the twins.

THIRTY-EIGHT

Sands drove as quickly as the small, twisting roads allowed, hoping and trusting that Google's algorithms were sending her the quickest way. The red numerals of the clock on her dashboard almost mocked her with the speed they ticked away, every minute that passed closer to the midday deadline for the twins' death.

Despite her warning the operation was still unfolding at Ian King's flat. Twenty-four armed officers had first surrounded it before eight burst through the front door, only to find the place empty. Now, based on Sands' instructions, the entire operation was being packed up and was on its way to the farmhouse. But this all meant they were at least half an hour behind Sands.

11:44. The dashboard clock ticked another minute closer.

"Tell me what you know about this guy," Sands asked the MID's radio operator on the rare occasion she was able to get through. She listened to the scratchy answer.

Ian King was twenty-four years old. An only child. When he was eighteen his father, John, had rolled his quad bike down a steep slope and been killed. Six months later his mother had also died, of stomach cancer. This double tragedy had left Ian, who at that point was living in Salisbury, to run the family farm and abattoir alone. For the last two years he had apparently done so, though there had been concerns it had become too much for him, concerns that had grown when he'd isolated himself and refused to allow visitors. Ian King hadn't kept the abattoir running after his father's death, and now the farm was also apparently no longer functioning. It was not known how King made ends meet.

"Hold on, I've got Golding on the other line." Sands cut the operator off and switched the call.

"Ma'am, he's nuts," he said. "He's totally crazy. I'm getting the messages decoded and Sterling's been feeding him everything, telling him what to do, how to do it, but basically feeding these insane delusions. As far as I can make out he believes he'll be transported back in time if he kills the twins today. He's going to sit on some high council of ancient Egypt."

"Anything else?" Sands said. "I've got the incident room on the line again. Is there anything else you can tell me?"

"Be careful," Golding replied. "If you're going in there, just be damn careful."

Sands reconnected with the incident room.

"Ma'am, I have Commander Black here. He's saying you're not to go onto the property until armed officers are on—"

Sands ended the call. She decided she'd run into a patch of poor reception just before that message was relayed.

THIRTY-NINE

One of Ian King's beliefs was that, as Sekhmut, he had been part of the team working on the capping stones – the high-quality white limestone that covered the more utilitarian building blocks of the pyramid. Although this particular theory was not well developed, he understood he had done so while his twenty-first-century body was asleep at night. The dreams he had experienced, of leading a team cutting and transporting these stones and fitting them into place, were not dreams at all, but visions of a different reality elsewhere in time. In his waking hours he liked to indulge this fantasy. Indeed, he often spent whole days engrossed in this delusion, filling in details, rewriting the script so that it fitted exactly with what he desired most. He knew, for example, that he wasn't just liked and a little feared as a team leader, but also greatly respected for his strength and his wisdom. He knew he had a wife – a voluptuous dark-haired beauty named Soe – who was also coveted by his co-workers, but who loved him, and only him, with an intensity never seen before or since.

He believed also that Soe would bear him two children – twins, of course – and that night, twenty thousand years in the past, these children would be conceived. It would be the first time that either Ian King, or Sekhmut, would lie with a woman.

The immensity, the weight of all this, was dizzying.

His watch beeped softly, breaking the spell. He glanced at it, wiping away the blood to see the screen. There was a message.

Seeing it was written in code he climbed the stairs to the room his father had kept as a study. Once filled with mundane details of running the farm, the computer's hard drive now contained thousands of videos and images of pyramids and ancient Egyptians. Its desktop image was a composite, built from several pornographic websites. A bare-breasted, dark-haired beauty with vaguely Arabic looks. It didn't take him long to copy and paste the message into the same website that Erica Sands was using at about the same time.

Ian, have sent you some visitors. I trust you will make them feel at home, in your own unique way. But I wanted to give you time to finish your work, so I've sent them to the flat, not the farm. Take care, And give my regards to Ra.

He felt nothing for a moment, and then a sudden white rage. Roaring, he punched the wall as hard as he could, his fist hammering through the miserly thin layer of plaster that hid solid brick. His knuckles cracked and split and his blood flowed over the dirty brown stains left by the chicken. But he felt no pain. *Visitors.* It could only mean Sterling had betrayed him; he'd feared he might. He'd sold him out, given his name to the police.

Well, no matter. Sekhmut calmed down as quickly as he had become enraged. For all of Charles Sterling's so-called brilliance, it was actually Sekhmut who had outsmarted *him* – Sterling wouldn't be travelling to Egypt. It wasn't Sterling who had been chosen. He remembered writing to Sterling after watching a documentary about him, and then discovering on the internet that he occasionally took the time to respond to letters. He remembered the thrill when Sterling had written back, not once but many times, and how their correspondence had grown. Eventually the man had told him of his role, as a messenger, a channel from the past, and had taught him how to pass messages secretly. King had understood very little of what Sterling told him, had failed completely to make sense of the complex mathematical papers he had made him use to code and decode messages. And yet he'd been grateful for the guidance.

But this wasn't the time to reminisce; he had to concentrate. There would be no second chances. If he failed in his sacrifice, the world would still come to an end, and he would die with it. His only chance to escape the death that every living creature on this version of the world faced was to complete his mission and travel through the pathway, back in time. He blinked, reread the decoded message. Considered.

The second time around things didn't seem so bad. If the police went to the flat they'd be too late. Perhaps Sterling hadn't given him up after all, but was merely playing with what little time remained to him. For a few seconds Sekhmut imagined the police, wearing body armour and helmets no doubt, creeping around the perimeter of the flat where he'd lived when his parents were still alive. Well, let them play with their primitive toy guns.

He switched off the computer and, still holding the knife, walked down the stairs, and out into the courtyard one more time. Then he opened the door to the former abattoir, where he'd imprisoned the twins.

FORTY

The GPS showed the blue trail of her route ending up ahead. Despite the chequered flag, all she could see when she got there, on the far side of a large field, were the tin roofs of a set of buildings tucked into a wood. The only entrance appeared to be a track closed off by a large steel gate. She also saw a wooden box, the type country people sometimes use to receive their post. She slowed to read "Kingston Farm". Underneath someone had painted in red:

Strictly Private. KEEP OUT

She stopped and got out, to discover the gate had been secured with a heavy chain and padlock. She looked around. She was halfway up a small valley, on a very quiet road. To her right, beyond the farm, a thick wood cut her off from a view of the hilltop above. On the other side, the land dropped away. She stared at the buildings. She couldn't see much, but they still managed to emit an aura of decay and dereliction. She knew it would be stupid to go any further but she was running out of time. According to his website, Ian King planned to murder the twins in less than ten minutes.

And so with regret she put her boot on the gate and began to climb.

As she got closer to the buildings the sense of decay grew palpably, and it was accompanied by the smell of death. Glancing into a shed she saw several carcasses of cows, their black and white pelts lying like rugs over the racks of their ribs. A few chickens ran about. It was easy to see which of the buildings was the farmhouse, and there were lights on, which drew her nearer. The back door was open, leading through a small utility room into a kitchen.

She stepped cautiously inside, glancing around. At once she saw a pyramid scratched into the wall. It reached the ceiling, and the floor was still littered with picked-out pieces of plaster. All around it were home-made attempts at hieroglyphics. Not well done.

She picked up a screwdriver from the work surface, holding the blade outwards. She remembered – it was impossible not to – that this man had executed his victims, coldly and without hesitation. And the gun he'd used hadn't been recovered. And yet she sensed from his surroundings a vulnerability, a duality between cold-blooded killer and something else, something sadder. She made a calculation, and decided to bluff.

"Ian?" she called out. "Ian King? It's too late. It's over. The police are here."

Silence.

She kept going, through the kitchen into a darkened stairway. She flicked on the light, not liking how the darkness gave King an advantage over her. At the top she saw three doors, all closed.

She chose the first, pushing it open and edging in.

It was a bedroom. Filthy.

"Ian?"

Nothing. There was an aspect to the silence now that suggested the whole house was empty, but she had to be sure. She turned back into the hallway, tried the next door.

Another bedroom, but this one was used as a study. There was a computer on a desk, on its screen the very same website she'd used to decrypt the book code. On the wall someone had pinned a sheet of paper contained step-by-step instructions for how to use it. She blinked, recognising at once her father's handsome script.

Another door led off this room, perhaps a bathroom. Sands called out towards it, "Ian? Ian King? It's over. You need to tell me where you are."

Suddenly she heard a scream – a child's scream. It came from outside the house, and she glanced out the window to see the long, low building that sat across the farmyard. It had an ugly, squat appearance and metal rails led to its entrance, from where a little light escaped. Sands didn't hesitate. She ran down the stairs and outside. When her feet sank into the sloppy, wet mud, she nearly slipped, but made it to where a concrete ramp led downwards.

Another scream sounded out, then a man's voice. "*Shut up! Just shut up.*"

"Ian? Don't do this." Sands ran down the ramp into the murky interior, but up ahead, further inside, she could see the yellow of electric light. "Ian, this is the police. You're surrounded. Give it up."

Sands slowed as she neared the light. The building was shaped like a funnel and she remembered what it had been designed for, to force animals into single file so they could be slaughtered in an orderly line. But it also made a perfect trap.

"Ian? Are you there? Do you have the twins with you?" She tried to force her voice to carry a weight of confidence she didn't feel.

"Who are you?" A voice came ringing out from somewhere deeper in the building. It sounded wary.

"I'm with the police, Ian. I've come for the twins. You need to let them go."

A pause, and then, still confused, "You're not supposed to be here."

Sands had reached the end of the first part of the funnel, where a short corridor led to a larger space from where the light was shining. She edged along, protected by the wall, until she reached the entrance. Then, mouthing a silent hope he wouldn't have the gun, she stepped forward into the light.

It was one of the most horrific sights of her life. Inside the bare, concrete room a man stood staring at her. He was dressed bizarrely, a leather tunic and some sort of skirt, his face and neck smeared with blood. One of his hands was injured and bleeding. But the other held a 9mm semi-automatic pistol. He lifted the weapon, briefly showing it side on so she could see it, and then aimed it at her face. Sands flinched involuntarily but didn't move, and for a second they were locked together. But he didn't fire.

Sands took her eyes momentarily off the gun. Behind the man the two twins were tied up on a dirty double bed, a combination of blue baling twine and silver tape holding them in place. In front of them a video camera stood on a tripod, wires trailing upwards to an overhead power socket.

Sands' brain flooded with information, with everything she had heard about this man as she drove here. Everything she'd taken in about the house. There was no way she knew why, no time to analyse, but for some reason sympathy was her default reaction.

"Why Ian?" she said, not daring to move. "Why are you doing this?"

"You wouldn't understand." The man shook his head as he spoke. He looked older than his twenty-four years, his yellow hair receding fast from the front, escaping from a ponytail at the back. "How many of you are there?"

"Try me." Sands ignored his question. "Tell me what this is about. I want to help you."

Ignoring her the man shifted position, expecting an army of police officers to come swarming in behind Sands at any moment.

"Are you here alone?" There was a hopeful note to his voice.

This time she responded, telling a calculated lie. "There's a team of armed officers outside. I'm the negotiator. It's over, Ian."

He screamed out now, a howl of pain, then he turned away and beat the grip of the gun into the palm of his injured hand, as if he needed the agony it must have caused him. Sands watched, expecting the weapon to discharge every time he struck it. When he stopped she stepped quickly forward but he became instantly alert again, swinging to point the weapon at the head of the nearest of the twins.

"Don't come any closer." He shook his head. "I'll do it. I've done it before."

Sands froze. She put up her hands. "I believe you. But you don't have to do it again."

A battle seemed to be raging inside him. His face contorted and his body twitched; the only part remaining still was the arm holding the weapon. His eyes darted to his wrist, to an expensive watch out of keeping with the rest of the outfit. Sands saw the eyes of one of the girls – she was alive, awake, watching in terror.

"No. It's too early." King was speaking under his breath now, grunting. "It has to be at twelve, *exactly twelve*." Suddenly, he swung back to Sands, pointing the gun at her again. "You have to give me time. I need more time. Just a few more minutes."

Sands felt totally exposed, now a metre into the room. She

tried not to look at the ugly barrel of the gun aimed between her eyes.

"What happens at twelve, Ian? Why is it so important?"

"Just a few more minutes," he mumbled again, but then his voice grew clearer, his eyes focused on her. "You wouldn't understand." He laughed. "You can't understand this." He shook his head. And Sands now remembered Golding's words. *He's totally crazy... he believes he'll be transported back in time if he kills the twins today.*

Suddenly he swung the weapon back to the twin. "Get back, don't come any closer or I'll shoot her. I'll do it." Again, the mumbling. "Just a few more minutes. I just need a few more minutes."

Sands shifted the weight from one leg, ready to step forwards again. "You don't have to hurt her, Ian. You don't want to hurt her, I can see that."

"It's not hurting, I'm not hurting. I'm not hurting anyone. Don't you get it? Don't you see?"

Sands tried to keep her voice calm. "Explain it to me. I want to understand."

King snatched another look at his watch, his face troubled by what it told him. Sands checked hers too: 11:57.

"What happens at twelve, Ian? Please tell me. Why do you think you have to hurt the girls at midday?"

King shook his head, not in disagreement but as if he were fighting to dislodge his thoughts. "The children don't matter. It doesn't matter if I shoot them, they won't exist in a few minutes. They won't exist, you won't exist, I won't..." He turned to look at her, his eyes wide and staring. "They're the key to the portal. They have to die at twelve, exactly twelve, and that opens the portal." He glanced at his watch again, fell silent.

"I told you you wouldn't understand." He spoke glumly now, as if the fantasy was too difficult to maintain in her presence.

Very gently Sands angled her wrist so that she could see her own watch. 11:58 now, the seconds dropping away.

"Where will you go?" She spoke calmly.

King didn't answer.

"Egypt?"

"You wouldn't understand."

"I went to Egypt once," she continued. "When I was a girl." He twitched. He was interested, suspicious.

"Where in Egypt?"

"Cairo." She didn't know where she was taking this, but sensed the need to make him talk. "I wasn't much older than those two are now, but I remember the pyramids. How impressive they were."

King scoffed at this. "The way they are today is nothing. You should see them as I have."

"You've been there too?"

"I haven't *been there*. I live there. I work there. I lead one of the teams placing the capping stones. The greatest team." King spoke proudly. It seemed to change him.

"That's wonderful," Sands replied, trying to guide him gently back towards reality. "That's incredible. It shows you're a craftsman, not a murderer."

At the word "murderer" King stiffened again.

"You're a craftsman, not a killer. This isn't the real you."

"Shut up." King shook his head, adjusted his grip on the gun. He glanced again at his watch. Sands eyes flicked to hers.

"Ian, this is wrong. They don't have to die."

"Stop calling me that. My name is Sekhmut."

"Sekhmut, Ian, it doesn't matter what you call yourself, if you do this it's still murder, and that's not you."

He took two or three deep breaths, the gun still steadied on the girl bound to the filthy bed. "It's not murder. If you really want to know, I'll tell you. The part of me you see here is one half of a twin. The other half – my true half – is a man named

Sekhmut the Great, who lived in Egypt – who *lives* in Egypt, but twenty thousand years ago. At precisely midday a portal will open. The Great Pyramid at Giza will be revealed for what it truly is, a tunnel through time, yet it will admit only a few, chosen people. I am one of those people, but I can only travel there by making a sacrifice. Only the death of this child will open the portal." He looked at his watch. "In exactly thirty seconds." He cleared his throat.

"I told you you wouldn't understand." He laughed suddenly, turned away and placed both hands on the gun, waiting the last few seconds.

Sands considered rushing him, but in all his madness he was handling the gun as if he'd been trained. He'd easily squeeze a shot into the girl before Sands got to him, and he'd probably then be able to turn the gun on her too. Her only option was to keep him talking.

"So what happens? You shoot them, then what? Will there be a burst of bright light, and you vanish?"

He didn't move. "Something like that."

"And they'll die? Two innocent children."

"I told you. Everything here dies. This version of the world will cease to exist and time will be rewritten from twenty thousand years ago. I said you wouldn't understand."

Sands blinked, trying to think. Her brain was making connections faster than she could understand them, Throwing out ideas. Without knowing how, or why, one idea stuck. She spoke without thinking.

"Well done, Sekhmut. You've passed."

She took a step forward, trying to project a confidence she didn't feel. It was as if the pressure was off; she was dead anyway. She held out her hand. In response he swung the weapon back onto her. When he didn't fire she took another pace forward.

"You've passed, Sekhmut. Congratulations. I've come here

now to reveal the real plans." Walking right up to him, for a second she thought she could simply take the gun from him but her nerve failed. The sight of the weapon, just a few feet away now, stopped her. She was so close she could smell him.

"What test? What plans?"

Sands forced a smile, the plan she'd already put into action feeling stupid now, doomed to fail, a dumb way to die. But there was no backing down. "I'm not really from the police. And there's no army of officers behind me. But then you never believed that, did you?"

He was silent.

"It's just you and me, Sekhmut. And I've come to tell you the children must not die. Not anymore. They want me to take them instead."

He stared at her as if trying to ascertain whether she was speaking the truth.

"That's not the plan."

"The plan's changed. Give me the gun, let me take the children." She reached out but he shook his head.

"Why would they change their minds?"

"They didn't. It's only your plan that's changed. They wanted to see if you were loyal, worthy." Sands tried to imitate the language she'd heard. "You've passed, Sekhmut, this is wonderful news. You've passed your test, now you need to prepare for what comes next. Give me the gun." And then, breaking the near silence in the underground room, his watch alarm began to sound.

Beep, beep. Beep, beep. Beep, beep...

King's face froze. He swung the gun towards one of the twins. But he didn't fire, he simply stared at the girl, his fingers anxiously moving on the grip. "How can I trust you? How do I know you're not the police?" The alarm continued to sound as he spoke.

"Because I'm here at the appointed hour. The police know nothing of this. They don't understand."

"*You* didn't understand. I had to tell you."

"No, I had to be sure you knew. I needed to be sure you'd carry out our instructions no matter what. It's essential you obey us, whatever we say."

"I am. I do understand. I will do."

"Then you'll give me the gun. That's the real plan. They don't want the twins harmed."

The watch stopped. There was a new silence in the room.

"You've..." He turned to stare at Sands. And she saw in his eyes a connection to reality that hadn't been there moments before. A realisation that she'd tricked him into missing the important moment. "You distracted me..." He glanced around the room, as if still expecting it to begin to dissolve around them. But the grey concrete walls stayed exactly as they were.

"It didn't end." Sands kept her eyes on his. "The world didn't end. I said you could trust me." Very gently, she reached forward until she was touching both the gun and his hand. He did nothing to stop her, and carefully she pulled his fingers from the grip. A moment later she was holding the gun. "Why don't you sit down?" Sands eyes darted to a chair by the wall. "I'm going to untie them now. I'm going to untie the twins."

FORTY-ONE

Ten minutes later there were shouts from outside, and then the first three ARU officers came clattering down the ramp, helmets on, their MP5 submachine guns readied to fire. But they stopped when they saw Sands sitting between the twins on the bed, loosely cradling a pistol. At the foot of the bed was the frightening, bizarre figure of Ian King, his head lowered, crying. They took it all in quickly, but still took no chances.

"Drop the weapon!" their commander yelled. "Get down on the floor!"

Sands waited until their own guns were trained on King, then held the weapon out, grip forward, and placed it carefully on the bed. Then she put one arm around each of the twins while the ARU officers roughly forced King to comply, pushing his face down onto the abattoir's concrete floor, where his tears moistened decades' worth of dried blood.

Sometime later, someone – Sands thought it might be Beth Chang, but by then the shock of everything was overwhelming her – took the twins away. Sands had already established that they were unharmed, although they had barely eaten or drunk for several days.

King had been removed too. Arrested, searched and then led away. The room was checked in case it concealed other weapons or booby traps. His weapon was made safe and then taken away in a metal box the ARU carried for such purposes. The ammunition went into another box. Both were labelled, the beginning of the long and complex investigation that would have to take place.

Sands left the building soon afterwards, helped up the ramp by one of the ARU officers. Somehow they'd got their trucks through the top gate, and now the farmyard was filled with police cars and minibuses, blue lights everywhere. She was told to sit down in one of the cars.

She hadn't been there long when Detective Golding got in and sat next to her holding a sheaf of papers. After a long silence, she glanced over at him.

"The decoded letters between Sterling and King. I thought you'd want to see them."

She didn't look at him, nerves all over her body were still firing randomly, sending fear signals deep into her brain.

"What do they say?"

"It all comes from Sterling. Not the other way around. He tells King to find some twins; it didn't matter who, they just had to be twin girls. He tells King to take them and tie them up and video them. And he tells him what website to use. And it's all wrapped up in this insane idea that the world's gonna end, and King'll go back in time and be this character in ancient Egypt. It's totally screwed up." Golding held out one of the transcribed messages. Sands didn't take it.

"What about the other murders? Lindham? His family?"

Golding drew a deep breath. "We're still missing some messages, but it's the same. Sterling told us King tipped him off on when the murders would take place, but in reality, he tells King who to target and when to do it."

"Jane Smith as well?"

"Yeah. It's like Sterling realises he can manipulate this guy and send him on this insane killing spree. But why? What's the point? Is he such a fucking psychopath that just causing mayhem is the point?" He ran his fingers through his hair.

"I don't know," she said. "Why did they use the code?" Rational thoughts were beginning to filter through her over-alert brain. She tried to follow them. "Whose idea was it? How did they communicate the idea to each other? I don't see how they used it. Why did they need it?"

"They needed to talk to each other without anyone knowing what they were saying," Golding replied.

"No. That's not it. That can't be it. They had to agree on using Sterling's old article as the key. King knows nothing about mathematics, so this must come from Sterling, but he still has to tell King to use a code. He probably has to write the damn papers that King is sending him, and just get King to make the number grids with the messages coded in them. But how the hell does he do that? How does he send the key to the code before they've agreed what the code is?"

Golding clicked his tongue. "I don't know."

"Nor do I."

"There's enough to charge him," Golding continued, after Sands had fallen silent. "Sterling, I mean. Aiding and abetting in the murders of Lindham and his family, kidnapping the twins. Smith too. I don't know if..." Golding stopped and raised his hands in the air. "I don't know if you want to be involved in any of that, or just move on. But that's how you've got to look at this." He turned to face her. "You stopped him. You beat him." He looked hard into her eyes.

For a moment she held his gaze, but then she shook her head suddenly. "I didn't. I lost." She shook her head, angry now. "Because I still don't understand."

"Maybe there's nothing to understand," Golding suggested. "Maybe he's just crazy too."

Sands shook her head. "He's not crazy. He's an incredibly high-functioning sociopath. You've seen what he's achieved, all from that *fucking* cell. There must be a reason for it. There has to be." Her thoughts were clearing, if only slightly. "Jane Smith was revenge. For Caroline Smith reporting him, or maybe for his failure to kill her the night he raped her. He couldn't reach Caroline because she was in Canada, so he decided that killing her sister was punishment enough. But the others? Lindham? Sterling didn't feel threatened by Lindham. It was Sterling who gave us the tip. He made sure he was drawn into this. Why?"

"I don't know."

"Have you heard from the prison?"

"The prison? No."

She looked pained. "I need to speak to him. I need to know what this was all for."

"OK," Golding said after a long pause. "If you like I can go with you. Whenever you need. I don't know if he'll talk but..."

She nodded, grateful. "Let's go now."

"Erica... ma'am, you can't. You're in shock. You're still shaking. You look like you haven't slept in days, and you..." he paused, smiled grimly, "frankly you smell like shit. Take a few hours. Have a wash. Reflect on the fact that you've stopped him. You saved those girls' lives."

Sands screwed her face up and rubbed her eyes. But when she dropped her hands again she shook her head.

"No. We have to go now. Something here's still not right."

FORTY-TWO

Sands let Golding drive, retracing the route she'd taken earlier. Blankly, she watched the road slip by, reliving the tension that had been gripping her. But although she tried to force her brain to rehearse what she'd say to Sterling, her thinking felt sluggish, her brain exhausted. Golding put a call in to the prison and McDonald agreed to meet them at the gate. He parked the Alfa carefully and led the way to the entrance. A gust of wind blew leaves and a light rain towards them.

"Detective Sands. Please." McDonald led them through the first layer of security and towards the metal detector. "Can I say first of all that I owe you an apology."

"What for?" Sands asked.

"I'm aware now that Sterling has been guiding these murders himself. I want you to know I based my assessment of him on the psychiatrists' reports. They believed he'd changed, that the prison process, and the time he'd spent here, had changed him. But it seems he fooled them all."

Sands stared, confused. What did he want her to say? No harm done? She settled for meaningless platitudes. "He's a sociopath. They should have known he's incapable of change."

McDonald nodded. "I'd hoped that wasn't the case. But I was wrong, and I apologise."

Sands swallowed. She still felt the after-effects of the huge dose of adrenalin that had surged through her body, and it felt like the worst hangover of her life.

"Sure. Whatever."

McDonald led the way down towards the lift shaft that led to the underground section of the prison.

"What do you hope to achieve? Seeing Sterling now?"

"I want to ask what this was all for. I still don't understand."

McDonald nodded. "And you think he'll tell you?"

Sands stopped. The question connected for the first time. And something else too. "Maybe." She started walking again. "I think he somehow *wants* me to know. He could have done all this without getting me involved. There must be some reason for that. I think it's worth trying."

"OK." McDonald called the lift and the doors opened. "If you don't mind, I'd like to watch as you speak with him. Over CCTV."

"Sure." Sands glanced at Golding. "You can wait there too. I should speak to him alone."

Golding nodded silently. They got in the lift and began to descend.

The lift slowed and the doors opened. Sands breathed in the dry, stale air of the underground part of the prison. Up ahead was Barney Atkinson's little office with its banks of CCTV screens. The door was open but the big man wasn't there.

"Where's Atkinson?" Sands asked.

"He was feeling unwell, and when we tested him he returned a positive Covid test. As you can imagine we have a very strict policy here for anything infectious."

Sands let this information sit in her mind, but she didn't connect with the problem it implied. "OK." She glanced at the screens, the largest of which showed Sterling lying on his bed as if sleeping, or perhaps meditating. She still didn't know what she was going to ask him, but she had to trust and believe that the words would come when she was face to face with him.

"Let's go." She forced her legs to drive her forward. Away from Golding, away from McDonald, feeling their eyes on her back as she moved down the corridor to her father's cell.

He didn't move as she approached, even when she came right up to the glass and looked around his cell. He lay on the bed, looking away. Not moving.

"Sterling?"

Nothing. No movement, no clever comment. No victorious smile.

"Sterling, can you hear me?"

Still he didn't move, and Sands felt... something. Concern she supposed, when she noticed his chest was barely moving. His green and yellow jumpsuit was still.

"Sterling? Can you hear me? Are you OK?" She turned to face the camera, knowing McDonald and Golding would be watching closely. "Get down here. I don't think he's breathing."

Golding was the first to get there, but the door to the Perspex cell was locked. McDonald arrived soon afterwards, concern written deeply on his face.

"I need to get this door open," he said, almost to himself, but Sands put her hand on his arm.

"Careful, this could be a trick."

McDonald nodded. "I have to go back to the control room. I'll get some staff."

It took a few minutes, while Golding and Sands waited outside Sterling's cell. He continued to lie still on the bed. Sands noticed other details. He had pulled the blanket up around his neck, in a way that, the more she looked at it, seemed wrong. They heard footsteps and the director returned with four uniformed officers. One of them held the keys to Sterling's cell. Another carried a taser, armed and ready for use.

"Has he moved?" McDonald asked.

Sands shook her head.

"He's breathing. Just," Golding said.

"OK." McDonald nodded to the prison warden but spoke to Sands. "We need to open the cell."

The first officer slipped the key into the door and unlocked it, slowly pulling it open while keeping his eyes on Sterling, but the prisoner didn't move. Two officers entered the cell. They approached Sterling.

"Be careful," McDonald cautioned, from outside.

It didn't look as though the officer needed to be told. "His eyes are closed. He looks unconscious. I can't see any signs of breathing."

"Has he got a pulse?" Golding asked.

The officer looked unhappy with the question, but placed his hand gently on Sterling's neck. It took a long time for him to reply. "Yeah. It's faint though. Can barely feel it."

"OK, let's get the prison doctor down here. And get some more bodies down here. Until we know what the hell is going on."

But then Sands realised it wasn't the blanket around Sterling's neck that was wrong. It was his *hair*.

Suddenly she moved forward into the cell. Placing her hand on Sterling's shoulder she roughly pulled him around so that she could see his face. And then she stood back, both hands over her mouth.

"Oh shit," she said. "This isn't Charles Sterling."

FORTY-THREE

As it always did, the bell rang at 7:30, waking Sean Nutt from his sleep. But he didn't move, hoping his mind would return to the dream. He'd been walking on a slightly altered version of Clapham Common. The leaves on the trees were turning the golden colours of autumn, and he could feel the tug of the grass at his feet. But more than anything he was aware that he wasn't alone. In his hand he held the soft, precious hand of his seven-year-old son, James. Chattering, always chattering, usually about his beloved West Ham United Football Club. Sean screwed his eyes more tightly closed, trying to bring the image back, the feeling of those little fingers, gripping onto his. But it was drifting. Slipping away.

Replaced by the grey-painted brickwork of the cell, the grey steel-frame bed, the grey blanket that itched against his skin.

Moments later he was fully awake, accepting that the dream was gone. And from directly below he heard an all-too-familiar sound. He didn't look as his cell mate, Mark Armstrong, emerged from his bunk and lumbered heavy-footed to the toilet they shared, just a few feet away. Armstrong was a big man, barrel-chested and carrying a heavy gut, but no one could accuse him of not being regular. Every morning, five minutes after the wake-up bell, he would settle himself on the john for his morning shit.

Some of the cells had a shower-curtain type arrangement that could be pulled around the toilet to provide some privacy, but they were flimsy and tended to break. When they did, the prison didn't have the resources to fix them. For cells like Sean and Mark's, where the curtain was long gone, the etiquette was for the man not using the toilet to keep their eyes averted and to make no mention of what was happening. And that's what Sean did now, trying not to listen for the drop and the splash. But etiquette did nothing for the smell.

As Armstrong strained, Sean thought again of his son, but as he was now, all grown up, with his own life. James had a wife now, a kid of his own. Milestones that Sean himself should have been there for, but had forfeited with the choices that had put him in this place.

There had been time too, in recent months, to think about those choices. His parole hearing had at first loomed ahead of him like a distant deadline, with its promise of possible freedom but threat of disappointment. He hadn't got his hopes up. Everyone knew Category A prisoners like himself never got granted parole the first time around. They were bastards like that. It didn't matter how well you'd behaved, how much you kissed arse or how convincingly you claimed to have changed, they'd keep you in for a few more years, just to be on the safe side, or to prove the point that they were in charge of your life. But Nutt went through the motions anyway; there was little else to do. He prepared a statement, setting out where he'd live if released, and how his son had agreed to support him. He added a letter to the victims of his crimes, apologising for his actions, and demonstrating that he'd really considered how his actions might have impacted them. And he'd thought about it too, putting himself in their place and thinking how it must have felt to see a masked man burst in brandishing a shotgun.

It was wrong to say he'd had an epiphany, to claim that he'd seen the light – life was far messier than that. But *something* had changed. Enough that, after nine years inside and with the hearing approaching, he felt a sense of hope that maybe, this time, things would go his way.

But when the panel convened and he sat down before them, that hope evaporated. They were brusque, eying him cynically, clearly looking down on him and not believing that his words of regret were genuine. The entire hearing took less than twenty minutes, and though the result would come in writing, as Sean was led back to his cell he had little doubt what it would say.

It came a week later, and for several hours Sean had been laying on his bed with the letter under his pillow – where it was now – not daring to open it.

He had been right, of course. The parole board hadn't seen in him a man ready to start afresh. They hadn't believed his protestations of regret. But sometimes these things just didn't matter. Political pressure on prison numbers tended to work in a cyclical way. The politicians wanted the prisons full, to show how tough they were on crime. But if the prisons got too full, the costs spiralled out of control, and then the politicians wanted to empty them, just a bit, to show the public how good they were at cutting public spending. And so, when Sean Nutt came to open the envelope, the news was unexpected. He was to be released, after serving nine years of his sixteen-year sentence.

That was just under six weeks ago.

Keeping his gaze away from Armstrong – now wiping with one hand, and picking his nose with the other – Sean found himself looking around the so-familiar confines of the cell. How many times had he woken up here? He didn't know. How many times had he stared at the bars on the window, the heavy iron door, locked shut, and wished this day would come? The last day.

And now it was here.

FORTY-FOUR

"OK, Sean, you have your *sheet* in order, no?"

One of the new wardens had come to fetch him. A man named Sinta from Venezuela. He was so green he hadn't learned how to swear properly, but Sean liked him. A lot of the older, tougher jailors were retiring from the service, being replaced by immigrants like Sinta, who didn't mind the long hours and low pay.

"Yes boss," Sean replied.

After breakfast was his final exercise time. It was raining, but only lightly, and Sean shuffled around a few final laps, finding time for a few last words with some of the guys who'd helped him out, or vice versa. Quiet goodbyes, each knowing they may never see the other again. And then it was back to his cell for just a bit more time. He made a pile of the few belongings he was taking with him; the rest he'd already given away.

"OK then," Sinta went on, dangling his keys. "Time to go."

"Yes boss," Nutt replied, keeping his eyes respectfully averted. The habit to refer to the wardens as boss was deeply ingrained. More than that, it was simply true – they were the boss.

"Guess this is it, then," Armstrong said, apparently emotionless.

"Guess so." Nutt nodded, and then he surprised himself by going up to Armstrong and giving the big man a bear hug.

"I'll see you on the outside. Two years, yeah? You'll make it."

Neither man really knew if this were true.

"Don't come back, huh?" Armstrong said. "I see you again, I'll kill you myself."

"I don't plan on it."

"OK, OK, we do this? Or no?" Sinta shook his keys.

Nutt took a last long look around his cell. Then he stepped into the corridor.

He waited while Sinta locked the cell door behind him, then followed along the iron walkway towards another locked gate. The cables of the CCTV camera placed above it were encased in steel to protect against projectiles. Sinta spoke into his radio, waited while the camera buzzed and focused, then the radio cracked.

"Arm."

Automatically Nut held out his left hand and Sinta scanned the electronic tag fastened there. Finally he pulled out his own large, iron key and unlocked the gate. Again Nutt followed. Already away from the part of the prison that felt familiar.

"Where we going?" Nutt asked.

"Holding cell first," Sinta replied. "Make paperwork, then we issue you outside clothes, and give gate money."

Nutt listened only vaguely, as if this were happening to someone else, not him.

"How long's it all take?"

"Takes as long as it takes, no?"

Nutt looked around him as they walked. Had he ever been to this part of the jail before? It suddenly seemed incredible just how small his world had been. His cell, the communal area between the two wings. The exercise yard, and then a handful of other places. And yet the jail itself was enormous, huge areas of it as unknown to him as a foreign land, despite the years he'd spent there. They passed more security gates. Another warden who Nutt didn't recognise yawned as he checked his name against a list on a clipboard.

"Put him in that cell."

"No. *I've* got that one. HP coming in for exercise," another guard interrupted, striding confidently toward them. He wore twin crowns on his shoulders, the mark of a Principal Prison Officer, outranking the other two. And "HP" meant high profile – usually one of the freaks kept in the underground cells buried somewhere deep beneath their feet. All the inmates knew about them, hardly anyone ever saw them.

The second warden studied his clipboard, confused. He looked reluctant to challenge his superior. "That's the last holding cell."

"Well I need it," the PPO said before turning to Nutt and sighing. "Who is this anyway?"

"Prisoner number 9657, Sean Nutt, due for release today, sir."

Unimpressed, the PPO inclined his head toward the open door of the cell, improvising a solution. "Put him in there. I'll help you process him."

Nutt was led into the cell and left there alone for half an hour with the door locked, before it clanged open again.

This time both Sinta and the PPO came inside. Sinta seemed about to lock the door again behind them, but the senior man stopped him. "We'll be done in five minutes. Then you can take him out of here." The PPO began removing items one by one from a clear plastic bag.

"Release papers. You need to sign these with the two of us watching. Then we'll issue your gate money. We'll get you some civvies in a moment, then you'll be outta here. But first you gotta take this Covid test." The man smiled coldly. "Standard bullshit procedure."

He pulled the plastic test kit from the bag and tossed it casually to Nutt. At once Sean began to unpack it. For months, during the height of the pandemic, they'd had to do daily tests. He pulled out the little stick and pushed it up one nostril, twirled it around, then did the other.

The PPO waited, watching to make sure he did it right, then pushed the papers towards him. "Right. Now sign these while you're waiting."

Nutt signed without reading a word. Nearly a decade in this place had bred an obedience to authority in him. He just felt more comfortable doing exactly what he was told. When he was done he simply stared into space, waiting for whatever came next.

"Oh, for fuck's sake!" the PPO exclaimed suddenly. He'd picked up the plastic test kit and was studying it, shaking his head. "Two fucking lines. You've got bloody Covid mate. Maybe you're not getting out today after all."

For the first time, Nutt felt a shaft of panic. "I feel fine. I'm not ill." Nutt looked from one man to the other, then the open door. "What about my release? I'm still getting out aren't I?"

The PPO had a hand pressed again his brow, as if he didn't need this hassle, but then the hand dropped and he shook his head. "Alright, calm down. This ain't changing anything. We don't have time for that." The PPO regarded him unsympathetically for a second, then turned to Sinta. "You've had your jabs, ain't you? He's probably infectious as fuck." He raised his eyebrows as if bored by the whole procedure.

But Sinta's reaction was completely different. "Infectious?" he asked, looked at Nutt with genuine fear in his eyes.

"Yeah, I guess."

"*Hijo de puta!*" Sinta swore suddenly, stepping backwards away from Nutt.

"Woah, what's your problem?" said the PPO.

"I can't go near him. *Mi esposa*, my wife, she's..." – he seemed to be searching for the right word – "Immuno-suppressed," he managed at last. "If I get it and pass it to her, she could die. Everyone knows this." Sinta looked shocked.

Nutt broke the ensuing silence. "What about me? Are you still gonna let me go? I'm not ill. I don't feel ill."

"Keep your mouth shut, prisoner," snarled the PPO, and Nutt was quiet at once. The PPO turned to Sinta. "Alright, calm down. Maybe you don't have it yet. You were only with him a few minutes. Did you get close? You touch him?"

"No." Sinta shook his head but his wide eyes told another story. "Not really, but I still have to take him out."

The PPO sighed, pondering for a moment. "Alright, go get us a couple of masks. I'll walk him. Whole thing's fucking fake anyhow."

"You are sure?" The relief was written all over Sinta's face. "I say, when I start working here. I tell to the management, I cannot risk getting infected, because my wife."

"Yeah, I'm sure. Fucking hell." The PPO muttered to himself as if he were bored of the whole exchange. Then he turned to Nutt. "You're still getting out. We've had enough trouble with fucking Covid in here. You go infect whoever you want on the outside. Now get undressed. I'll get you some clothes."

Sinta scuttled out, returning a few moments later wearing a face mask and tossing two more on the table before loitering a few seconds and then scampering away. The PPO watched him go, then turned to Nutt. "Well fucking put it on, then! And get the rest of your clothes off. I'll fetch some civvies."

He walked out, shutting and then locking the door behind him. And Nutt undressed, by habit taking off his underwear too, so that he stood waiting bollock-naked but for the cloth mask covering his face.

He shivered as he waited, but it didn't occur to him that anything about this series of events was off. He trusted the PPO would come back when he was good and ready. He trusted he would be led through the remaining layers of security and to the exit of the prison. Where he'd finally be free. But Nutt was quite wrong about that.

The key grated in the lock and the door swung open. The same PPO marched back in, closed the door and locked it. There was nothing unusual there, but what he was carrying did cause Nutt to frown.

"Put these on."

He tossed a set of bright green and yellow overalls towards Nutt. The same sort the HPs wore, underground. He hesitated.

"I said put them on."

"What about my civvie clothes?" Nutt began. "I thought I got jeans—"

"I said *put 'em on.*" The PPO shut him down.

Nutt's frown deepened, but he did what he was told. He kept his eyes averted from the PPO as he unfolded the overalls, noticing that the number on the back didn't match his own. He wanted to point that out as well, but he knew better.

He stepped into them, pulling them up to his waist, then found a way to ask what was going on. "Do I get changed again before I get out?"

"I wouldn't count on it."

Before Nutt could respond to the PPO's comment, the big man had crossed the floor of the cell to reach him, grabbing his bare arm. Nutt felt a pinch on his muscle and then gasped in astonishment when he saw a hypodermic syringe in the officer's hand, its needle already embedded in his arm. And then his vision grew foggy. His legs unsteady.

The PPO pushed the chair beneath him just in time as his knees collapsed from under him and the room went dark.

FORTY-FIVE

"This isn't Charles Sterling," Sands said for the second time, after nobody had replied. "And if this isn't him, where the hell is he?"

No one knew what to say. "Where is he?" she demanded again. "Is he on exercise? Has he changed cells? Please don't tell me he's fucking escaped."

It was quickly established that Sterling hadn't moved cells – such a thing was unheard of in the underground section of the prison – and it was confirmed that the number on the back of the man in Sterling's cell matched Sterling's prison number.

"He *can't* have escaped." McDonald's eyes blinked in his now chalk-white face. He turned to Sands, earnest. "Are you *quite* sure this isn't Sterling?"

"Are you damn well kidding me?" Sands lashed out now. "Just *look* at him."

Finally, McDonald moved. He ordered his officers to check the other underground cells and then, breathing shakily, he initiated the prison's emergency escape protocol. A klaxon began to sound, a low, wailing noise that echoed around the walls.

"What happens now?" Golding asked.

The director glanced at his watch. He was visibly shaking. "All the prisoners will be returned to their cells, counted and scanned, all the doors locked. The external prison doors have already been sealed shut. No one gets out until I give the order to release them."

"How about roadblocks?" Sands asked.

McDonald paused, as if on the verge of telling her they weren't needed, but then he nodded and issued the second protocol over the radio.

Sands listened coldly. "You'd better get a doctor down here for whoever this is."

The search revealed nothing, but the director hadn't mentioned how the protocols he'd initiated also cut power to the lift shafts serving the underground cells. It took half an hour before it was turned back on, in which time all the prisoners on the main wings had been checked and secured. None were missing. There were no other reports of anything untoward.

The first part of the mystery was solved when the prison doctor finally arrived.

"I know this man," he said as he quickly checked his vital signs. He seemed stable.

"Who is it?" Sands asked.

"I gave him a medical exam just yesterday. A parolee, due for release today. I think his name was Nutt."

Once they had a name, a picture began to emerge of what had happened, but still little of it made sense. They found a major clue back in McDonald's office. Daniels the technician was working in the meeting room, still trying to figure out how Sterling had managed to access certain internet sites without being seen. "There's something here you should see," he called out.

"What?" Sands asked, beginning to read what was on the screen.

The technician took a deep breath, but was interrupted by Sands. "*Jesus Christ.*"

"What?" McDonald said, agitated.

"He was moving money?" Sands ignored McDonald, turning to Daniels, who nodded, then shook his head.

"Not money exactly. He was moving Bitcoin." He glanced at McDonald, technically his boss. "Bitcoin is a public ledger where all transactions are recorded simultaneously on every computer running the network. That way it's impossible for anyone to falsify entries. But it also means anyone can see every transaction made. Sterling made two transactions today while we thought he was looking at waterfalls."

While he was speaking Sands continued to check the computer.

When Golding asked, "Can we see who he paid it to?" Daniels shook his head.

"No, just the wallet address."

"What does that mean?"

Daniels replied, "Transactions are routed to and from wallets, but you can't always see who owns a wallet. They can be completely anonymous. The only way we can know that Sterling controlled this wallet was because the transactions were carried out from the IP address of the computer in his cell. No one else could have done it."

It took Golding a while to process this. "Do we know how much he sent? Was it a lot?"

"Yeah," Daniels said. "Actually, we do know that." But he didn't go on. His face had also gone white.

"Well?" McDonald demanded, when he failed to continue.

"He made two transactions." It was Sands who finally spoke, her voice stripped of emotion. "In one he moved 181 Bitcoins. The second one was bigger. That's for just over sixteen *thousand* Bitcoin."

"So is that..." Golding asked in the end. "I don't know how much that is?"

"At current exchange rates, 181 Bitcoins is worth around nine million pounds. Sixteen thousand is just shy of one billion."

"Jesus Christ," McDonald exclaimed.

The second clue arrived when they discovered that Sean Nutt had been released, as per schedule, earlier that day. Although of course he hadn't been, as he was currently lying in the hospital wing after being discovered unconscious in Charles Sterling's cell. Nothing in the records seemed out of place, but CCTV footage made things a little clearer.

"He's wearing a mask!" McDonald asked as they crowded around the screen. "Why's he wearing a mask?"

"Is that him? Is that Sterling?" Golding looked at Sands. She ran her hand through her hair.

"What the hell is Barney Atkinson doing there?"

They watched on the screen as Atkinson, in his PPO uniform, marched another man, dressed in civilian release clothes, into the prison's exit hall.

FORTY-SIX

"Nice day for it," the rear desk-guard said. He was staffing the low-security exit to the prison. In addition to staff arriving and leaving for work, it was used for prisoners on day release or at the end of their sentence. The last line of security between the prison and the outside world. Nonetheless, everyone who left by this route was checked, and their names recorded.

The prisoner's eyes, above his mask, looked cautious.

"I said it's a nice day for it. Being released, after..." – the guard checked his paperwork – "nine years. Nice to see a bit of sun." He inclined his head to the window, where a shaft of early afternoon sunshine kissed the surrounding moorland.

"Another happy customer, huh Barney?"

Barney Atkinson grunted a half-acknowledgement and began to unlock the handcuffs binding him to the prisoner. Even on his release date a prisoner remained a prisoner until every protocol had been completed.

"So... Nutt, Sean. Step forward to the scanner."

The prisoner did so, lifting his arm so the machine picked up the tag around his wrist. When it beeped the guard checked his screen. "Prisoner number?"

"9657, boss," he answered automatically. He wore a new pair of jeans and a baggy sweatshirt.

"That's good... Lose the nosebag."

"Sorry boss?"

The guard pointed to the man's face and waggled his finger. "The nosebag. Your facemask. Take it off please."

"He just got a positive Covid test," Atkinson interrupted. "Guvnor insists he wears it."

"Maybe, but he also insists I check everyone in and out this door. So lose the nosebag, please."

It looked for a second as if Atkinson might protest further, but the prisoner was already raising his hands to remove the mask. But as he did so he was hit by a fit of coughing. Four or five times his chest racked as the noise filled the small room. He tried to keep his hands in front of his mouth, but the plastic barrier in front of the guard was still speckled with moisture.

"Sorry boss," the prisoner spluttered, turning away to cough again.

"Alright, alright. I get it, you're dying. Well at least that explains why you're looking so miserable on such a happy occasion." Again he looked at Atkinson. Barney gave a half-smile.

"So..." He typed quickly into his keyboard, then removed a large machine from a drawer below his desk.

"Quiz night on Tuesday, Barney? We're gonna be looking for revenge."

"Sure."

"Put your arm in here please." The guard addressed the prisoner again. "We'll get that tag off... and then you'll be free to go."

The prisoner put his arm forward again, and this time the powerful magnets began to align inside the mechanism in his bracelet. It always took a while.

"Might as well sign me out as well," Atkinson said.

The guard looked up in surprise. "Early shift?"

"Not feeling great. Hoping I don't have the damn 'rona too." Atkinson gave the prisoner a dirty look, as if it were his fault.

"Oh shit, I hope not. Say, I still don't get how you knew what the longest river in Venezuela was. Who knows that?"

"I guess I'm just smarter than I look." Atkinson scanned his pass as the guard's attention returned to the electronic tag around the prisoner's wrist. The clasp released and the tag came off, clattering loudly onto the desk. The guard picked it up and tossed it into a plastic bucket at his feet. The prisoner rubbed his wrist, as if unused to the feeling of having nothing there.

"Well that's it, Mr Nutt. It's 1p.m. As per the terms of your parole you are now officially a free man." He pressed a button and the electronic door sighed and opened. Fresh air came flowing into the room. "Bus stop is just past the end of the car park."

The prisoner nodded stiffly. He picked up his bag, and took a step outside.

Then the guard called after him, "Oh, and try not to come back. Too soon anyway." Again he smirked at Barney, but Atkinson wasn't looking. He had his eyes on the CCTV camera.

"Say, I seriously hope you're gonna be alright for Tuesday." The guard sounded worried, but his expression eased when Atkinson looked back at him.

"Don't you worry, Paulie. I'll be there."

And Barney Atkinson stepped out of the prison into the fresh afternoon. But Sean Nutt had already disappeared.

FORTY-SEVEN

Roadblocks were set up on all major roads leading from the prison, while images of Sterling's face were circulated to every police force and out to the airports and ports. But Sands' only hope was the officers who'd been sent to check passengers boarding flights to all non-extradition countries. But that hope soon faded. It turned out thirty-three countries had no extradition treaties with the UK, which meant nearly two dozen flights leaving London's airports that day and a handful at regional airports. That alone would have been difficult to handle, but the possibility of Sterling boarding a connecting flight opened up hundreds more. Maybe they would get there in time. Most likely they wouldn't.

Meanwhile a raiding party was sent to Atkinson's house. He lived alone, having split with his wife two years previously. It was no surprise to find it empty. What was unexpected was the note left for his colleagues:

We live in a deterministic universe, where every action is the result of those that come before it. Every step we take is not our

choice, but the inevitable consequence of factors beyond our
control. There is no such thing as free will.

"What the hell does that mean?" McDonald asked.

Sands replied, "I'd say that's the excuse given by one of your officers for accepting nine million pounds for helping Sterling escape." Phoning Commander Black, who was helping coordinate the police's response, she asked him to send more officers to the airports.

And it was here that the breakthrough came. Too late, just as Sands had feared.

It wasn't Sterling who was identified from CCTV footage, sitting nervously as he waited at the gate for a direct TAM flight to São Paulo, but Barney Atkinson. But the flight was already over the mid-Atlantic, well out of British airspace, where Sands or Black, or anybody else for that matter, had no jurisdiction. A start was made on a request to detain Atkinson when the flight landed, but abandoned when it was clear it would take at least a week to be acknowledged by the Brazilian authorities. Atkinson had slipped the net.

FORTY-EIGHT

Sands drove slowly for once as she and Golding made the trip through the rolling Purbeck Hills towards Langton Matravers, and the old stone schoolhouse that Robbins had turned into his home. She felt unsettled, but not immediately threatened, by the new reality of Sterling's freedom. His priority would surely be to escape, first the area and then the country, and there seemed very little chance that, if he were successful, he'd ever risk his hard-won freedom by returning. She glanced up at the sky where, far above them, an airliner was passing by, and Sands wondered what he was doing right now. Was he in the air somewhere? If so, what was he looking down at? What was he planning to do? And how would he react to the passengers and aircrew? She had no idea if he'd kill again, or whether he'd really meant it when he claimed he'd changed.

"Are you OK?" Golding broke her brooding silence and she turned to look at him. There were lines on his face she couldn't remember from when they'd first met: the job was ageing him. She nodded unconvincingly. "They got Ronnie Biggs in the end."

"Huh?" Sands frowned.

"The Great Train Robber. He hid out in Brazil, but eventually they got an extradition treaty and brought him back. And even when he was there they made his life hell. So don't worry. We'll get him."

"I'm not worried," Sands replied. Suddenly, she felt sure of it. "He wants me to come after him. He wants some great game where the two of us chase each other around the world, him leaving clues and me chasing them down. But I'm not going to. It's not going to happen. He killed his family, and I'm all he has left. And he thinks this way he gets some sort of relationship with me. Even if it's insane." She turned to look at Golding. "I'm not going to look for him. I'm not going to try to get him extradited. I don't care how he's treated, in Brazil or the Dominican Republic. Or Qatar or wherever he installs himself, waiting for me. He's gone and I don't care. More than that, I feel at peace, for the first time in my life. He's gone. And I'm not going after him."

When they arrived in the village Sands slowed down to observe the few people on the pavement as the Alfa slid quietly past. An old lady was pushing the groceries she'd bought in the village shop in her trolley bag. A couple of long-distance walkers were striding along wearing thick socks and hiking boots. The woman carried a bright red backpack and was holding a map. The man glanced into the car as Sands drove by, an admiring glance which she ignored. They passed a pub, The King's Arms, which looked as if it had been there for centuries. A sign offered real ale and "Rooms Available".

"You fancy stopping off when we've seen Robbins?" Sands asked, keeping her eyes on Golding until he answered. "I could really use a drink."

He spent a moment trying to read her expression. Then he seemed to give up, and simply nodded. "Sure."

. . .

The tyres crunched the gravel outside the old schoolhouse, and they both got out. The sky was darkening, both with the approach of night but also as a thunderhead of cloud approached from the west. Weather was rolling in, and the night promised storms. Sands rang the buzzer for Robbins' flat then stepped back, glancing at the single illuminated window above them. When no hallway light came on upstairs to suggest he was coming down, she rang the bell again. Then the downstairs light came on in front of them and Robbins' housekeeper appeared at the door.

"Good evening Mrs Hartley," Golding began, "Is he in?"

"You've missed him, I'm afraid. He's gone out."

"To the pub?" Golding asked hopefully, but the housekeeper shook her head.

"No," She glanced out of the doorway at the sky. "I'm afraid he's gone down to the pool again." She looked troubled.

"The pool?" Golding frowned and glanced at his watch. "He told us he goes down in the mornings. Every day at eleven."

"He does, but sometimes, when there's a storm coming, he likes to go down then as well. He likes to swim in the pool and then be washed clean by the rain." She shook her head. "I worry about him though. He'll catch his death, not to mention how slippery it is down there, all the mud..."

"OK. Thank you. I'm sure we can catch him another time..." said Sands, flashing a tired smile and picturing the pub they'd passed, wondering whether there was a log fire. She could use an hour sitting by an open fire.

"...but at least he's not alone this time," the woman went on.

The ground suddenly shifted under Sands' feet. Nothing definite, just the arrival of a potential threat.

"Not alone?" Sands sensed how Golding had stiffened along with her. "Who's he with?"

"I don't know, I didn't catch his name, but the professor said he was an old friend. A nice man though, very polite..."

Golding pulled out his phone and began searching through it, telling the housekeeper he'd like her to the identify the man from a photograph, but Sands pushed his hand down.

"There's no time. We can call for back-up on the way." And she turned and began running to the footpath that led down the hill.

She wanted to sprint, but it was almost a kilometre through the field and down the path to the pool. She considered driving, but though the track was passable for a Land Rover or 4x4, it was blocked by a heavy, padlocked wooden gate. So she paced herself, hearing Golding's heavy breathing beside her. They vaulted a fence, slipping slightly in the mud on the other side. Eventually they came to the brow of the hill where the path sloped down towards Dancing Ledge. The pool itself was still out of sight, tucked in and hidden under the cliff.

"I can't see him," Golding said.

Sands simply kept running, increasing her pace. It still hurt to move fast because of the crossbow bolt and bullet wounds she'd received a couple of years before, but she'd got used to ignoring the pain. Soon they were on the downhill section that led to the ledge.

They arrived at the bottom of the hill, where there was yet another stile and the path became rocky. There were no climbers here this time, chased away by the threat of rain. The light was dying too, already reduced to a narrow slit of pale yellow on the horizon, bordered above by a thick bank of dark cloud and below by the grey vastness of the ocean. Sands took the rocky, uneven steps two at a time, trying not to think about the consequences of a slip here, which would see her tumble down onto the main platform of Dancing Ledge. Behind her she heard Golding half-slip and swear under his breath. But they both got down safely.

Then there was a choice. They could move to the edge of the upper ledge, where they'd be able to see down to the lower part where the pool was located, but from where it was impossible to descend further. Or they could run directly down but would be unable to see the pool until the last minute. Sands chose the latter, running and then scrambling down over the rocks. Finally she stood on the lowest part of the platform, the pool still hidden by a bend in the cliff. She turned to help Golding descend the last few rocks, then nodded.

"Be careful."

It looked at first as if they were the only ones there. There was no light, and the approaching night had made the platform so gloomy that it seemed deserted. But they walked – looking about them cautiously – towards the pool. And then Sands saw. Something, dropped by the edge of the water. A towel perhaps? A robe? She touched Golding's arm and pointed, feeling his muscles tense. On one side the cliff offered countless shadows and hollows where a man could hide.

There was a noise. Sands spun to stare into the darkness of the cliff face, her eyes searching left and right, boring into the dark seeking any movement, any glint of light. But then she realised the sound hadn't come from the cliff but had bounced off it, an echo in the darkness. She left Golding behind, breaking into a run.

In the near night, the water of the pool had taken on an inky, oily blackness. It hadn't occurred to her as they'd descended but there wasn't a breath of wind – a perfect calm before the storm. She could see the absence of wind on the surface of the water, the sky above reflected perfectly in it. But she didn't look for long as her eyes then took in a pile of clothes dumped by the side. And then she saw it wasn't just clothes but the slumped figure of a man, the whites of his eyes reflecting the low light.

He swallowed painfully, looking at her.

Sands moved across to the man – unmistakably Jeremiah

Robbins – but remembered to glance around as well. No one else in sight.

"Are you hurt?"

In response Robbins looked down, pointing with his eyes to where his hands were covering his stomach, and when he moved them Sands saw an inky darkness there too. Then she realised the pool wasn't just still from the lack of wind; a film of blood was billowing over it, spilling freely from the professor's wounds.

"Sterling?"

He nodded, his breath laboured, as if each inhale and exhale carried a pain he wouldn't bear for much longer. The only other sound was the soft sigh of waves kissing against the rocks.

"How long ago? Is he still here?"

It took Robbins a few moments to answer, but Sands gave him the space. She still hadn't stepped forward and dropped down to check the man's wounds. Instead she stayed still, focused on her peripheral vision, ready to react to any movement left or right.

"Five minutes. He has a knife."

Golding was beside her now, his eyes wide as he took in the scene. Sands turned away, letting Golding attend to the wounds. She scanned the cliff face, just metres away and hidden in shadows. It was impossible to penetrate. Sterling could have been anywhere.

"Keep pressure on the wound," Sands said, continuing to stare into the blackness of the cliff face. Could she see him, in this light? Or would he suddenly be upon them? She didn't know. "There's back-up coming. They'll send a helicopter." But she knew from the sheer amount of blood on the water and pooled in the depressions and fossil imprints in the rock-floor that it was hopeless. No help would come in time. And not for her or Golding either if Sterling attacked.

But then suddenly there was a light. Above them. Not from the upper of the two ledges of the former quarry, but from the grassy ledge of the hill, high above them now, that led back to the village. It was a torch, shining out and down, seeking them out, and after sweeping this way and that it found them, blinding Sands. And then the light turned around, illuminating the man holding it. Allowing them to see him. Sterling. Then abruptly it flicked off.

"Stay with him, I'll go after him," Golding said at once. For a second Sands wanted to argue, but she sensed the futility of it. Sterling had a fifty vertical metres head start, and the route itself was much longer. They would have to scale the lower and upper parts of the cliff just to reach where Sterling was now and by the time they got there he would have disappeared into the night.

"Be careful," she said to Golding as he moved away, but her chief concern was the rocks. Sterling, she knew, was gone.

She crouched down to inspect the wound in Robbins' stomach. Stupidly she hadn't taken her own flashlight from the Alfa, but she used her phone torch to see how badly he'd been injured. His stomach was exposed – he was wearing only his bathing trunks and a long towelling robe – and the hands clutching his stomach were covered in blood, with more leaking and pulsing slowly through his clenched fingers. When Sands moved the light to Robbins' face she saw fear in his eyes. Acceptance too.

"How bad is it?"

"The helicopter will get here in time."

He began a pained laugh, then stopped when it clearly hurt too much. "You're a worse liar than your father."

Sands rocked back on her heels. She eased his hands away and pressed her own over the wound. She felt the warmth of his blood.

"Don't call him that." She adjusted her position and,

noticing Robbins' shoes beside him, wedged one behind his head, trying to make him more comfortable.

"What's this about? Why did he come for you?"

It seemed Robbins was too far gone to answer any questions, so Sands continued herself.

"The code was meant for you, wasn't it? He knew we'd ask you to help us decode it; you were on the database of cryptography experts, and probably the only one good enough to decode it. When did you break it?"

Robbins coughed suddenly. Sands felt droplets of blood on her face. "Not long before you did." His voice was weak. "I thought it might be my paper. I should have tried his earlier work, but I guess I was afraid to do so."

"Why?" Sands pressed. "What were you afraid of? What happened between you two?"

He seemed to want to speak, but couldn't do so.

"Back when you and Sterling worked together, Caroline Smith came to see you. She told you that Sterling had raped her, tried to kill her, but you did nothing. Why not?"

"I made... I made a trade."

"Sterling's work? His work on prime numbers? You saw its value, what it could become, and you told him you wouldn't go to the police if he worked with you?"

For a moment he stared at her, his face illuminated by the phone light. He nodded, almost imperceptibly. "I assumed Caroline was exaggerating, or embarrassed about sleeping with him. I never thought Sterling would actually hurt anyone."

"So you stole his work? Pretended it was yours? And you became fabulously wealthy? All the while he rotted in prison?"

"He rotted for what he'd done. And I gave him money. When it became obvious that Bitcoin would succeed, a large portion of my early investment went to him."

"And now he's used it to escape. Why did you come down with him here, tonight?"

"What choice did I have? If he wanted me dead he'd find a way. I chose to get it over and done with, in a place of my choosing. Better that than have him hunt me down, or live in fear for the rest of my life." Robbins winced. He was slipping away. "He'll go now," he managed to say. "He'll hide out somewhere abroad and try to restart his life. I believe that. You mustn't try to catch him." He shook his head painfully as his attention was caught by a light in the sky to the east. With it came the rhythmic thump of helicopter blades. A searchlight flicked on, still far away, but dramatically illuminating the rocks below as it searched for the ledge. They turned to watch for a moment. They both knew it was too late.

"I remember you, Erica. You were a strange girl. Precociously intelligent, and yet sweet with it." The noise was louder now as the helicopter flew closer. It seemed unlikely it could land in the quarry itself; the steep, overhanging sides would be too close to the rotors, but it might be able to land on the hillside above. But to then get a stretcher down the rocky path, and carry Robbins back out again would take hours. Time he didn't have.

"I remember you here. We came *here*. Your mother. Caroline. Charles. Happier times."

He tensed suddenly, as if experiencing a spasm of pain. When it passed, he sounded weaker. "Don't do it, Erica. Don't go after him. It's what he wants. And he's untouchable now. He doesn't care who he hurts, and he's got access to more money than you can possibly imagine. You don't understand what opportunities that level of wealth opens up. If you chase him, he'll use it against you. Please don't give him the chance."

Suddenly they were bathed in bright white light as the helicopter found them with its searchlight. It moved closer, and the strong, hot wind from its downdraft whipped at their clothes and hair. For a few seconds Sands felt angry, tempted to wave it away, but then she realised it didn't *need* to land. It increased its altitude to reduce the downwash and began to winch a stretcher down.

"I'm not going to make it, Erica," Robbins said, his words hard to make out above the din of the machine above them. "You may as well call it off. But just promise me you won't go after him? Don't hunt him. Don't seek him out. Just live your life. Don't give him what he wants."

Sands was distracted for a moment as the stretcher came lower. She could see a man descending with it, and then his boots touched the ground not five metres away.

"How bad is he?" he shouted, a man dressed in the overalls of the air sea-rescue.

Sands glanced down, but she didn't need to. She felt it in her arms where the blood no longer pumped, where there was no more tension in his back.

She shook her head.

"You're too late. He's gone."

A LETTER FROM THE AUTHOR

Dear reader,

Thank you so much for reading *The Trap*, I hope you enjoyed learning more about Erica Sands and her father. If so you'll be pleased to hear that more books are planned in this series! If you'd like to join other readers in keeping in touch, here are two options: Stay in the loop with my new releases with the link below. You'll be the first to know about all future books I write. Or sign up to my personal email newsletter on the link at the bottom of this note. Here you'll get bonus content, a free novella, and get occasional updates and insights from my writing life. I'd be delighted if you choose to sign up to either – or both!

www.stormpublishing.co/gregg-dunnett

If you enjoyed this book and could spare a few moments to leave a review that would be hugely appreciated. Even a short review can make all the difference in encouraging a reader to discover my books for the first time. Thank you so much!

Join other readers in hearing about my writing (and life) experiences, get a free novella, and other bonus content. Simply head over to my website at www.greggdunnett.com

Gregg

f facebook.com/greggwriter

Made in United States
Orlando, FL
10 September 2024

51313257R00182